THE SILENT MONUMENT

Shobha Nihalani

tara press

The Silent Monument
Shobha Nihalani

Tara Press
(Trade Division of India Research Press)
Flat No. 6, Khan Market, New Delhi - 110 003
Ph.: 24694610; Fax : 24618637
www.indiaresearchpress.com
contact@indiaresearchpress.com;

2011

10 9 8 7 6 5 4 3 2 1

ISBN : 978-81-8386-099-4

Printed for India at Manipal Press Limited, Manipal.

Acknowledgement

Many people helped me on my journey to become a published author. I owe them my deepest gratitude.

To my husband Bhagwan, whose advice has been invaluable. To my daughter, Heenu for her honest and insightful suggestions and to Nitin, my son, for his imaginative twists and out-of-the-box ideas.

I am grateful to The Hong Kong Writers' Circle, where I honed my skills. Lawrence Gray, Diana Kwok, Mio Debnam, Ken Kamoche, Jane Wallace, Gillian Bickley, Sam Ferrer, Mohyna Srinivasan, Tammy Ho Lai-ming, Jeff Zroback, and many more Circle members have been a source of inspiration. Leela Devi Panikar and Atiya Bansal have been my writer buddies and sources of moral support, thank you both. Nury Vittachi makes writing seem so easy, and over the years his advice has been priceless.

Special thanks to The Hong Kong Women in Publishing Society. This group of dedicated and intelligent women has provided me with insights into the world of publishing. Many great friendships have grown from my decade-long association with the Society.

Magne Hovden of Ancoral, my Scandinavian literary agent, believed in my writing and always gave friendly encouragement. And Per Jacobsen, head of EC-Edition, thank you for your enthusiasm in taking on *Karmic Blues*, and for translating and publishing it into a beautiful book, *Kaerlighedens bla Safir*.

My gratitude to the team at Tara Press/India Research Press. For believing in me, Anuj Bahri. And I am grateful to Sharvani Pandit, Sanjana Roy Choudhary and Debbie Smith for their editorial assistance and numerous valuable suggestions.

Inspiration for this book came from many sources. Shri P.N. Oak, *The Taj Mahal is a Hindu Palace*, Lustre Press Pvt. Ltd *Delhi Agra Jaipur The Golden Triangle*, Lonely Planet Guides, and my wild interest in conspiracy theories.

Other books by Shobha Nihalani

Karmic Blues
NINE unknown (*in preparation*)
Unresolved (*in preparation*)

Kingly power is like a cruel bolt of thunder,
Let that fade away like the blood-red sky at dusk,
Let just one eternal sign remain like sadness in the sky,
Wasn't that all you'd ever asked for?
The glittering jewels
cast their spell
like an eternal magical mystery
But even if that does vanish,
Let just one tear drop roll down the cheeks of Time
The pure light of Taj Mahal.

- Rabindranath Tagore

Prologue

Reporter Parag Saxena checked he was alone before tugging the timber beams that blocked the corner of the small doorway on the riverbank. No one visited the east side of the five-hundred-year old monument by the river Yamuna or noticed its crumbling wall. The moon was incomplete and its glow formed shadows on the recessed windows, arches and slender minarets of the pearly white marble structure with its gold-topped dome. Captivated by the impressive sight, Parag paused for a bit. He stared in awe at the ancient mausoleum that had hidden secrets for centuries and his pulse raced in anticipation. The Indian Institute of Archaeology had turned a blind eye or was intentionally silent about it. No effort had been made to dig deeper, below the surface, where the murky truth lay, lost in the bosom of the ancient monument for centuries.

The worker involved in the reparations of the monument had warned him about the consequences if he was caught. There were 'official people' watching, he had said, when Parag had bribed him to reveal the entryway into one of the hidden rooms, one of twenty-two. Finally, when the man was satisfied with the weight of notes greasing his palm, he told Parag about the access to the corner chamber. It was by the Yamuna, fewer chances of being noticed, and the best part was that there were no security guards at night.

The secret rooms in the basement of the burial site were boarded up and hidden from public view. Parag, however, had done his research and finally found someone from the Institute ready to talk and reveal the true story. His informant had provided him ten black and white grainy images of some very peculiar facts that were shockingly obvious. Parag had what he wanted but now he needed to see the truth for himself, and it had to be inside the monument.

Parag bent low and squeezed through the opening. He stepped into complete darkness. Kneeling down, he touched the floor, it was smooth. Parag paused, listening, trying to figure out the echo of the scuttling sounds. Coarse fur grazed his hand, he pulled away quickly. He stood up. Crap, he loathed rats.

Slivers of moonlight streamed in through the triangle, forming jagged white lines on the stone floor, interrupted by the rodents scurrying around. It was suffocating inside, and a wet muddy smell filled his nostrils. He waited for his eyes to adjust to the darkness before he switched on his flashlight.

Rooted to the spot, he stared wide-eyed.

'God!' he whispered, and his voice reverberated against the stone walls. He cast the beam in different directions; it illumined dozens of idols, some huge, staring at him with large stone eyes and some tiny sculptures. Moving quickly, Parag held the torch between his knees and worked his camera, his flash exploding repeatedly. The rats were all over the place, racing around the statues, coming out from every nook and cranny. Parag shuddered; he could almost feel their cold clawlike feet across his arm, over his neck and down his back. He shook his shoulders to get rid of the feeling.

As he scanned the chamber, their beady eyes warned him to keep his distance. 'Don't worry, I won't bother you, if you don't bother me,' he said with more confidence than he felt. He peered ahead, only the area within the circle of light was visible. He scanned - idols, sculptures of warriors, maidens, sentinels and animals, were scattered around the chamber. Ancient works of art.

Parag's face was slick with sweat. He wiped his face with his forearm. Fear was a slow nagging pressure in the pit of his stomach, but he ignored the feeling. He picked up one of the statues and studied it. The grey stone piece was intricately carved, bold eyes, wide forehead, and a small hole for a mouth. He realised he was holding a piece of history in his hand, probably as old as five hundred years, maybe more. Then he noticed the tiny black wormlike creatures squirming out from the stone mouth. Terrified, he dropped the piece. What was this place?

Parag scanned the area again; the air was thick and no matter how much he wiped, sweat continually trickled down the sides of his face. His neck and back were drenched. There were countless statues, like bodies strewn on a battlefield and all seemed to have tiny snakes emerging out of their orifices. Parag stepped back, blinking away the ugly sight. He was not just scared, but consumed by an overpowering sense of panic that knotted his neck muscles. The flashlight trembled in his hand casting an eerie glow and the eyes of the stone statues seemed to move, focussing on him.

Parag knew these ancient objects were not meant to be there. The fact that they existed inside this monument would become the biggest 'breaking news' of the century. It would rock the very foundations of ancient Indian history. And big news meant colossal danger. He felt stupid coming here alone in the dead of night.

Parag had to leave. He stepped back slowly, afraid the rodents would jump on him when he turned away from the statues. He paused in front of a particularly large idol in meditative posture. In the mouldy darkness, the outline of the stone man was imposing. The statue seemed to watch him with anger, with an energy that seemed to demand his reason for coming. He was trespassing inside sacred grounds, but not quite. The chamber was eerily incomplete. Neglected for centuries, it was best left undisturbed.

Parag took another step back, lost his balance and fell to the floor. He scrambled to regain his composure but dropped the torch. 'Shit,' he muttered.

Moving quickly to avoid the rats and the slimy creatures lurking inside the statues, he searched frantically for the torch. Then he saw the bones. It was a hand clasping a metallic object. He didn't see the rest of the skeleton, just the carpal wristbones with all the five phalanges intact, encircling what seemed to be a dull gold baton. The rest of the skeleton wasn't visible. The hand must have belonged to an artisan, one of many who sculpted this monument, Parag surmised. In the old days, kings chopped off hands of artistes so that they would never recreate such beauty. He shuddered at the very thought. The bones lay hidden next to a jug-sized brass bell. Parag knelt further. The object must have been held in a death grip. But he just had to tug gently and the bones crumbled to pieces. He pulled away as dozens of tiny black snakes glided away into the darkness. Parag picked up the long circular artifact and brushed away the dirt and grime.

It looked like a short curtain rod with thick knobs at both ends. The ends were oval in shape and seemed like gold, felt heavy too. The pipe-shaped stem between the gold holders was solid and had intricate floral designs, quite similar to the motif on parts of the Taj. There was also an engraved insignia. His pulse raced. He had made a valuable discovery, this looked like a royal relic, he guessed from the Mughal era, or even before that. Fervently, Parag tried to open one end. Perspiration trickled down his face as he fidgeted and twisted hard. After some effort, it gave. He removed the oval end and shone his light inside the golden tube. His heart thumped, it wasn't empty. Parag turned it upside down on the palm of his hand, very carefully, he slid out the content. It was a rolled up sheet of yellowish waxy paper held together by a red string. *A scroll.* He handled it delicately, turning it over and noticed another insignia stamped in the centre. It was the sun – a symbol of royalty clan.

This was precious.

Definitely an ancient document, Parag realised excitedly. He didn't dare unroll it, afraid it might disintegrate in his hands. He returned the scroll in the holder and reattached the top. This was a piece of evidence of Mughal history, and it seemed authentic. He clutched the artifact, wrapped his hand around it like the bones.

Parag's heart boomed in his ears, his hands were clammy. Despite the excitement of the discovery, the fear was back in full force. The only other time he felt this nervous was when he had covered the late prime minister Rajiv Gandhi's visit to Tamil Nadu; the day the latter was assassinated by a suicide bomber. The LTTE terrorist, a woman, bent to touch Rajiv's feet and then detonated the bomb. Parag was some distance away, but his colleague had died in the blast. Why did the memory of the incident enter his mind? He wondered.

Parag felt uneasy in the silent tomb, watched by the statues with deep secrets. He had hit the jackpot finding this rolled-up document, thrown in the corner of the chamber, attached to the skeletal hand. He was impatient to unravel its mystery, to read the five-hundred-year old message. But not yet. He had to get out of this godforsaken place first. Afraid the ancient relic might get damaged, he wrapped it carefully in a kerchief. With trembling fingers, he zipped it inside the long pocket of his cargo pants.

It was then that he noticed the shadow cutting the slivers of moonglow in the chamber. The menacing dark silhouette of the turbanned man was as large as a demon from the ancient scriptures.

Parag realised the enormity of the risk he had undertaken. A deep sense of terror clutched at his heart. He licked his lips. His mouth felt dry. He had to find a way out. Desperately, he pressed against the back wall to check for any exit. All he felt was cold slippery blocks of stone. No partition or sign of secret doorway. Parag leaned against the wall and slid sideways.

'I saw the opening in the wall so I… I, came inside….' Parag said in Hindi hoping the intruder would let him pass. He had to buy time, he switched off his flashlight and removed the camera slung around his neck and waited for the man to leave or give way. He didn't. The man blocked the exit like an ominous ghoul. Slowly, Parag moved towards an oval stone structure, sliding his hand across the smooth dome, stood behind it. The intruder didn't respond; instead he clicked his torch and flooded the room with white light aiming it directly at Parag. A thousand scampering claws scuttled into the shadows.

His light was blinding, Parag held up his hands to block it. 'I was just taking pictures. I will leave now,' Parag murmured, heading towards the exit slowly. The camera hung from his left wrist. He took two steps, when suddenly the man came forward in giant strides.

'How dare you enter these sacred grounds? You think you can play with fire and not get burned?' the man's guttural voice echoed as he pulled Parag by his collar. He grabbed him in an elbow squeeze and tightened it around his neck.

'Let me go, I have done nothing wrong,' Parag croaked, as he struggled against the vicelike grip. He couldn't breathe and his vision was becoming fuzzy. Parag tried pulling at the man's arm but the assailant just pressed harder.

'Your camera, give it to me. Are you going to show the world these pictures?' The attacker pulled it off his arm and let go with a shove. Parag fell to the floor. He gasped, acrid air filled his lungs, sputtering and heaving, Parag breathed deeply. This was his chance, with every ounce of strength, Parag crawled towards the opening. Then just as he thought he would escape, the monster yanked him hard, turned him around and rammed a tight fist on his jaw. Parag felt the sharp effect of his punch as he went sprawling to the floor and banged his head against one of the stone statues. He lay there stunned. His head pounded, and he felt dizzy.The back of his head was wet. Blood. He could feel the throb where his skin had split. He decided to reason with the man, his only chance to get out. 'I only came to find the truth. You understand, don't you? You see what lies beneath this monument? Such beautiful sculptures and art, it's all hidden. But it must be revealed to the world'. Parag said, his voice strong with passion.

The assailant paused and stared, Parag could see a pulsating vein in his forehead. The man's eyes were wild and blood shot. Parag realised he didn't have a hope in hell of getting out of here. The crazy man wasn't going to let him go that easily. Death was breathing down his neck, and as the thought filled his brain, he broke out in cold sweat.

He thought of Manzil, his wife. Countless times she had begged him to stop taking risks. This was supposed to be his last foray. He was going to settle down and write columns.

Please give me a chance.

The madman ignored his explanation and picked up a rat by its tail. The rodent struggled, its red eyes glowing in the darkness. Parag tried moving further away. The man grunted.'You like to take pictures of what is dead and gone? You like to show the world what existed centuries ago? Why?'

Parag shifted uncomfortably.

'Answer me!'

Parag thought quickly and responded. 'Because...because...these are historic facts and need to be revealed to the public.'

In the attacker's hand, the rat continued to squeak helplessly. The man gave him a cold smile, 'Rats are also trespassers, you know?'

Parag shook his head. 'No, no....' he pleaded. The man was totally crazed. Parag wished he was in another place, as far away from here as possible. Away from this horrible moment. The perfect place was at home with his Manzil. The thought of her facing a sickly situation like this terrorised him. Her life would be at risk now, especially with all the other damning information he had collected.

What had he done?

The sadist was dangerously close, he swayed the rat in front of Parag's face. He edged back slowly, but the monster was getting closer. His head hurt like a bitch, his swollen lips throbbed and he tasted blood. He knelt and clasped his hands together. 'Please, I beg you, let me go.' The man was towering over him holding the struggling rat. Parag begged, 'I promise on my heart I won't breathe a word to anyone. I won't tell anyone I was in here.'

'Too late. You are like this rat, crawling in places meant to be kept silent.' The madman pinched the rodent's neck until it went limp. He came close to Parag's face and he could see the sweat glistening on his forehead.

'Eat this!'

Parag stared in horror. 'Please, don't do this. You want money, anything, I promise I will give it all to you. Just let me go.' Tears streamed down Parag's face, he clutched his hands together. 'Let me go and I will forget about this place. I swear on my life.'

'Not until you swallow this rat.' The attacker was enjoying himself. 'This place is forbidden and no one leaves without punishment. You are a fool to think I will let you go.' He grinned; but it was full of hatred, his eyes glowed bright like the rat.

'God help me,' Parag whined. He was leaning against a statue; he felt a cold slimey wetness slithering on his neck. Violently, he brushed it away.

The sadist guffawed. 'God? Which God?' He laughed loud and hard, bending over and then he moved closer. Parag's attention was focussed on the dead rat he dangled in front of him. 'Open your mouth.'

'No!' Parag said loudly. The man removed a knife from his pocket. The blade glinted and in a swift move severed the rat's head. The head fell to the floor, and in minutes it had been dragged away by the other creatures. Parag shuddered. No, he didn't want to be left in here. The man swung the decapitated rat above Parag letting the blood drip over him.

'It's smaller now, you can swallow it.'

'Please, please let me go, I beg of you.' Parag felt himself lose control. A strong acidic smell filled the air.

The assailant gave him another hard knock under his chin and Parag felt his head reel as the shock of pain reverbated through his jaw.

'Don't make me angry. You make me angry and I will torture you until you will beg for death.' The madman's voice was tight with rage. He opened the palm of his hand and again dangled the rat in front of Parag's face.

There were sounds outside the chamber, distant voices. Parag called out. 'Help me, help me,' he shouted, but his voice was feeble. The voices were coming closer.

'You bloody hypocrite!' The man whispered. He pressed Parag's nose and his mouth fell open. He shoved the dead rat into his mouth. Parag's scream was locked in his throat, his eyes were wide with horror, he tried to remove the dead creature from his mouth, but the man held him down, and covered his mouth. The rat's blood poured down his throat. Its fur rubbed against his teeth. Parag choked, and his stomach heaved. The madman held his nostrils.

'Suffer the indignity of this death. But I will leave you outside. You don't deserve the status of being in this burial place, it is fit only for kings and queens.' The madman said gruffly as he checked if there was anyone outside.

Parag felt his life slipping away. He closed his eyes, letting death claim his senses. The odour of the dead creature in his mouth filled his nostrils and his body reacted, he dry heaved, jerking forward and backward.

'Why don't you just die?' The madman let go of his nostrils and pulled him closer to the doorway. He plunged the cold blade through Parag's body. Twice. Parag felt nothing at first and then the pain came in sharp waves, biting into his stomach like claws.

The madman took hold of his legs to drag him out. Parag was barely conscious of the wetness of his blood spreading, and spilling out of his body, dripping down the sides and in the light of the moon, he thought he saw the tiny black snakes swarm over his blood. He felt himself weakening as the pain claimed his senses. The rat still hung from his mouth, its tail protruding. He didn't even have the strength to push it out. The dead rat wasn't the last thing he wanted to feel before he died. He wanted to be like one of the unfeeling statues. Thoughts flashed through his mind, and his heart twisted in despair. Manzil – his wife - the love of his life. Tears stung and he blinked. Her smiling face was etched in his mind. He wished... there was no point, he resigned to his fate.

Parag never prayed before, but in the last moments of his life, as he was dragged out of the chamber, he opened his eyes for one last time and stared at the ancient stone statue and prayed. The dead rat fell out of his mouth.

Fifteen minutes later, a teenage boy approached the body lying by the Yamuna. Quickly, he searched Parag, inside his shirt and the many pockets on his cargo pants. The boy found the film roll in the small pocket near the dead man's ankle. And when he checked higher up, he felt the bulge and found the golden artifact. It was partially muddied and tinged with blood.

Before dawn broke from the east, the thief hurried away from the ghostly stillness of the Taj Mahal.

Agra
May 2009

Chapter 1

Agra: 200 km south of Delhi

'C'mon, pick up! Why won't you answer?'

It was just after ten in the morning. Manzil Saxena's increasing sense of uneasiness slowly turned to dread. She dialed Parag's cell phone yet again. Nothing.

He had promised he would be home in two days, it had been five and she had filed a missing person's report just the day before yesterday. She paced thinking about the work he was involved in. Shit, she said, over and over again. The police were not to be told anything, Parag had warned her. But she didn't care, she was getting anxious with every passing minute. Twice she had called the police station to check if they had heard anything. Nothing, they had said. She knew the business of being a reporter, Parag liked to dig deep and draw out deadly facts. The phone rang. She pounced on it. Wrong number.

Her heart raced, she had to go to the police again. But first she had to think carefully about what to say. Parag had definitely been breaking some law last night.

Manzil sank in her seat. She felt an enormous weight burdening her shoulders. She wished Parag hadn't given her the key to the locker. 'It's all in there – pictures, letters, and the contact details of the informant.' He had said, adding, 'Be smart. Be careful.'

Manzil sniffed. *Smart and careful – what have you been up to, Parag?* She unlocked and rotated the steel handle of her Godrej cupboard. Clothes hung from hangers, and some folded neatly on the shelf. Below and towards the interior on the right, a segment of the steel wardrobe was concealed. Manzil felt inside for the sliding metal door. She found it, inserted another key and twisted clockwise twice. Manzil slid open the door and felt an increasing sense of fear. She wasn't sure what to expect. Kneeling down, she peered. The small rectangular safe was stuffed with papers and files. Parag was a messy guy, he should return home and sort out his stuff. He had said if he didn't call or worst didn't come home for longer than a few days she should open the locker and burn everything. Manzil shook her head in frustration. *Burn everything?*

She removed the contents and dumped them on the worktable next to the bedroom window. A file containing ten black and white images with the official rubberstamp impression of the Indian Institute of Archaeology, the IIA, caught her attention. The pictures were of the Taj Mahal from various angles, some zoomed in on the spire at the top of the Taj and others were pictures of the carved inlay of the marble. The octagonal burial chamber consisted of two white tombs decorated with a floral arabesque design. To differentiate between the tombs, the Queen Mumtaz Mahal's cenotaph had a slate design while the Mughal King, Shah Jahan's had an ink-pot to signify that the wife should be a slate for the husband to write upon. These were in close-up.

Despite the poor quality of the photographs, the beautiful monument still took her breath away. Manzil recalled her moments at the Taj with Parag. As newly weds, she had insisted on visiting the monument at dusk. It's so romantic, she had said excited. The overwhelming structure had taken on a pinkish hue and glowed like pearls. Manzil was so taken by the magical quality, she had become teary-eyed, while Parag looked at her amused. It was quite possible that those who hadn't experienced love before would have felt the emotion at the mere sight of the grand mausoleum. A verse inscribed on the tomb honoured the architect of the Taj – "*The builder could not have been of this earth. For it was evident, the design was given him by heaven.*" Manzil couldn't agree more.

Parag was working on a special assignment on the Taj Mahal. And while she had gushed at the beauty, he studied the technical aspects of the workmanship.

And while she had oohed and aahed, he had groaned and muttered under his breath. He interviewed dozens of people for a lead on his controversial story and Manzil aware, yet unaware by shutting her mind to the fact, knew he would one day get into trouble.

'You can't keep doing this kind of work, Parag,' she had told him once, when he came home with a nasty cut on his lip, and a black eye. 'It's dangerous. You are talking to conmen, terrorists, politicians, dons. What if…?'

'I thrive on it, Zil,' he said, while she nursed an icebag on his face. 'This is my passion. Part of who I am. Also the reason you love me, agreed to marry me.' He smiled. And that was that. She melted when he gave her one of his dazzling dimpled grins.

A few days ago, he had been overly excited about his new discovery. He was out till late for one of his meetings. When he came home, she saw the gleam in his eyes, the eagerness to write the story. 'This is big, Zil. I've hit a goldmine. This is not about the rumoured treasure in the Taj, this is bigger. The information I have discovered is going to rock the very foundations of our heritage,' he had said. 'There is one more thing I need to do before I put this out. I need to go and take some photos.'

Manzil was uneasy. 'If this is so big, then it must be just as dangerous. Please, let this one go.'

'I can't, Manzil. It's almost done. After I've written this piece, which I have to word very carefully, I will sit back and watch jaws drop in shock. I promise this will be the last assignment then I'll just report on Bollywood, and the size of actors' mansions, okay?' he laughed.

Manzil agreed reluctantly, but she had tried to dissuade him. 'You have enough material, just write the article, and forget about the photos – send someone else.'

'No Zil,' he said firmly. 'This one's mine. All mine.'

Manzil spread the pictures, these were from the IIA. Parag didn't need pictures he could have just used these.

Then she noticed the description and a little notation at the corner marked 'top secret.' No wonder he couldn't use these photos. There was more: IIA documented reports, official letters from other archaeologists, and research that Parag had printed from the internet. When she read the letter from a professor of archaeology based in America, her heart was racing.

'Amazing!' she whispered. Parag was indeed sitting on a really big story.

It was then that she received the phone call. It was the police. And, Manzil's world collapsed around her.

It was dusk, when she returned from the police station. Manzil sat on her sofa, listening to the sounds of the outside world. Normal sounds. Her neighbours' voices filtered through her quiet apartment. She heard Kanta's stream of angry words. She was probably yelling at her three children to finish their homework, while she cooked to feed her expanding family. Manzil recalled a conversation at the door when they bought vegetables. Kanta had warned Manzil about having children, 'unless you have the mindset of a saint'. Manzil had planned to have one, Parag wanted two. 'Hum do, hamare do,' he joked, referring to the Indian government's family planning slogan promoting small families with two kids. Outside her apartment, she could hear the maids chatting with the bread vendor. Manzil ignored the doorbell. She didn't need anything.

Tears streamed down her cheeks. She sat staring into nothingness. Wondering what her next move should be. The world was speeding and she was stationary, in a hopeless void. How would she survive without Parag, her love, their life?

When Inspector Yadav had asked her to come to the station, she knew something terrible had happened to Parag. She expected her husband to call and apologise for not letting her know where he was. Instead, the police had called and his disappearance had turned into a horrific reality. *Please come to the station immediately,* the grim voice had said.

Inspector Yadav had a very angular face and a fit physique. The constables were respectful in his presence. When she was led to his office, he looked at her with cold eyes. He didn't look like the kind of person who smiled much. His lips were set in a tight line, as if his life was a series of bad news. He aimed to be gentle in his tone, but it didn't have the desired effect. He ended up sounding morose.

A body was discovered by the riverside, he explained. And he told her about the senseless act of violence perpetrated on the body. She had remained composed. Clearly, he wasn't used to talking to women about death. He had asked her if there was anyone she could bring with her, a relative to lean on. She had said no. She would come alone.

Then, he started asking about her husband. Mostly about possible enemies, Parag's purpose of being by the Yamuna late at night and his current assignment. All this, while the other policemen watched her surreptitiously.

Manzil knew nothing; she had responded softly, eyes downcast, unable to look at the hard faces and their mud brown uniforms. Why were they wasting time on these questions, she had wondered. Parag was alive. They had found someone else's body. Manzil's heartbeat was a desperate mantra – he's alive, he's alive - somewhere out there. She would return home and he would be waiting for her. Recently, he hardly got home before ten at night.

Yadav led her to the morgue. While he spoke gently, Manzil didn't turn away when he asked her to identify the body. 'The body' he had said, but, they were sure it was Parag. Could have been someone else but they had to verify with Manzil.

Her thoughts buzzed: It's not him, it's not him, it's not him.

Manzil had filed a missing persons report and they had to eliminate every possibility, Yadav said. There was nothing on this body, not even a watch, when the police checked him at the banks of the Yamuna. Only she would know, could determine if it was Parag.

The face was dark grey; his lips were swollen and blue. There were fine scratches on his cheek. There was pain in his expression. And regret.

Parag!

Two years of blissful married life and they were going to plan a family.

The past reeled her back. They had met in college and fallen in love. Parag had been the one reason she believed that there was good in this world. He was passionate about being a writer and he succeeded by becoming the top investigative reporter for the *Hindu Times*. He had revealed corruption in the municipal level of government. With evidence, he had carefully put together a news item of a minister's son financing a prostitution racket. He had a nose for news, the editor had said. He was their star. The circulation of the newspaper had tripled since he had joined them.

Manzil was a chartered accountant for a small firm. She was happy and more in love with Parag after five years of dating. And after marriage, she continued working part-time but was keen on starting a family.

Despite the comment made by the executive director of a multinational Fortune 500 company, that 'no daughter of mine would marry a two-bit newspaper reporter,' Manzil defied her father and married Parag.

Parag is dead. The words finally penetrated the memories that temporarily buffered her pain. *Parag is dead.* The finality of it crushed her, and she doubled over as if in pain.

In a daze, she didn't know when and how she reached home. From the moment she had nodded at the sight of the body, Inspector

Yadav had led her out of the morgue. He had whispered a few words but it didn't seem to register. Manzil nodded mindlessly. Now she was at home.

Manzil entered her room. She was staring at her reflection in the mirror. She closed her eyes tight and let the last of the tears run their course. After washing her face, Manzil turned on the computer to type out her resignation letter.

She had to deal with Parag's unfinished business.

Chapter 2

Anwar Hussain wiped his mouth with the back of his hand after he had downed two glasses of lassi. The yoghurt drink soothed his burning stomach. He was nervous. Elbows on the table, he scratched his wiry red hair as he waited for his boss, Khanbaba, to speak.

'You did well; this is a lesson to Deva and his inquisitive minions. Why didn't you search the man?' Khanbaba asked, speaking in such a soft voice that anyone would be fooled that he was talking to his son. Rotating the gold rings on his chubby fingers, he made it obvious that he wore his money. Khanbaba's large bulk and the chains of gold around his neck - a signature trademark - commanded respect, which circling waiters greedily offered.

The small dhaba was an indent in the side of the road, with dirt parking and stones to boundary the area. The aroma of lentil-battered fried food and garlic chutney hung in the air. To the left was a circular brick tandoor over which stood a sweaty cook, wearing only a singlet, already slapping the rotis on a smoking convex pan. The two-lane narrow road was busy with trucks, bullock carts, cyclists and villagers balancing baskets of vegetables on their heads. Many of the vehicle drivers veered into the dusty stop to grab a bite.

A lorry, balancing a pregnant load wrapped in sack cloth, roped down and threatening to burst, turned sharply into the parking area. The truck came to a sudden halt raising a cloud of dust. Khanbaba sneezed twice and muttered an obscenity under his breath. Anwar watched the driver slam hard on the breaks, switch off the engine, jump out of his seat and rush towards the yellow concrete structure that bore the sign 'Toilet' in big black uneven letters.

Anwar returned his attention to his boss. Khanbaba slurped his fourth cup of tea. He had a chubby round face, which looked even more youthful with his paan-stained red lips. He could have passed off as a jolly fat man, easy-going and fun-loving. But, Khanbaba, Anwar knew, was just the opposite. As soft as he was on the outside, the boss was hard as rock on the inside. A few years ago, Anwar's friend, suspected of two-timing the sect, was whacked to death by Khanbaba's gold cane.

The underworld survived on trust. Members of sects, who did not give a hundred per cent to their sect lords, were destined to die. Anwar was prepared to die a martyr, not an unfaithful servant. And the reason was a treasure hidden in the Taj. Khanbaba had made sure that his people were keeping an eye on the area by the river. And anyone who dared infiltrate the monument from that side was destined to die.

'Khanbaba, I heard someone approach and I had to leave the body by the river and run. I didn't expect the camera to be empty.' Anwar felt his voice turn into a whine. He leaned forward, waiting for the dreaded attack or a second chance.

Khanbaba didn't care about the time or the place – even in the crowded dhaba, sitting cross-legged on a rope bed, he wouldn't think twice of killing Anwar. Resting between them, the aluminium plate of chilli pakodas on a wooden plank had turned cold.

Khanbaba pursed his lips, and pressed his fingertips together. He looked at Anwar through red-rimmed eyes; his gaze was intent, as if reading his thoughts. Anwar's scalp beaded with sweat.

'You kill someone and then you don't search him? I find that not just useless, but completely stupid, the intruder might have found a clue.' Khanbaba's voice had a slight accusatory edge; it felt like a prod from a knife.

The heat of anger rose to his jaw, and Anwar bit down hard. 'There was nothing inside, Khanbaba – it was another one of those chambers filled with stones. The kind that needs to be left undisturbed, hidden,' He said calmly.

'I see. Next time make sure you are careful about your actions. If what is hidden comes out, it will be bad for everyone, do you understand?'

Anwar nodded. But the flame of rage surged within him, burning his stomach again. Anwar took a deep breath and looked away. 'Khanbaba, I have some very good news. I have discovered who has taken the film roll,' he said, with a grim smile.

Khanbaba narrowed his gaze. A tiny tear leaked from the left corner of his eye. 'You have too much fire in you, Anwar. Be careful or it will burn you. By the month end; I want everything, whatever the dead man had on his person, belongs to me. I don't want to know how you find it. You get it or you die a traitor's death, you hear me?' His voice was so soft; it had an almost lulling effect. But the words chilled Anwar.

He nodded and got off the rope bed. 'Salaam, Khanbaba,' Anwar said, slipping his feet back into his shoes and headed towards the toilets. Behind the concrete sign, the roughly built four walls without a roof, was further away from the dhaba than he realised. It was a deserted area, with only a dirty stream infested with larvae. The muddy banks were lined with garbage.

As he approached, Anwar could hear the lorry driver, who had raced towards the toilet earlier, singing a popular song as he washed his hands. Anwar entered and stood behind him quietly. When the man looked up into the mirror, he noticed Anwar's reflection.

The man smiled in greeting, but before he could say anything, Anwar bashed his head against the mirror. The driver stared in horror at the cracked mirror, his reflection split into a dozen triangles. He turned to face Anwar, 'What the...'

Anwar's head was hot, he felt his insides bubbling with rage, he could feel the throb in his chest. He slapped the man and then grasped him by the sides of his head, pressing hard. The injured driver struggled, scratching his attacker's hands, desperately pulling them away. 'Leave me alone!' he screamed. 'What have I done to you?'

The more he yelled the more Anwar hit him. The side of his head split, the driver's face was covered in sticky rivulets of blood. Still the bloodied man fought back. He pushed and scratched desperately, crying and shouting obscenities. 'Leave me, please. I have two small children,' he sobbed.

Anwar kept hitting the man's head against the wall until he was nothing more than a ragdoll. The anger dissipated, Anwar let the man drop to the floor, his face was a pulpy mess; one eye stared unseeing at Anwar and the other one swollen shut.

Chapter 3

Old Delhi

Three of Deva's thugs waited outside the temple at the corner of Deva's den. They knew that Deva must never be disturbed when he had organized the ritualistic worship. Ramu, the youngest, but tallest of the three, had heard about the wrath of Deva. Rumours were that he used a trishul to stab a man who dared interrupt him during his prayers. Deva had the fieriness of Lord Shiva and a faith that was as unshakeable and mighty as the Himalayas, or so he claimed and Ramu believed him.

Deva was aware of the threesome pacing outside the temple, but ignored them. He would talk only when he was ready. Deva joined his palms together and listened to the droning sounds of the Rudram mantras. They had a hypnotic resonance and were believed to be the perfect pitch and vibration to connect with the Lord. Properly attired in a cotton dhoti, Deva, bare-chested except for a holy string that crossed diagonally across his body, a metal talisman around his upper arm, was ready to perform the pooja.

Four saffron-robed priests, trained in the art of reciting the ancient Sanskrit slokas sat perpendicular to the deity. One of the priests moved to sit cross-legged in front of the idol, while the three continued their chant.

Sprinkling small amounts of rosewater on a marble disc, the holy man prepared for the ritual. First he scraped the sandalwood stick on a flat stone disc, until the rosewater turned to the colour of marigolds. From time to time, he added strands of Spanish saffron, which Deva had specially bought for the purpose. The worshipper was focused on the task at hand as he worked purposefully at creating a thick cream of gold-coloured chandan. When he was satisfied with the consistency, he transferred the tilak into a tiny silver bowl.

Deva picked up a silver pitcher filled to the brim with cow's milk. Standing reverently over the lingam, with both hands holding the pitcher he gently poured the milk over the black stone while the priests continued their droning chorus of the mantra. The recitation of the powerful five syllable *Namah Shivaya*, was believed to energise certain parts of the mind, elevating the spirit to a higher level.

Deva applied three lines of the gold tilak across the dome-shaped stone. With the third finger of his right hand, he pressed a large tilak on top of the stone and applied more on the hood of the silver five-headed cobra that curled around the lingam.

Deva bowed low and whispered passionately.

The ritual was far from over; Deva's men continued to wait outside. The priests stood up to complete the final part of the Monday prayer.

On a silver tray, a cotton wick dipped in pure ghee burnt brightly, and on a mound of rice, the camphor squares created dark smoke as the pungent flame grew tall. The priest circled the *aarti* clockwise, rang the bell and blew the conch to appease the Lord. After it was over, Deva bowed low, then waved his palm over the sacred flames and touched his forehead and chest.

The milk concoction that washed the lingam was poured into a small silver glass. Deva dispensed a small amount in the palm of his hand and drank the *amrit*, and then emerging from the temple offered it to the waiting men. The three held out their right palm, supported by their left, and drank the liquid nectar, blessings that were supposed to cure all ailments, and wash away all sins.

Inside the temple, the priests continued their meditation. Eyes closed and bodies still, they were absorbed in another world.

'You have news for me?' Deva asked, as they headed towards the shade of a spreading banyan.

'The reporter was murdered and his camera stolen.' The youngest of the three, Ramu said. 'Luckily, the reporter had removed the filmroll and hid it in his pocket.'

'Did you see who did this?'

'It was one of Khan's men – Anwar.'

'That cold-blooded killer! The reporter must have suffered a tragic death.' Deva commented. 'What did you do?'

'I waited until the killer left and then searched the dead man's pockets,' Ramu said. He handed Deva the filmroll and bloodied scroll. 'I found these.'

He studied the objects, but his attention was on the scroll. 'This looks very old,' he removed one of the knob ends, and extracted the contents, carefully he unrolled it. He looked at it trying to make sense of it. He noticed the symbols of the sun and other motifs. He shook his head, rolled up the scroll, returned it to its holder. He was silent for a few minutes, eyes closed.

'You didn't find anything else, gold coins or rubies or diamonds?'

'No,' Ramu said honestly. Deva could tell when he lied, and a hard slap or two was the punishment, some other liars got worse. He noticed the trishul leaning against the wall and shuddered. Ramu had heard talk of Mughal treasure hidden somewhere behind the Taj. And Khanbaba's men were watching the place, just as carefully as Deva's. As far as Ramu figured, it was all rumours. If there was any treasure it would have been looted by now.

Then suddenly Deva looked at each of them. An idea struck him. 'This time we follow a different route. The information on the ancient letter might be of some use to the fanatics.' He turned to

Ramu, 'show these to the reporter's wife. I am sure she will want to take revenge on the people who killed her husband. She will go to the press. Offer her your assistance and protection, Khanbaba's men are aware that something was found, they will want to destroy it and kill her. It's better it is not in my possession for the time being. Let intelligent people deal with this. Let the widow be the one to make public what is being found inside certain monuments,' he said. Ramu knew the scroll meant more than just a piece of old relic for a museum, it carried some information that seemed to bother Deva. He didn't press further, but the reason for keeping an eye on the Taj had taken on a new meaning. It wasn't just about a rumoured treasure.

'Ramu, I want you to be my eyes and ears. Where ever the widow goes, you go, whatever she does with these... ancient things, you tell me, understood?'

Ramu nodded.

'One more thing,' he turned to his other two minions, 'call that digger archaeologist. He has become careless.' Deva said with anger smouldering in his eyes.

Chapter 4

7a.m. Manzil's Apartment, Agra

Parag had died because of those pictures, those letters. This thought circled Manzil's head as she sat up in her bed. Her heart skipped a beat. She glanced at the worktable where she had left the papers lying scattered. It was careless of her, she should put them away. But she dreaded handling them. Should she inform Inspector Yadav? No, she realised. The police were corrupt and the information too sensitive.

As she dressed, she wondered what Parag would have done. He had met an archaeologist last week, according to his notes. A Mahesh Bhakti. He was the last man Parag had met. This Mahesh Bhakti must have given Parag the evidence. She would find him. But first she would meet the editor of the *Hindu Times* and show him the information Parag had collected. And he could help her decide what to do with it.

The insistent doorbell distracted Manzil, but she didn't rush to the door. Must be one of the vendors. She tried to eat something, a toast and tea, she was unable to swallow even that. The emptiness in the house ate at the core of her being. *Parag, why did you have to get so involved? Why do you care so much about the truth or the lies?* She whispered, hoping he would hear her pleas. Manzil didn't want him to rest in peace yet. He had to guide her and tell her what to do next.

Anger replaced the sadness, when the doorbell continued its insistent buzzing. She didn't want any eggs, bread, detergent. *Damn it.* She yanked open the door just as a boy's finger poised above the doorbell.

'Yes?' Manzil asked impatiently, sure that he had the wrong house. He didn't look like a teenager nor did he look like an adult. He was skinny and his long limbs gave him an angular look. His hair was an untidy mop and his face square and the skin still smooth as a child's, except for a few stray tufts of hair that darkened his upper lip and chin. He hadn't broken into adulthood yet.

'I have news about your husband. He left something for you.' The stranger said without offering an introduction.

Manzil stared at him for a minute and then she shut the door in his face.

The bell was insistent, accompanied by knocking and muttering. It continued for two minutes. The boy-man was pushy. She might as well open the door and tell him to get lost.

Manzil was suspicious, but also curious about what he knew. 'Tell me quickly, I haven't got all day,' she snapped.

'My name is Ramu. I saw your husband at the Taj, near the riverside,' he said almost begging to be believed.

'So why are you here?' she demanded, keeping the door only slightly ajar. The boy's shirt hung haphazardly outside his loose jeans. He searched his trouser pockets and pulled out an object.

'Recognise this?' he asked, holding it close to her face.

'Where…where did you get this?' Manzil did recognise it. She took the silver-plated ring. It was Parag's – his wedding band. She had the same one; only hers was slimmer. She looked on the inside and saw the inscription that proved it did belong to her husband. 'To my love, my life, forever.' It said. 'How did you get this?' she asked, tears smarting her eyes.

'Let me in and I will tell you everything – show you what your husband found,' Ramu insisted. She held the ring tight in her palm, still unsure.

'Okay,' she whispered and opened the door slightly wider to allow him in. Ramu darted inside, before she could change her mind.

His eyes skimmed the hall and rested on the mug on the coffee table.

'Can I have some tea?' he asked.

Manzil nodded silently and went to the kitchen. She didn't think he would rob and kill women without reason. But then again, she thought, what was there to live for. Each moment, knowing Parag was dead, felt like a fresh wound. The pain seared her heart.

Ramu followed her. There was a small stool by the kitchen cabinet, Ramu perched like a bird with both his feet on the edge of the seat. It was her seat. Manzil often sat there in the evenings, waiting for Parag to come home.

'What do you want to tell me?' Manzil asked as she added milk to a cup of water. She opened a packet of biscuits and placed the plate next to him.

From his cloth bag, Ramu took out a roll and placed it on the counter. Then very gently, he withdrew a slender rod. It looked ancient, dusty.

Manzil picked up the object, it was heavy, the colour dull gold. She rubbed a corner, and it gleamed. Seemed like real gold. She gasped. It was a striking artifact. She noticed intricate etchings, very elaborate, very delicate with the symbol of the sun in the centre. The distinctive knobs at both ends had etched patterns too.

'What's this?'

'Your husband had this in his pants,' Ramu said, as he ate the biscuits two at a time.

'You stole from my husband?'

'If I didn't take it the police would have, and then you would have never seen it. Ever.'

The tea bubbled and almost spilled over. She turned down the gas in time.

She studied the objects. The filmroll probably had more evidence. She picked up the gold relic.

'Open it,' Ramu said.

She pulled one end, it didn't budge, then she tried the knob-shaped plug on the other end. It gave.

'What is this?' She looked inside, 'there's something there,' and gently slid out the rolled up paper on the counter. She studied the roll of waxy paper. Her heart thudded with excitement, this seemed like a very ancient document. She noticed another royal seal.

'This is very strange...' she murmured.

She unrolled the scroll with trembling fingers. The handwritten document was in a language she couldn't understand.

'What does it say?'

Ramu shrugged, 'Don't know,' he responded, his attention on the tea still brewing on the stove.

The roll of paper was unusual in texture; old and parts of it yellowed with age. There was a splattering of rust-coloured drops along the length of the scroll. Manzil let go abruptly, turned away and checked on the tea.

'Why are you here? Why are you giving these to me? Why do you want me involved?' She demanded angrily.

'Can I have some tea, please,' Ramu said.

Manzil ignored him. She took the scroll and began checking it carefully. From the corner of her eye, Manzil noticed Ramu hop off his perch and deftly pour the tea through a strainer into a mug, he helped himself to two more spoons of sugar, and stirring it quickly, returned to the comfort of his seat.

Manzil couldn't recognise the script, but the flowing loops of ink formed words, and held a heavy meaning to it. It was a royal document of some sort. There was a signature at the bottom and a date, but it was smudged. She had read in school history about messages passed between kingdoms or rulers through such scrolls. She would have to find an expert. The scroll was authenticated by a formal seal, a symbol of the sun and another symbol scripted above it.

Ramu slurped noisily. 'Nice tea,' he murmured.

'What do you want me to do with this?' she asked.

'To do what your husband would have done.' Ramu looked like one of the many shoeshine teenage boys at the Chandni Chowk corner. Bright eyes, suppressed energy with spindly arms and legs. Yet there was a strength about him, and scars on his arms, as if he had been in fights, seen suffering and knew about death.

'Write about it? I'm not a reporter.' Manzil responded, exasperated by his focus on his tea and biscuits than his reason for coming to see her.

'I thought you may want to follow in your husband's footsteps. That's what Deva said. Anyway, you are the smart one, been to school-college and all. You tell me what I can do to help you,' he said.

She looked at him in frustration. *He is making no sense. And, who is this Deva.*

Parag had collected a lot of evidence, and he couldn't have managed without help. She recalled Parag saying he had a source inside the IIA who wanted to help reveal some secret about the Taj. What if the scroll was further proof?

Manzil faced a hard fact: her life was in danger too. She couldn't go to the press with all the information yet. If she did, she could become a target. And the Taj, besides being a national heritage, was sacred. Whichever way one looked at it – it was a sensitive issue.

Manzil had to verify that the scroll was indeed a genuine ancient document. And not some touristy fake.

'I don't think you can help me further,' Manzil said, turning to Ramu as he slurped the last drop of tea. 'Thanks for all of this, you can leave. I will decide what to do with them.'

'You misunderstand. I am also here to be your bodyguard. Deva knows everything, he asked me to be your shadow, in case there is trouble.'

'Who is this Deva you keep talking about?'

'A great man, helps poor people, does a lot of cleaning up.' He smiled, 'There's lots of garbage on the streets, and he helps those who work for him and gets rid of the others...' he said suspiciously. 'He is the one who knows all and helps all. He said your life is in danger and I must protect you. He knows many stories that are spreading in the city, and they are not good.'

Manzil didn't like the way someone else was calling the shots in her life. 'Sounds like a great man. Why does he think I'm in danger?'

Ramu looked at her as if she was being deliberately stupid. 'The wife of a renowned reporter working on a very controversial story, is bound to be in danger. Especially when her husband is killed.'

Before Manzil could respond, the doorbell rang insistently.

Ramu leapt from his perch, 'Make sure no one knows I'm here,' he said, and scooted to the nearest bathroom.

'But why?' Manzil asked, as she headed towards the front door. She opened it.

It was Inspector Yadav.

Chapter 5

Mahesh Bhakti recalled the night he had waited at the corner of the narrow alley in Paharganj for Parag, the now dead reporter. The situation had become complicated, he realised with irritation. Mahesh wished he could turn back the clock and cancel their plan to meet.

Mahesh had been ordered to visit Deva. And the archaeologist knew Deva's wrath would be unleashed on him; that Deva will find fault in the way the information had been transferred to the reporter. Mahesh couldn't alter the events that led to Parag's death, but he could certainly prepare his side of the story.

While he made his way to the don's den, he recalled his meeting with the reporter.

Mahesh had met Parag on a new moon night; he recalled the sequence of events clearly. The weather was muggy with an overwhelming odour of wet earth that he felt smothered. He sucked on the bidi and then flicking it into the gutter nearby, waited in the darkness. The guy was late. Mahesh paced restlessly. He pulled out another smoke from his pocket. Stupid reporter had better be there soon or he would leave. Diagonally across, the streetlights cast a soft yellow glow onto the paan shop. It was bustling even though it was close to midnight, men, some with busty women clinging to their arms, laughed boisterously at the paanwalla's bawdy jokes. Drunks sat on the pavement in a stupor and some stumbled past holding a half empty bottle, crooning, as though straight out of a cheesy Bollywood film.

Mahesh stepped off the curb to leave and that's when he noticed Parag walking tentatively towards him. The fellow didn't fit in that part of town: lonely men's hangout. Parag's neat pressed shirt with a squeaky clean collar looked out of place in the neighbourhood. Oh and the shoes, the man was wearing foreign-made sneakers. Where did he grow up? America? Mahesh looked at his own kolhapuri slippers. They suited his elegant feet and the hot sticky weather.

'You're late,' Mahesh whispered harshly. He plucked the bidi from his lips, stabbed it against the wall and let it fall.

'Sorry, the damn bus broke down and then the bus driver….'

'Never mind,' Mahesh interrupted. 'Here's the packet. I'm not doing this out of the goodness of my heart. I expect this information to be used and published, right?'

Parag nodded.

'One more thing,' Mahesh had threatened. 'This could cost me my job. You better keep your mouth shut about your source. Or else….'

Parag nodded, he looked around. Barely anyone noticed. He took the packet. 'Yes, I know or else I'm dead.'

Mahesh arrived at Deva's sprawling house. It was surrounded by a brick wall, and he knocked on the side gate. The bodyguard nodded and let him in. Mahesh saw the weapon tucked in the thug's belt and his cynical smile to match. Mahesh wondered, for the hundredth time, why he got involved with this lot of people.

In one area of the square courtyard, young boys were being trained in wrestling, another group of older boys were learning how to read and write, and a third, the most pathetic of them all, were the maimed beggars. Their appearance was pitiful, but they laughed and talked loudly as if their lives were complete. These were Deva's followers, thugs and ruffians. They received food and shelter and protection. And in return, they gave Deva their earnings and their complete allegiance – including indulging in unlawful activities. This was the deal. And no one was allowed to leave Deva's broad network of businesses. The illiterate, street boys, beggars, and those who had nowhere to go, were given a ray of hope, a chance at life and basic necessities – food, clothing and shelter, if they became a part of Deva's clan and followed his twisted ideologies.

Mahesh knew that Deva was both good and evil. But definitely didn't want to witness his evil avatar. Mahesh was led into the room by another one of the bodyguards that circled the den outside. Deva was listening to some classical music on the radio. His eyes were half-closed as the music resonated with impossible notes of a raaga that chased the tabla's intricate beat and fingerplay. 'Wah, wah!' he exclaimed, his hand slapped his knee to the rhythm of the old classic '*Laga chunari mein daag*'. It filled the room with its achingly soulful notes.

Mahesh remained quiet, he didn't want to interrupt the don, well-known for his quicksilver temper that usually resulted in severe damages that ended up requiring medical attention. Mahesh sipped on cold rose sherbet served by a young boy. He waited patiently for the seven minute song to end. The singer with the magnetic voice had obviously been classically trained and was reverently called Ustad. Such musicians had the status close to god. Through music they were believed to touch the divine. No, not just music, in fact the ultimate aim of every Indian art form was connecting to a higher power, Mahesh reflected.

Today, the music did not stir his soul. Ordinarily, Mahesh would be moved to tears by the end but his mind was restless, unable to focus. Again his mind drifted to the past, he wished he had not met Parag that evening. The reporter had come from Agra, after a gruelling five-hour journey by bus. He said he had been careful that no one knew where he was going, or whom he was supposed to meet.

Should he tell Deva what had really happened, Mahesh wondered. The song ended abruptly and what Deva said caught his attention.

'You digger,' Deva roared, pointing an accusatory finger, 'what had you promised me and what have you ended up delivering? You have been careless and foolish. Your purpose was to feed the reporter information on a possible treasure in the Taj, and his job was to make it public and force the government to do something about it, which in turn would have led you to snitch on the IIA, and get me access and we would have found the treasure first. But nothing of that sort has happened, instead... instead, you have created a new problem.'

Mahesh was stunned at the man's plan, which incidently wasn't the original plan at all. Mahesh was supposed to leak information that the government had chosen to keep secret. That was all. Where did the information on treasure come from? What was he talking about? As far as he knew, those were just rumours. 'What is this?' Mahesh asked, surprised at the outburst.

"You have given Parag useless information and now it has fallen in the wrong hands. You idiot, that reporter died because of you!' he shouted. Deva was sitting erect, hands on hips.

Mahesh looked appropriately shocked. 'The reporter knew from the first time we met that the information I would give him could prove fatal. He was playing with fire. He insisted on asking too many questions from too many people. I am not the only one involved. Parag contacted me saying his newspaper and some American magazine would be publishing his articles next week and needed some more proof. I gave him the confidential information. I risked my job. What do you expect from me if the reporter got careless; I had already warned him,' Mahesh said in defense. It was important to justify his reasons. Deva was a powerful underworld don and Mahesh didn't want to be his next victim.

'You fool!' Deva stood up, fists clenched. 'That reporter found something even more precious than the pictures. He found proof – some document, a letter with the stamp of the symbol of a royal. A scroll! It clearly has links with some secret hidden in the Taj. I am sure of it!' He stamped his foot and faced the veranda. His followers were swarming the courtyard. They paused to look up. He addressed them, his back towards Mahesh.

'My fellow believers, because of its foundation: Universal oneness or '*Vasudeva Kudumbakam*',' he closed his eyes and seemed to enjoy the roll of his tongue on the words. 'We worship the ideal in the idol, the formless in the form,' Deva's voice suddenly took on a pitch that hurt the ears. He turned towards Mahesh. 'So how dare you forget your duty towards me? ' he said and raised his hands in the air as if calling to the gods for help. His eyes were huge in their sockets. They stared at Mahesh with the intensity of a laser beam.

Below, in the courtyard, Deva's men listened respectfully and when he was done, they returned to their tasks, unperturbed by their don's commentary, which was completely unrelated to the issue at hand, Mahesh realised.

Many years ago, Mahesh had approached Deva for help, and he was still demanding payback. Mahesh should have known better than to deal with a don. It was a small matter, a wayward policeman had caught Mahesh in the act of prostitution and he wanted money to keep it quiet. The policeman blackmailed regularly. Deva was the only one who could set the cop straight. And stop the drain of his bank account.

Mahesh did a double take. Did he hear right? A scroll? A piece of ancient proof? This was an important archaeological find, more relevant than even the pictures of the Taj. Mahesh's heart drummed with excitement. He had to have the scroll. This matter was more important than any rumoured treasure, the scroll was the treasure. And if the scroll contained information related to the origins of the Taj, then that would be something worth killing and dying for.

'Where is the scroll now? Can I take a look at it?' Mahesh asked excited.

'I have sent everything to the reporter's wife,' Deva said.

Damn!

Deva drank thirstly, the rose sherbet dripping down his thick chin in little rivulets. He set the steel glass down with a bang. 'You have failed me. The widow will not let her husband's death go in vain. She will follow in his footsteps. If she is a true wife, she will make sure all of her husband's work is rightfully revealed, as he would have wanted it. And you will continue to find information on the location of the Taj treasure.'

Mahesh cursed under his breath. He wanted to argue with Deva. The crazed man had just given away a precious piece of artifact to someone who had no knowledge of its value. Mahesh had first right to it. He desperately wanted to see it, to analyse it. Deva should have realised that it was better off with him. This would be a once in a lifetime opportunity for an archaeologist. And the fanatic had gone and given it away. Mahesh wanted to shout a few expletives, but he held back. Deva had three guards in full combat outfit within spitting distance. One gesture from Deva and Mahesh's body would be riddled with bullets.

Mahesh paused, pretending to think. 'Deva, my life's mission is to bring the truth to the public. To make sure every single Indian is aware about our rich heritage. But the dead reporter ruined everything. His wife might not be able to do justice to this information; in fact she might just throw it away.'

'Don't defy me! She will take revenge. Her husband's death wasn't accidental and she will make sure the world knows what he was working on. I've sent someone to show her the ancient letter, and be with her at all times for her protection,' Deva shouted.

'But Deva...' Mahesh stopped mid-sentence. Deva's anger was evident in the throbbing vein on his forehead. Mahesh squirmed. He wanted to exit in one piece.

'You failed me,' Deva said in a dangerous tone. 'Go away and don't even think of interfering in my business again.'

'Please Deva, it is crucial that I check this document. It is a very valuable ancient relic – if it is real..,' Mahesh's voice trailed when he saw the guards lift their weapons. Deva flicked his hand as if he were a fly. 'Go away. Only when you have something substantial, show me your face again.' He wagged a finger in his face, 'And remember, stay away from the woman. Understand!'

Mahesh nodded and left quickly.

Chapter 6

Inspector Yadav prided himself on being a very good judge of character. He had inherited his father's skills, a brave police officer in the investigative wing of the CBI. His father had died trying to nab the don of a local drug ring; he also knew that a minister's son had been involved. All the senior officer had to do, was find proof so that the Indian justice system would put the politician's son behind bars. Yadav senior died from a single gun shot wound to his forehead execution style, before he could find concrete evidence. Everytime Yadav thought of his father, he knew his spirit was close to him, guiding him.

Yadav could tell right away that Manzil Saxena, the dead reporter's widow, was sitting on a heavy secret. It seemed to physically weigh on her, he felt she might just crumble to the floor. Sure she acted brave but he could tell that the visit to the police station had been hard on her. Women were not prepared for grisly details of death or violence, Yadav sighed, moreover the presence of a police officer, was generally considered the harbinger of bad news.

Yadav had filed the report on Parag Saxena, as a botched robbery. He kept the file open. Although, he knew it was pointless since the murderer would never be found. But there was something about the case that didn't quite fit the circumstances surrounding his death. Yadav's instincts niggled him. Parag's killing was more than a simple robbery. He was involved in something far more dangerous.

The autopsy report clearly indicated that death was a thrust by a curved knife, not the regular garden variety, he was told. The kind warriors carried with them. Yadav didn't think there were anymore Rajput or Mughal warriors remaining in this day and age.

He would leave the case pending for further investigation and check on Mrs Saxena. He had an excuse; she had called twice to check when her husband's body would be released. Instead of calling her up, Yadav decided to visit her.

'Inspector? I wasn't expecting you,' Manzil stammered as she stepped back.

'I'm sorry if I'm interrupting something, Mrs Saxena,' he replied coolly, 'I only came to tell you that we can release . . . your husband, I mean his body . . . tomorrow morning.'

She looked up at him, and didn't move. There was guilt written all over her face. He might as well take the opportunity to investigate. 'Am I disturbing you?' Yadav said, stepping closer so that she would take the hint and let him in. Manzil moved away to allow access. He sauntered slowly through the living room and then into the kitchen, noticing every detail as he passed. He heard water running in the bathroom. 'Is someone else here?' He turned to her.

'No, no. I mean yes – it is the cleaning lady. She is washing the clothes,' Manzil said, clearly nervous. She indicated the living room. 'Would you like some water?'

'Are you alright, Mrs Saxena?' he asked, pausing.

Wearing a simple white salwar kameez, she looked vulnerable and seemed distracted, something was on her mind.

Just tell me.

'I'm fine. Still…still adjusting … to my husband's death,' she murmured, looking away.

'I understand. It was a bad situation.' He said glancing suspiciously towards the locked bathroom. 'Actually, some tea would be nice, Mrs Saxena.' When she turned away, he followed. 'Maybe I will join you in the kitchen,' he said.

'No. It's okay, please have a seat,' she pointed to the sofa. 'I will bring it to you.'

He ignored her request. 'I would like to ask you some questions if you don't mind? Easier while you prepare the tea, no?' he asked, watching her. A thin film of sweat shone on her forehead.

'Okay,' she mumbled, hurrying to the kitchen. The woman was definitely hiding something.

'Mrs Saxena, what was your husband doing at the Taj alone, and that too so late at night?' Yadav leaned against the counter and folded his arms across his chest.

Manzil poured some milk into a pot with a slight tremble. 'My husband is...was an investigative journalist and liked to take his own photographs. He wanted some photographs of the Taj at night.'

'When was the last time you saw or heard from him?'

She added half a cup of water to the milk and turned on the stove.

She paused to think. 'About five days ago,' she said confidently. From a steel container, Manzil plucked some tea leaves with her fingertips and flicked them into the pot. Her back was to him. 'Sugar?'

'No.'

She returned the jar to the shelf and purposely kept her back to him, watching the brew boil.

'Mrs Saxena, your husband didn't contact you for those five days and you didn't think there was a problem?'

'My husband's work is such that many a times he would be away working for long hours, days, sometimes weeks. I assumed..'

'It is best not to assume anymore, Mrs Saxena.'

She was quiet as she poured the tea into a mug and handed it to him.

'Thank you.' Steam rose, and he placed the mug on the countertop.

'Your husband was seen talking to workers fixing the exterior wall of the Taj. Do you know anything about that?'

'No.'

'What about his contacts? Do you know anyone he was in touch with regularly?'

'No.'

'Did he tell you when he would be back?'

'No.'

Manzil's answers were becoming abrupt.

'Did he say he was working on a special assignment? Anything that might have been risky?' Yadav noticed the newspaper haphazardly covering some papers. He pushed it aside and noticed the grainy photos of the Taj.

She looked at him as if he was intruding on her privacy. 'He worked on many different projects at the same time,' she defended. Clever answer. Yadav smiled and then picked up his mug of tea, 'Must be cool enough.' He sipped and then gulped the rest. He placed the empty mug in the washbasin. 'Your maid is taking very long in the bathroom, isn't she?' He said, looking out of the window.

'Yes,' Manzil shrugged. 'Lots of clothes.'

'These photos aren't very good for a professional. Were these taken by your husband?'

Manzil hesitated, 'No. It belongs to a friend of his. Hoped he could do a better job.'

'I see,' Yadav said. He realised she wasn't going to reveal her husband's secret mission. Maybe she was really clueless, but there was something not quite right. He didn't want to intimidate her. She was facing a tough situation. Better to befriend her. Not become an enemy.

'Mrs Saxena, I am very sorry about what happened. We have to do this sort of questioning to rule out any other possibility of foul play. Your husband was famous – people know him by his work. We have to be sure this wasn't anything other than just an unlucky day for him,' he said with as much softness he could muster into his voice.

She just nodded. But there was a glint of a tear forming in her eye. Yadav smiled uncomfortably, he knew how to handle the hardiest criminal but he didn't know how to handle sobbing females. It was time to leave.

He placed his card on the counter, it had his contact numbers. 'If there is anything you need or if there is any problem . . . call me. Any time. It's my direct line and mobile number. This city is a tough place for a woman by herself. Be careful.' Inspector Yadav gave her an assuring smile, as opposed to the stern expression he had maintained throughout. He hoped to put her at ease.

'Thank you very much,' Manzil said almost in relief.

Yadav headed towards the door. 'By the way, do you know what the initials 'MB' stand for? I found a small piece of crumpled paper in your husband's trouser pocket with MB and a smudged phone number on it, any ideas who this person is?' He didn't miss the sudden look of recognition flit across her face. She knew. For a moment, she seemed to want to tell him something, hesitated, then she looked at him and shook her head.

'No, I don't know,' she said, as she opened the front door for him.

He stepped out of her apartment, pressed the button for the lift, and before she could shut the door, he added, 'Be careful. And remember you can call me anytime. Day or night.'

She nodded, trying to smile. The lift door opened and noticing the uniform, the liftman jumped up and offered a broad salaam.

Yadav nodded.

Inspector Yadav did not look conspicuous as he popped chana into his mouth from a coned paper holder. He waited by the paanwala's shop diagonally across the road from Manzil's building, next to the bus stop. He watched people enter and exit but he wasn't interested in the residents. He paced. Fifteen minutes later, he smiled. Yadav knew he could trust his instincts. He saw Ramu exit the building and hurry towards the bus stop.

Deva's minion involved in this matter – this must be big.

Chapter 7

Delhi

A product of the British Raj, the Indian Institute of Archaeology (IIA) came under the aegis of the Department of Culture and was responsible for archaeological studies and preservation of heritage sites. However, a lack of funds had turned it into nothing more than a record-keeper of the many ancient monuments dotting the country. The employees were easy to bribe and archaeologists ready to sell any precious discovery to the highest bidder.

The headquarters of the IIA was a dilapidated six-storey building with three broken windows. The glass had been patched up after a few goondas had thrown stones at the IIA office. They were protesting against the institute's discovery of ancient Hindu writing, almost imperceptible, on a stone wall of a mosque fifty kilometres north of Ahmedabad. The protesters claimed it was fake.

The patched up windows were a constant reminder that Indian archaeology was dangerous business.

Director-General Rizvi slapped his table with the palm of his hand, before he stood up to pace restlessly. There was just a square foot of visible space on his wooden table. The rest was covered with thick files packed with protruding papers. On the furthest end of the table, where assistant director-general, Dass sat, Rizvi's tarnished brass nameplate sat right next to the miniature Indian flag balanced on a plastic stand.

'Did you read the news report about an unidentified body by the Yamuna? Coincidence or what? Just when there's repair work at the Taj, people become obsessed with the rumours. As if we are trying to hide something. The back wall of the Taj has been vandalised countless times. Damn it, we can't even afford extra security.' Rizvi complained.

He paced like a caged lion, unable to take even three strides across his small office. A narrow bookcase was wedged between the corner wall and the window. It was teeming with books on archaeology and heritage. Besides these, the lowest level of his shelf was packed with hard-backs on management; it was located close to the ground almost as if he was embarrassed by his need for such books.

'Now this dancer Kanyadevi is spilling her earnings in our direction and in return, expects information about our discoveries. Who the hell is she anyway? Is she spying on us? Is she selling us out to foreigners? We already have to answer to the government and now her!'

The Ministry of Culture had allocated a pathetic amount of money to the Institute – Rizvi wondered how the seventy thousand ancient monuments would ever be protected or maintained with it. Presently, to protect as many as three thousand monuments, they could only afford gatemen to watch two monuments at a time. How foolproof was that? And they couldn't even afford a damn security guard, just a paan-spitting watchman. Rizvi could only guess that the heritage sites were being plundered, or worse still, desecrated by derelicts.

Dass sat across his boss's work table and sipped the strongly brewed tea, India's answer to espresso coffee, served in tiny glasses. He observed his boss's emotional outburst, Rizvi's ears turning a bright red and his flushed cheeks slowly acquiring a hint of rouge. Dass had known him for fifteen years and over the years, their professional relationship had developed from mutual respect to friendship. Rizvi was beginning to show signs of ageing, his receding hairline and expanding midriff made him look inefficient, as if he was lazy and sat around all day drinking tea. But Dass knew better. His boss supervised, walking up and down the corridors, checking every workplace, followed up on projects and current dig sites. He was mentally and physically agile, and as a result overstressed. The bottle of antacids were more than just table decor.

'Don't worry. The reparation work of the plinth wall has been completed, we poured cement over the timber support beams to make sure it stays in place and to keep away snoops drilling holes and spreading conspiracy theories. We've faced a lot of bad press recently. The dead body is only going to add fuel to the fire burning in the hearts of fanatics and treasure hunters.' Dass withdrew a white perfectly ironed handkerchief from his pocket and polished his glasses. He hesitated then continued, 'But if you want, we can spy on this female and check what she is up to, I can arrange it with Rana.'

Rizvi looked at him incredulously; his eyes riveted. Red veins criss-crossed the whites of his eyes. 'Spy on her? If she finds out, she will cause a scandal,' he said, his voice rising in pitch. 'Don't we already have enough to deal with? Government cronies are breathing down our necks – they don't want unrest. They have their politics, to please everyone on their agenda. They ask us to shut up and now when a pretty female dancer waltzes in, they want us to open our mouths and spill our guts?' Rizvi was behind his desk and leaned forward as spittle splattered white specks on the leather pen stand with the Air-India logo on it. He sat down heavily in his seat.

Dass didn't speak immediately but when he did, his voice was calm. 'Think about it this way, Rizvi.We might be able to use her to our advantage. She might understand our predicament and be our voice to the government. You and I know that the Taj is trouble. Even though we officially announced that the book about the Taj, claiming the mausoleum was full of hidden treasure and idols of another culture, was a pack of lies and the evidence fabricated, the monument has caught the fancy of the press. Any small inference with the Taj seems to explode... expand into something else,' he said, raising his eyebrows meaningfully.

Rizvi swivelled his chair and picked up the glass paper weight from his desk. 'The government has asked us to keep a distance from the monument. But how can we disclaim any rumours unless we seal off the Taj, perform tests, and invite specialists in epigraphy, numismatics and allow for an objective conclusion. We need the government's sanction,' he said, pointing his thumb at the president's picture hanging on the wall behind his desk. It was between the picture of Mahatma Gandhi and the geographical map of India.

'Yes and they are going to hand this to us on a silver platter – just before elections. That's a joke,' Dass grinned. 'I can imagine the leader of the Congress party orating about equality and secularism to all castes and religions while here we are busy questioning what lies beneath the Taj. That's going to make them look like hypocrites.'

Rizvi smiled. 'Yes, as if politicians don't habitually lie through their teeth now! But politics aside, we have to focus on all the other monuments and heritage sites that need our immediate attention. As far as the Taj is concerned, we have to, maintain it, conserve and protect it.'

'The "pretty female dancer" might be just the touch we need. In fact, she is the epitome of our country – devi-like, with no specific religious inclination, and exports our culture abroad.'

Rizvi looked exhausted, dark circles around his eyes; obviously he wasn't getting enough sleep. He grabbed the bottle of antacids, twisted the top and shook it until two tablets fell into the palm of his hand. He popped it in his mouth and chewed. 'Dass, we have to learn marketing and to sell the importance of our Institute otherwise there is no way of protecting all those heritage sites. Don't you think it's time for us to get some respect for what we do here?'

He took one sip of his cold tea and pushed it aside.

'It's not a new situation. Everything costs money and we need more funding. The recruits need training. And there aren't enough experienced diggers around. Besides that, we need new equipment. We have asked for money a dozen times but received a pittance.'

Dass smiled, 'You know what, the countless sadhus in ashrams all over India preaching the spiritual texts market their religions through the media, and know how to sell themselves. We should learn from them.'

'Unless you want to consider hiring a publicist – costs additional bundles of money - for Indian archaeology and heritage, we have a job to do as protectors of our heritage sites.' Saying this Rizvi gulped down a glass of water.

Dass had a faraway look. 'Maybe it's time to change. I've heard rumours of the far-reaching effects of a non-governmental organisation...'

Rizvi looked at him sharply, 'NGO? Does what?'

'Its main objective is to protect the country from interfering dons and self-proclaimed self-righteous bigots. Some powerful businessmen, educators, intellectuals, and well-connected Indians are members and offer funds and support. This outfit has a large group of supporters from colleges and universities. Some trained by retired colonels to fight, if necessary. They are quite widespread with volunteers in every village. They are not afraid of underground organisations. Their sole objective is the preservation of historical facts and archaeological treasures. And, more recently, the evasion of religious conflict.'

'That is a fairytale. I've heard about it. I don't think it could be that powerful,' Rizvi grimaced.

'Its popularity is increasing. I have a reliable source, Rana has told me about their meetings at certain locations. In fact, the rich and famous are promoting the NGO. And I think the dancer is part of this organisation,' Dass said. 'I believe there is more to her than meets the eye.'

'So, this is good, isn't it?' Fingertips joined together, Rizvi eyed his assistant.

'It might be. I'm not sure. We need to find out more. Our work here is being compromised by lack of support. Maybe it's time for outside help. We need to work as scientists – objectively. We've had too many skewed ideas from thugs who add fuel to the fire of religious sects.' Dass said frankly.

'You are right. We can't handle all this ourselves,' Rizvi drummed his fingers on the table. 'We are suppressing our own heritage, there is so much to show the world and yet we hide because bigots are going to kill each other.'

'Rizvi, we have to stand our ground,' Dass said, trying to pacify him. 'We will be objective and discuss facts not fabrications: and rumours should not be given any attention.'

The intercom buzzed. 'Yes?' Rizvi asked, pressing the speaker phone.

'Superintendant archaeologist Urvashi on the line from Ajmer, sir. She says it's urgent.' The secretary's metallic tone insisted.

'Put her through.'

He picked up the handset. Rizvi's greeting was abruptly interrupted by the shocked expression on his face. He looked at Dass and raised his eyebrows. Dass waited for his boss to finish. He was pacifying the caller and offered to send more people to help. He specifically said more men. Dass smiled. He knew what was going on. Women as archaeologists were still not readily accepted.

'Same stupid problem?'

Rizvi nodded. '"A female archaeologist faces aggravation and insults from the local panchayat". That's what the newspapers should publish. Not the tiring rubbish on sectarian conflict. Urvashi is one of our best. It's frustrating for her to work with people who have no respect for her, just because she is a woman.You are sending some men?'

'Yes. I will arrange it right away.' Dass stood up to leave.

'Let's try to do what is right for the IIA. Especially where the Taj is concerned. We need to put this matter to rest once and for all,' Rizvi suggested.

Dass headed for the door. 'We can try. We need time, money and resources. Many monuments pre-existing the Mughal reign and not of Muslim origin became part of the Muslim heritage during the Mughal rule – the Hindu influence on architecture cannot be dismissed.'

Rizvi sighed. 'The artisans hired during the Mughal rule were Hindu, therefore the influence would be visible in some carvings and for this we are facing unnecessary bigotry.'

'In those days, precious stones and gold were used to decorate monuments, it was part of the culture, and there's no hidden treasure. It's been looted over the years.' Dass added.

Rizvi raised his hand, 'Our duty is to protect and maintain the archaeologically rich cultural heritage of India. If we get involved in the age-old sectarian squabbles, there will be no end to the problem.

Dass smiled, 'I think this NGO may be our valuable ally. Rana is a good man. Like he has done before, he will keep an eye and keep us informed.'

Dass was a tall man, disciplined by the army, and three wars after India's Independence. He had learnt very early on that emotions got in the way of objective decision-making and he didn't think the Taj was such a big issue – it just carried too much emotional baggage. The whole love angle was the reason for its fairytale and people always liked to destroy fairy tales.

Chapter 8

Liege, Belgium

It was Kanyadevi's twentieth performance, but her first in a foreign country. The stage was lit, and the backdrop was an ancient Indian temple. It was touching to see that the foreigners had taken so much effort to recreate an authentic atmosphere.

Kanyadevi's heart beat wildly, and she felt the familiar thrill of facing an audience. As she waited in the wings, Kanyadevi checked that her long braided hair, intertwined with fake jasmine flowers, was securely pinned to her waist belt. She didn't want it twirling around her neck when she performed. Her eyes were deeply lined with kohl, to highlight the expressions of the dance. She pressed the thick red bindi between her eyebrows.

Kanyadevi had practised and perfected every movement of the Bharatnatyam dance before she had performed her initiation dance. A two-and-a half hour public recital. She still recalled that first time, and the feeling was pure ecstasy. Dance was her life and her religion. Her dance teacher, her guru, had taught her the importance of connecting with the audience. 'Be absorbed in your dance, and yet be aware of the presence of others and let your emotions touch their souls. That is the secret of a good performer.' Kanyadevi mentally prayed to her guru.

The president of the Indian Expat Association stepped up to the podium. She was a silver-haired lady and wore a cream silk saree with a thick gold border. 'Please welcome the renowned Bharatnatyam danseuse from India, Ms Kanyadevi. Trained in the ancient art form by the distinguished guru Aishwaryadevi, an expert in classical dance form, Kanyadevi has performed at several major dance festivals in India. She has been awarded many titles including the prestigious Padma Shri and recently received the Central Sangeet Natak Academy Award. Kanyadevi has contributed her own concepts to the traditional style. Through her experimentation and innovations, she has produced and choreographed several highly appreciated dance dramas. Her passion for ancient relics and fine arts has focused her attention towards India's archaeological heritage. She is actively involved with the Indian Institute of Archaeology to promote and preserve the country's ancient cultural heritage. Performing for the first time in Europe, please welcome one of India's finest artiste, Kanyadevi.' The audience welcomed the dancer with an enthusiastic applause. The stage was set, lights dimmed and the musicians ready.

Kanyadevi closed her eyes briefly and then touched the stage, offering her respects, before she stepped on it. Gracefully, she moved towards the centre, bowed low and performed the namaskaram.

The musicians' tabla beat, harmonium notes, accompanied by a raaga singer and the band of bells strapped to Kanyadevi's ankles were the only sounds in the auditorium where an audience of two hundred watched, entranced by Kanyadevi's thumping feet and rhythmic movement of her hands, the mudras. Kanyadevi focused her thoughts on her expressions, and her body moved fluidly to express the yearning for her lover.

The stage was decorated with flowers and diyas. The huge fake stone statues displayed on either side, were as beautifully designed as the originals in the temples of India. Kanyadevi moved to the rhythm carved in stone. Her arms curled like a snake, and then across her chest. They moved above her head; then folded low at the waist. She swirled back, and then forward. Her hands were on her hips, her eyes expressed emotions, and her head, facing forward, shifted from side to side.

As the beat changed, instinctively she let her body sway in tune with the earth, the Gods and her soul.

In her mind, Kanyadevi was dancing in the darkness of an ancient temple. She heard the bells chime gently, and in her mind's eye, the fires clung to the wicks desperately making the dancers on the wall move as if in a frenzy and Kanyadevi moved with them to the Tantric dance. Her feet floated, seemingly above the ground.

Kanyadevi tuned out reality, and sunk in the depths of her mind. Nothing else mattered.

This is what complete peace was all about. This was what the saints preached and the sadhus searched. Aligning the mind to a focused intensity, completely absorbed, she understood the meaning of bliss, the joy of no joy, detachment from all attachments. And Kanyadevi experienced this ecstasy with each dance performance.

As the rhythm of the tabla increased in tempo, Kanyadevi, slave to the music, eyes closed, intuitively made her way through the imaginary stone temple; the fire dancing in the oil lamps cast shadows all along the stage walls. The stone dancers seemed alive. Their faces in ecstasy, pure love, and magnetic rhythm moved the dancers' feet. In that aura, Kanyadevi felt her feet move to music as if possessed. She could sense it all, in every structural pose; she could hear the music and feel the energy like those undulating statues. She felt her heart soar to new heights, her body light; there were no sorrows, no worries. Nothing.

And then, it was over. Palpitating heart and breathing heavily, Kanyadevi crashed down to the present. She stopped, her body struggling to stay still in a closing mudra.

Two seconds later, the burst of applause filled the hall like a thunderstorm. Kanyadevi joined her hands in a namaskar, smiled and bowed repeatedly, facing every part of the oval hall. The minister of culture, the Indian high commissioner, and a few other dignitaries in the front row stood up. The applause grew louder as the rest of the audience followed suit and offered Kanyadevi a standing ovation. This time she waved to her audience, bowing again with a flourish.

Back in her changing room, Kanyadevi faced the lightbulb-framed mirror to start the process of removing her makeup, the heavy jewellery and stitched costume that took over an hour to put together. Kanyadevi had spent years learning the Bharatnatyam. It was a lot of hard work and required hours of practice of even the smallest movement. But she loved every minute. It was her destiny. And it helped dim the memories of her past...

Abandoned at birth, luck had everything to do with her survival. Kanyadevi believed that if her fisherfolk parents had not found her at the rocky edge of the southern-most tip of the Indian continent, Kanyakumari, she would never have survived the ocean's increasing tide. She was named after the town where she was found.

Few years later, when Kanyadevi discovered that she was not a fisherwoman's daughter, she understood why she hated the smell of fish, even though she had tried very hard to accept it. She also wished her parents had let her die.

Kanyadevi didn't have to be the incarnation of a goddess every full moon night. Her mother, to make more money, would dress her up as a Devi, which she looked like with her fair complexion and oval face. Villagers would come to her for blessings. They would kneel, or prostrate before her. Some would weep and wail their sad state. Kanyadevi felt helpless, she wasn't a goddess she wanted to tell them, just a little girl. But her mother would beat her after if she didn't act or talk as she had been taught. Hard-earned money came pouring in from distant villages when word spread that a Devi was in their midst.

When she turned thirteen and had her first period, they couldn't use her as a devi anymore – she was now considered soiled, unclean and impure to bless others. Her 'parents' were griefstricken and seemed to blame her for their poverty. 'You must work like we do. You must also find a way to make money, after all that we have done for you, we saved your life, you owe us,' they had said. Then one day 'Uncle' came to visit. He said he would take her to the city and find her a good job there. Kanyadevi nodded eagerly, the man's wide smile and roving eyes were discomforting, but she agreed to leave with him. He promised to send money to her parents. He had brought a big box of cashewnut milk-cake for her and her family. And her parents were very happy, they also received a thick packet of money. They spoke to her lovingly and wished her well.

The day before a full moon night, she left her hometown. With Uncle, Kanyadevi got on the rickety bus to Chennai. Next morning, when they arrived at the city bus station, Uncle woke her up roughly saying, 'you lazy bitch, I spent five thousand rupees to get you here, don't think I won't wring every paisa out of you,' he said with a viciousness that made her cry. Kanyadevi should have run away right there and then. Each time she thought about that precise moment in time, she felt a deep burning fire of regret, of not following her instincts to run and hide. Instead, she had stood next to him, trusting him, while he flagged down a taxi. That night he raped her. Kanyadevi remembered it clinically, she could look back now without getting emotional, earlier the memory would make her violently ill. She recalled how much she had fought back, how much she had screamed for every God to save her, how much she wanted to go back to being a fisherman's daughter. He slapped her a few times and then there was no strength left in her. Eventually she resigned to her fate, she was nothing but a ragdoll. 'Uncle' let his friend join him later. The man kept a knife by his side, within reach, as if taunting her to take it.

That day was etched in her memory for ever. After he had his way with her, he carved a letter on her thigh. She was branded for life, he had laughed. She couldn't forget the insult. The mark on her leg was now a pink knobbly scar, but it was a constant reminder of her bitter past.

Kanyadevi squeezed her eyes shut to block out the image from her head – but it never went away, and she knew it never would. The mark on her thigh ensured her past stayed with her.

The next three years were a haze of men who came and went. When the police finally raided the little outhouse, she managed to escape from a backdoor, and Uncle was jailed. Kanyadevi didn't run away. She knew where to hide and how to keep away from the eyes of her Uncle's cronies. She stayed on different platforms of a railway station until her Uncle was released from jail.

Three days later, Uncle was found dead in a gutter with a screwdriver in his eye and his head bashed in with a hammer.

Kanyadevi ran away, took one of the trains from Chennai to Puducherry and knew the first place she would choose to work would be the house of God. Simply because He abandoned her, she wanted to be in His face to show Him what had been done to her, what she had done in revenge, and how He never cared for her. The cathedral was a perfect place, and the dance academy next to it was an added bonus.

The first time that Kanyadevi ever experienced true bliss was during one of her dance practices. She recalled the most exhilarating feeling of peace, the rhythm of the beat, her body in tune with the music and a oneness within her soul. She didn't hate herself or the world anymore – dance was her salvation.

When nightmares led her to sleepless nights, she would leave the cathedral grounds and take a walk along the moonlit beach. It soothed her scarred mind, helped her to find solace and acceptance within her and as a result reconciliation with her situation.

On one of her lonely explorations along the seaside, she found the ruins of an ancient temple, She wandered inside, and discovered an ancient artifact wedged in the far corner of the sanctum sanctorum. She still had the biscuit-thin stone plate with Sanskrit letters engraved on it. She believed it was her lucky charm. A friend from the IIA had tested it and discovered that the stone plate was at least a thousand years old. The words engraved on it were from the Taitreya Upanishad, the ancient texts that predated the Vedas. It said: '*Yato vach nivartante. Aprapya manasa saha. Anandam brahmana vidvan. Na bibheti kutashchaneti*'. (*He who knows the Bliss of Brahman, from which all words return without reaching It, together with the mind, is no more afraid of anything.*) The meaning indicated the infinite possibilities of the mind: speech cannot define, nor can the mind feel, nor the intellect completely comprehend the Self which is the eternal. She felt calmed by its presence in her life. It was a sign that whatever she had experienced, and whatever she had become by her sheer willpower, had sculpted her to be a stronger person.

The stone tablet was locked away in Kanyadevi's vault. Since then she had became a collector of ancient sculptures and her active connection, including some donations to the IIA, had helped provide her with information about different archaeological sites.

With no real roots of her own, it was as if she was obsessed in creating her roots in the ancient culture of India. She returned to her hometown, Kanyakumari and bought a lavish bungalow. Someday the memories would wash away.

As she gained fame, and her passion for ancient Indian art became public knowledge, she was invited to join an NGO. When she attended her first Onyx meeting, Kanyadevi knew then that she was destined for bigger responsibilities in life.

There was a knock on her door. Kanyadevi snapped out of her reverie. 'Come in,' she said.

It was Raghu, Kanyadevi's agent. He wore plastic-framed glasses and a broad smile. Clutching his black bag under arm, he breezed in kissing his fingertips repeatedly, complimenting her performance. 'Madamji, you were superb. Even the *angrez* have appreciation for the great Indian dance. I have received so many offers – a very good one from London, to perform in the presence of the royal family. I can arrange it for you right away.'

Raghu had the energy of a buzzing bee. He was enthusiastic to the point where his unshakeable optimism was a welcome balm to her tendency towards melancholy. He chatted about how everyone in the audience loved her and how much Bharatnatyam was appreciated. He thrived on the flattery as if it was meant for him and not her. Kanyadevi enjoyed the adulation; it was gratifying to know that her years of practice and self-discipline brought pleasure to many. She was in control of her happiness, not letting it take control over her and make her a slave to it. She maintained a sense of calm within herself; a kind of detachment. And the dance itself was a path that would heal her soul.

'Raghu, what would I do without you. It is all your effort and hard work that has brought me here.' She said as she wiped the paint from her face.

He seemed to swell with pride. 'Thank you, Madamji. We still have plenty to do. There are so many wonderful cities in Europe to consider. But for now, I must leave you to rest. Tomorrow we dine with the minister of culture himself. He has extended a special invitation. I will see you later, Madamji.' Raghu grinned broadly. With a sprightly step, he opened the door and was about to exit when a delivery man blocked his way with a huge bouquet of tulips.

'Wah!' he exclaimed, 'Madamji, flowers for you!' He cried, signing the sheet and taking the bunch. He placed it on a stool next to Kanyadevi.

'Who is it from?' she asked, glancing at the beautiful flowers, while continuing to cleanse her face. The makeup was thick and the black kohl was the most difficult to remove. Kanyadevi smoothed the cotton on her face, using plenty of moisturiser to remove the makeup and protect the skin around her eyes.

'Strange,' Raghu said, holding the small card close to his spectacles. 'It says from "O" with best wishes, and congratulations. "*Ek raaz hai, ek tamanna hai, koi baat hai jo kehna hai. Kal milenge*". Is that a new Hindi love song, Madamji? Looks like you have a big fan.'

Kanya wiped her fingers swiftly. 'Give me that,' she said sharply. She read the card and immediately understood the message behind the lines. *There is a secret, a desire, there is something I must tell you. We meet tomorrow.*

'Raghu, I need to get back home. Please arrange the first flight out tonight.'

'But Madamji...' he stopped when he saw the steely look in her eyes.

Chapter 9

Kanyakumari, South India

Rana Singh watched the woman's house from across the quiet road. He sat alone in the white van waiting for the call; the voice of authority that would give him further instructions on whether to spy or confront. For now, he had to keep track of people entering and exiting the dark bungalow. Inside the compound, three coconut trees stood like sentinels guarding the house. The street was isolated except for mongrels that sporadically interrupted the calm of the still night. No one passed his vehicle, the dim street lights might be the reason why people didn't step out of their homes. It was a ghostly stretch of road with bungalows on both sides. On the other side of the road, through a large window, he could see a family of seven sitting at the dining table. Rana wanted to get out of the van and stretch his legs, but the residents might take note.

Rana sighed and stared at the mobile phone. He knew he would have to act quickly. He felt the carved handle of the knife in its sheath strapped to his waist. It was a gift from his grandfather and Rana carried it with pride. He never had a need to use it, yet. And hopefully, never would.

Rana was not told why Kanyadevi had to be monitored and he did not question those who had the authority to give him money when he needed it, under the table or above. He was smart enough to keep his mouth shut.

The waters of the oceans crashing against the rocks were audible in the distance. Three bodies of water: the Arabian Sea, the Bay of Bengal and the Indian Ocean met together at the southern-most tip of the peninsula. They blended easily, no one could tell the difference between the waters when they collided together. Indian history was the same, who could tell the difference when ancient art was steeped with various cultures. It was the empires that stood mighty and strong, while their kings ruled with passion.

They fought in the past, and now his bosses fought to hide the past.

Rana twirled his moustache. He didn't need to; his upper lip did not sport a long curved 'soup-strainer' moustache like the Rajputs. It was an unconscious habit picked up from his grandfather, the royal guard of Udaipur palace. Rana had spent more time with him than he had with his parents. As a child, seated on his grandfather's lap, he listened to stories of a bygone era when kings and queens were revered as gods.

Rana was proud of his heritage; he was as brave and as loyal as the Rajput warriors from long ago. His baseball cap hid his curly black hair. A turban would have suited him better. Hooded brows highlighted his intense charcoal eyes. His cheekbone and jawline seemed to have been chiselled by talented artisans.

Rana was a descendant of the brave men who had died fighting for the honour of their country. He prided himself on his ability to withstand the harshest elements of nature, the extreme desert heat of his land, while his bosses complained. Bred on wheat rotis and pure ghee, Rana, the third child, was the son of the earth. And he would die protecting his motherland. He wanted to join the army but had fallen short of the mandatory height requirements.

Rana worked for the IIA. The Institute comprised a mixed breed of archaeologists, heads of department and research students. He assisted the assistant director Dass. Rana was asked to keep an eye on particular sites, and the reaction in the surrounding area. When land was being dug up, people got curious, and especially more so when it was near a religious structure. And Dass liked to know what was going on before the press got wind.

Alongside the others, Rana toiled on the earth searching for ancient relics and travelled to do fieldwork. He had been part of expeditions from the foot of the Himalayas to the centre of the Thar desert. Across the length and breadth of India, he analysed, marvelled and questioned as much as they did.

Out on dig sites with a team of archaeologists, Rana had felt the texture of the earth change as he dug deeper and deeper. While archaeologists studied the objects, he was fascinated by it like it were a treasure hunt. Each mound of earth had a story that told of spilled blood and sacrifice. The archaeologists with their notebooks, pens, compasses and instruments whispered that Indian history had many untold secrets. They talked about it in hushed tones around campfires, as if the ghosts of those they spoke about would return from the graves to hunt them down.

They didn't understand that secrets were meant to be just that – *secrets* – and were best left buried.

Some ancient recoveries from the digs were priceless beyond words. They were lovingly carved and created. The hands of many slave artisans had been cut off so they would never be able to create such beauty again.

Rana knew Shah Jahan had done just that, after the construction of the Taj Mahal.

Lately he had sensed that his bosses had been extra careful over any sensitive piece of information related to the Taj. The secret seemed far worse than the rumours about Fatehpur Sikri, the fifteenth century deserted ancient city built by Mughal Emperor Akbar and Shah Jahan's grandfather. The great emperor had built it with dedication and had lived there for fourteen years. Suddenly he abandoned it and never lived there again for the rest of his life. Rana knew that it wasn't because of inadequate water supply, the reason that had been cited by historians; it was because of a spirit that had cursed the king. But that detail has never been mentioned in history books. Fatehpur Sikri with the beautiful gardens, grand hall and the tomb of the Sufi saint Chisti was nothing but a ghost city.

Rana's cellphone rang. The tune of the national anthem. He answered right away.

'Sir, there has been no activity since six p.m. today,' he told his boss.

'Good. There is no one in the house right now; she is in Europe. Tomorrow she has a meeting. Make sure you install devices in every part of the house.'

Rana nodded, 'Yes, sir.'

'Be careful.'

'Yes, I understand,' Rana said, 'I will do as you say. You can trust me, sir.'

Chapter 10

Kanyakumari

Rana darted across the road. Up close Kanyadevi's bungalow didn't look so large; it was centred on a large concrete compound with a rectangular carpet of green grass in one corner.

In one speedy move Rana scaled over the wall and crouched low. He waited. No dogs attacked him. Above, the three coconut trees swayed majestically, their leaves rustling hypnotically in the still night. Moonlight flickered through.

Rana stayed alert. He didn't hear any alarm go off nor the warning shout of a night watchman. He inched slowly towards the back of the house. A guava tree in the corner was heavy with fruit. Next to it a small concreted square structure housed the tulsi plant, the smell of sweet jasmine incense lingered. Rana darted to the side window. Easily, he unscrewed the hinge and pushed inwards. The opening was just large enough for Rana to snake his way through.

The living room was dark. Within minutes, Rana's eyes adjusted and he hurried towards a low table, an eye-catching piece at the centre of the Persian carpet. The coffee table was a Rajasthani engraved wooden door covered with glass and balanced on four elephant-shaped legs. The dancer must have paid a huge amount of money for it. He shook his head, he could have just picked one up for free, from one of the many sand and red clay homes in Chittorgarh, his village. Rana attached the tiny microphone to the vase, a small centrepiece on the table. Swiftly he moved through the rooms located at the four corners of the hall. Deeper into the back of the house was the dining room. There was an oval table made of darkwood, with eight high-backed chairs. The wood had been polished that day. The waxy petroleum smell was perceptible in the air. There were sheets of paper, face down, on the table. Rana picked them up. The words were indistinct in the darkness; he folded the sheet and put it in his pocket.

This was where the meeting was most likely to occur, he hazarded a guess. Ideally he would have preferred to stick the fly-shaped listening device in the middle of the table. But there was no centrepiece. Unsure where to fit the microphone, he decided on the wood panelled wall, closest to the table. He fitted it right next to the frame of M.F. Hussain's painting of naked featureless dancing women. Rana completed his task and exited the house.

He didn't see a slim camera fitted in the corner of the dining area that had caught him in the act.

Chapter 11

Kanyakumari

Dr. Annie Besant is one of those foreigners who inspired the love of the country among Indians. She declared in 1918 in her paper New India*: 'I love the Indian people as I love none other, and... my heart and my mind... have long been laid on the altar of the Motherland'. Annie Besant, born of Irish parents in London on 1 October 1847, made India her home from November, 1893. Dr. Besant, said Mahatma Gandhi, awakened India from her deep slumber. Before she came to India, Dr. Besant passed through several phases of life - housewife, propagator of atheism, trade unionist, feminist leader and Fabian Socialist.*

Dr. Besant started the Home Rule League in India to fight for the freedom of the country and to revive the country's glorious cultural heritage. She attended the 1914 session of the Indian National Congress and presided over it in 1917. An orator and writer with poetic temperament, Dr. Besant was a veritable tornado of power and passion. By her eloquence, firmness of convictions and utter sincerity she attracted some of the best minds of the country for the national cause. She was largely responsible for the upbringing of the world renowned philosopher J. Krishnamurti. Dr. Besant died in 1933.

After independence, the Home Rule League was revived and renamed the Onyx to carry on the work of freeing India from the stranglehold of religious dogma and communal violence. The renaming was purposely made to eliminate any religious connotations or political associations. Those who belonged to this group idolised the concept of unity in India. The O symbolises this unity.

Rana read the first half of the paper with interest. So this is what the dancer was involved with. His respect for her increased a hundred fold. The organisation would do what the government was trying to do in the last sixty years since independence. Yes, this is exactly what India needed. It was a worthy cause and he would gladly serve an organisation that was single-mindedly passionate about a united India. Rana smiled, he liked the sound of that – united India – he repeated it until he felt the strength of the words in his heart.

He continued to read:

The One India Week was instigated by Onyx. Saraswati Sen, a professor of anthropology, suggested the idea and the rest of the Onyx members followed it within their own industry. It worked. What started as a small movement by youth groups of the Delhi University where both Professors Gupta and Sen were teaching, developed into a mass-market advert of unity of the country. Noted film producer Satish Kumar was responsible for the promotions. The domino effect resulted in a bhangra hit number by a popular music director of the film industry. India idolised the film industry and the movies were the best way to change perceptions of the masses.

The universities and then schools around India picked up on the idea and followed it up with a 'Love thy neighbour' slogan. Soon there was a 'bhai-bhai' cult that developed in the slums of Mumbai.

But Onyx knew that these kind of messages had to reach the grassroots - rural India, where the recruitment of extremists took place and young boys came to the cities to cause havoc, working for sect lords, who used them for their purpose. There was so much more that needed to be done.

Rumours existed that the president of India was at one time a member of Onyx, but no one knew for sure. The elite eight didn't belong to any one religious group, but represented the wisdom of all the major religions. They believed in a sole purpose to counteract potential conflict and violence. Their motive was preservation of life and protection of valuable secrets that could affect national security.

'I salute you and your cause,' Rana murmured. He picked up his mobile phone and dialled Dass's number. This news couldn't wait.

Dass answered on the first ring. 'What's wrong?'

'Nothing.' Rana responded enthusiastically, 'I found some papers, looked like a report of the work of an NGO called Onyx.' He explained the contents of the papers he had found.

'The group must have got some information. It might be about the Taj Mahal. The members of Onyx must have contacted Kanyadevi for an urgent meeting.' Dass guessed. And then he added, 'Good work, Rana. This seems like positive news.'

Chapter 12

'I got your message, Satish. I came back from Europe just yesterday. Looks like our meeting has been compromised. We will meet at your outhouse. I will inform the others,' Kanyadevi said crisply. Her voice crackling over the phone.

'Understood,' Satish Kumar said, and hung up.

Satish Kumar, noted film producer's holiday residence on the outskirts of Mumbai, one of five around India, was the new venue for the meeting of the senior members of Onyx.

Khandala

The five men and three women were not seated in the opulently designed living room in black and white tones with splashes of red. Instead they were in the enclosed dining room, with high-back leather chairs. Known for his highly successful series of movies, Satish Kumar was an icon in the industry, a man with great influence and enough money in offshore accounts to retire in luxury.

'No servants?' Kanyadevi asked, sitting at the head of the polished rectangular rosewood table.

'None. I sent them away,' Satish replied. 'The coffee, tea and food is on the counter over there, help yourselves.' Waving his hand expansively, he indicated the long lacquer cabinet against the wall. Atop, a state-of-the-art coffee machine and a steel thermos containing brewed tea was set on a large tray. Porcelain cups and saucers lined another doily covered tray. And three fountain platters of sandwiches and other eatables decorated the rest of the long cabinet.

While the others helped themselves, Satish sat on Kanyadevi's left 'Guard dogs are in place. Alarm systems are functioning and security cameras are all on auto. The rooms have been searched for bugs. We are clean.'

'The last time this happened,' Kanyadevi said, ' our plans were foiled and the most famous face of our group,' she said turning to Satish, 'was severely judged in Bollywood as an extremist with connections with the underworld.'

'Have you got an idea who wants to sabotage us?' Saraswati Sen asked, placing her cup and plate on Kanyadevi's right. She sat down and proceeded to wear her wire-rimmed glasses. Her hair was pulled back and tied into a severe bun, stretching her skin so that her face looked wrinkle-free and her complexion flawless, making it difficult to gauge her age. Kanyadevi was sure she was the better part of fifty. Saraswati Sen's white saree bordered with red was immaculately wrapped around her body. Her pallu was starched and folded neatly over her shoulder. Saraswati was a professor of social anthropology and political studies, race and ethnic relations, and the feminist movement in India.

'Not sure who is spying on us, but I suspect the IIA. They are nervous about our actions which might put them in bad light. Not to mention the underworld dons out to shut us down if they even get a whiff of our existence.' Kanyadevi replied, brushing the thought aside, with the wave of her hand. 'Let's get on with the reason we are here.'

Seated next to Saraswati, Pritam Bhalla, editor of *Aaj Ki Khabar* had called the emergency meeting. Sliding a hand through his bald head, he began by saying, 'We have heard from a reliable source within the underground network about some new evidence.'

'Who's network?'

'Deva.'

He heard the sharp intake of breath.

'A scroll has been found inside the Taj Mahal, in one of the twenty-two hidden chambers. The reporter who discovered it has been killed. There are rumours of its contents, something exaggerated.' Pritam said grimly. The widely read Hindi newspaper had carried controversial news about many Indian heritage sites. Pritam gritted his lantern jaw suppressing his frank opinion of the situation. Scowling at the plate in front of him, he looked more like a pugilist than a tycoon, head of one of the largest newsgroups in India. 'I'm quite sure this is going to become a major source of conflict, and blood will spill on the streets. The odd thing is that Deva has handed the scroll to the widow, the dead reporter's wife. It must be some tactic to get her to authenticate the scroll. They think it will prove something.'

'Proof of what? Treasure? Seems odd that evidence is suddenly discovered after all these years,' Junaid Khan, a specialist on Islam in India, commented. A bright student, he advanced early in life. By the time he was in his forties, he was the associate director of the Department of Culture, Religion and World Affairs at the Delhi University. His specialty was religion and politics in Southeast Asia and the Muslim world, with specialisation on democratisation and violence. Junaid had published more than a dozen books, as well as several major policy reports for government and private foundations.

Junaid was well-liked in the intellectual circles and well-respected by the politicians. He had a way of discerning facts and creating a whole new perspective of any situation. And at the age of fifty-five, his words were worth their weight in gold. 'I'm sorry about how this may sound, but we must not assume this object is real,' he said, adjusting his square frames over his nose, 'The fact is that we have tried in many ways to solve the mystery of the hidden rooms, but we've never been allowed access despite numerous petitions to the Supreme Court and the government. The ease with which this was discovered makes me think that it's a lie and meant to cause an unnecessary ripple in society. One must not overlook the possibility that the scroll could have been planted to incite violence.'

'Yes, but we have to deal with this as if it is an authentic piece of evidence. People will believe what they see and hear, even if it is a fabrication,' Saraswati Sen said.

'Besides the scroll, some other documents and photographs are with the reporter's wife,' police commissioner Akash Sinha said. He grimaced as he sipped his coffee. He got another packet of sugar, tore it and spilled the contents in his cup. 'For some reason, Deva is ignorant of its value, or very smart. In this manner, he is off the hook if there is a bloodbath. Deva has one of his boys assigned to be with the widow at all times. Khanbaba's men are spying on the woman. This is a feud between the two rival dons, and the widow will be caught in the crossfire.'

'Actually, I'm surprised the reporter's wife hasn't gone to the press already, I would have imagined the first place she would have approached would be her husband's newspaper,' Pritam wondered. 'Any editor would jump at this news.'

'Pritam, you should keep track of this information through your contacts. I'm sure you will find out the moment the news hits the press.' Sinha suggested. 'As far as I know she has been quiet. She probably realises the significance of what she possesses.'

'She would probably want to have the scroll translated or analysed before attempting to meet the press.' Junaid pointed out.

'Translated?' Kanyadevi queried.

'If the scroll was from the Mughal period, during Shah Jahan's reign in the seventeenth century, it's most likely to be a Rajput language, Pahadi, or another dialect.'

Professor Gupta explained further, 'This is based on the theory about the origins of the Taj and how it was built, Shah Jahan received assistance from the Maharajah of Jaipur. But then again I could be wrong. I need to see the scroll before I can give any accurate information.'

The professor of Epigraphy and Ancient History, and expert on Aryan and Dravidian culture, Department of Classical Studies of

Delhi University was the eldest of the Onyx members and sat at the opposite end, facing Kanyadevi.

'We have to look at this as if it was the real deal,' Lavina Mascarenhas, the senior vice-president of the Asia division of a leading investment bank and author of books on colonial rule in India, said. 'We could be facing mass agitation at the wrongful portrayal of the Taj.'

'I suggest the best solution is to steal the scroll,' Akash Sinha said with a straight face, looking at Saraswati Sen and then at Gupta. 'You have contacts. The widow will most likely be coming to Delhi University to search for a translator. You can easily make a switch. This way we can keep the matter under control.'

'How can I switch something I have not seen before?' The professor asked.

'Then you have to convince her to give it to you.'

Kanyadevi knew it was imperative that the woman be contacted. 'We have to keep an eye on the widow. If the secret is out that she has some dangerous evidence linked to the Taj, then there are others who might be interested in what she holds.'

Sinha agreed. 'Inspector Yadav is keeping an eye on her. He has a deeper interest in this case. For him the reporter's death was not a botched robbery but a murder, he is looking for clues and keeping an eye on the woman's contacts. I will not give him the details but will mention that as a holder of the scroll, she is a pawn that will be used for certain destructive outcomes. He must protect her.'

'What if she doesn't bother to find a translator and just keeps the scroll and does nothing about it or worse still, destroys it?' Junaid asked.

There was silence.

'Then someone needs to advise her,' Kanyadevi said.

'How?'

The commissioner of police offered a solution. 'I will direct Yadav to give her Professor Gupta's contact details. In the sense, that if she needed to talk to a professor about her husband's work, it would be best to visit an expert.'

'That is a good idea,' the professor said, nodding. 'We will have control over the situation. Let us hope she doesn't go to the press first.'

'I will make it clear to as many newspaper editors as possible that if she approaches anyone of them, then whatever she has to offer is hands-off, and to contact me immediately,' Pritam suggested. 'But I cannot cover all grounds.'

Satish returned to his seat. He had jumped minutes earlier, edgy at the gravity of the situation, realising what it would take to tip it into a bloodbath. Heading to a glass countertop against the wall in the corner, he had asked, 'Who wants something stronger to drink?' Three of them accepted his offer. After preparing double pegs of whisky on the rocks for Akash, Pritam and Saraswati, he was now sipping his whisky as he ruminated aloud.

'What if... I have an idea that is totally...crazy... an out-of-the-box solution?'

'I hope its not the alcohol taking effect,' Junaid smiled.

Satish guffawed, sitting up. 'No, nothing like that. It's all about presenting the information in a certain way. We are facing a situation that may or may not result in violence. And since it's about the Taj, we have to address it in a more creative way,' Parag paused sipping his drink again. 'What if I make a movie on the subject? The general public is more open to ideas in movies than what comes out of politicians' mouths.'

'You are trivialising the seriousness of the scroll and its effect,' Lavina, the businesswoman of the year, said, she was facing the open window, as she puffed deeply on her cigarette. Her approach in the banking world earned her the reputation of a shrewd woman. She wore a neatly pressed blue suit and she probably had a dozen of the same in her closet. No one had seen her wear anything else. She appeared to have just stepped out of a board meeting. 'Your idea is not going to solve this age-old animosity that exists between ethnic groups. There is organised crime within these groups who get in on the act and add fuel to fire on both sides,' she said in a gritty voice. 'Even the One India Week lasted for that time: one week. They were back to simmering over petty matters the following week.' She turned to the window and exhaled.

Satish shrugged, 'I think it's an interesting approach – a better way of handle it on a mass scale.'

Junaid looked at them with concern, 'We have to keep an open mind. There is some truth in what Satish bhai is saying,' he said, gulping down his second can of Coke. 'I felt emotionally connected to the movie – *Munnabhai* – where a mob boss starts to follow the principles of Mahatma Gandhi. I think a lot of people connected with the sense of pride of their heritage. There was a sudden wave of what came to be known as Gandhigiri across the country. It was practically mass hysteria over Gandhian ideology. A kind of patriotism emerging from the grassroot, which is a healthy sign. The government promoted the movie, running it tax-free. Slum lords were putting up posters with Gandhi's words of wisdom. Students were helping old folks. Suddenly there was a surge of charitable acts, neighbours became more tolerant,'

'Yes, it did have an effect, but how long will it last?' Pritam asked exasperatedly. 'That's the problem. We take two steps forward and then, three steps back when communal violence breaks out.'

'And then the police gets blamed by both sides for unfair treatment,' Sinha added.

'For now, we are talking about the Taj, a world heritage site – anyone would be devastated by any new evidence. It will have a cascading effect. Next thing you know, all the ancient monuments and artifacts will be questioned. We don't want that kind of mass hysteria!' Lavina said.

'All this is getting quite pessimistic,' Kanyadevi said, 'We know the problem, and the effects, let's focus on finding a solution. And a movie is not the immediate solution. Frankly, we don't even know the contents of the scroll. It could be a simple order for marble from the makranas of Jaipur.'

Junaid was shaking his head, but before he could speak, Saraswati Sen raised her hand, 'Yes, but previous efforts in promoting peace haven't resulted in any permanent change. The ongoing propaganda of nationalism and unity amongst Indians is going to take a while to sink in. People involved have to drill home the message. It is a long term process. We have used our innovative techniques, but it has only managed to contain the fire of hate in isolated pockets. We still hear about squabbles here and there. Maybe this movie idea is a way to make a difference.'

'Bah! Our innovative techniques - the peace marches or sometimes we've used our trained army, and teachers in slums. But, we all know, mass awareness in this country will have a greater effect. If a movie works; then yes, let's do it. The message we want to extend is that the scroll, or any other discovery, is only an object that refers to a piece of history, but doesn't change the fabric of society. This will reach the masses: villages, the illiterate and the poor, where caste and religion is deeply ingrained. With this kind of a movie, we will be able to touch the hearts of the masses. The professor said.

Satish stood up to make another drink. 'I can already visualise the scenes. After sixty years of independence, I'm sure Indians will be open to new ideas – ideas of our country as a whole, not a divided nation.'

Junaid smiled, 'You may sound like a politician but you have a point. Patriotism does not develop by itself. We have to draw people's attention to the positives of India and not on the negatives. We have to change a whole mind set.'

'No doubt, films have had a huge impact on the Indian psyche – we have seen trends change and with it people change. It might work.' Lavina said.

Kanyadevi sensed a feeling of hope within the group. Too much had happened and the Onyx was unable to curtail the angry mobs on the streets. The group's silent revolution wasn't working. Talking to slumlords, to politicians, to teachers and scientists had little effect. They needed a stronger force, a powerful message that would touch the hearts of the people in every strata of society.

'We can discuss this idea further, but first I need to know what's going on within the IIA. I will make contact with some on-site archaeologists,' Kanyadevi said. 'I heard that there is a team heading to a location in Puducherry.'

'There could be a dangerous element within the IIA – a snitch. You should watch your back,' Pritam remarked.

'In the meantime, if anyone makes contact with the reporter's wife, we have to be informed quickly to decide our next step,' Sinha said, focussing on the immediate concerns. 'We need to protect this widow. She will become the most-wanted citizen of India.'

The meeting ended.

Chapter 13

Agra is a city teeming with life on the banks of the Yamuna, with the old and new coexisting in harmony. Serpentine streets, bustling bazaars, and characterless buildings form the obscure backdrop at the centre of which, the city's spiritual centre lies a shimmering white monument - the Taj Mahal. It stands out imposing and perfect. Ethereal against the dust and grime of the riverside.

Unlike the tourists, the locals know that the Taj is not the only monument that is powerfully beautiful, there also is the Agra Fort, centre of imperial Mughal power over India. Manzil imagined how it must have been in the old days. Five hundred years ago, the Mughals must have journeyed for days on caparisoned elephants with palanquins of gold and silver. Soldiers on horsebacks following complete with harems, cooks, slaves and armies between the forts from Delhi to Agra.

Today, it was a four-hour journey by train.

Manzil and Ramu made their way to the banks of the Yamuna. She edged slowly towards the river side. Kneeling down, she gently placed the earthen vessel, containing Parag's ashes, covered with a red cloth, into the flowing water.

'Rest in peace, my love,' she whispered, fighting back her tears.

Ramu paced along the banks, watching the surroundings, giving Manzil her private moment. The Taj Mahal loomed above them like a grand emperor watching over his subjects.

Ramu noticed a man watching them from a distance, quietly studying their movements. He didn't want to rush Manzil and in broad daylight, with policemen hovering around the area, Ramu didn't think the watcher would be stupid enough to confront them. Let him look.

'I think we should go,' Ramu said finally, when he saw that she wasn't doing anything but staring at the still waters.

Manzil stood up slowly; the wind whipped up and blew in all directions. The ends of her white dupatta flew; she tamed it around her neck, and covered her head.

'You have no respect for the dead?' Manzil asked with irritation, as they started up the slope.

'I do, but I have more respect for the living.'

They made their way towards the Taj. 'Why did you hide from the police the other day?' Manzil questioned the silent boy who walked with the wariness of a cornered animal.

'I'm a street kid, working for a man called Deva. Even if I'm not guilty of any crime, the police will find some riot to pin on me,' he shrugged his shoulders.

'What if I offered a solution to your nomadic life?' Manzil asked, 'I could help you get an education, a job... a better life.'

He had bright intelligent eyes and there was a worldly-wise air about him. He possessed a rebellious streak and a little bit of discipline and education would help calm him.

Ramu was quiet as if he had not heard her, then he spoke. 'We both belong to different worlds. When a boy has slept without a roof over his head all his life, a ceiling feels like a jail. For me, Deva is God. He saved me from the streets, from the bad boys who sell drugs, and kill for a few rupees. I'll do anything Deva says, I belong to him.'

Ramu moved swiftly up the steps towards the top flat marbled level of the monument.

Manzil wasn't letting him get away with that. She followed briskly and caught up with him, 'You have your own mind, you are not a slave, no one belongs to anyone without their permission.'

'I will do anything for Deva,' he said as if he hadn't heard a word she had said.

'So if this Deva tells you to kill on his behalf, will you?'

'Yes. No questions asked.'

After a cursory glance at the monument, Manzil felt goosebumps on her arms. It was visible, just like it was in the photos, but no one noticed, or cared. The interior was a perfect pentagon shape, the architectural style of Rajputs. The three domes could be considered representative of the trinity. As Manzil's eyes surveyed the edifice with a fresh perspective, she noticed other minor details like the shape of the flowers on the walls; they appeared as a symbol of another culture. Manzil's thoughts were a blur as more images carved in the stone formed shapes and symbols. Details raced through her mind. She didn't want to see them but thanks to Parag's work they were in her face.

'What difference does it make after five hundred years? It's still an Indian piece of history to be proud of,' she said softly, almost to herself, as she made her way to the centre, where the tombs of the two great lovers lay side by side. 'Why can't we just accept the way it has been told to us – a symbol of eternal love?'

In the *Padshahnamah*, the royal chronicles written by Abdul Hamid, Shah Jahan claimed to have built this monument. It took him twenty-two years and he arranged for the marble to be transported from makranas, the marble quarries of Rajasthan, with the help of Maharajah Jai Singh. The gemstones were brought in from various parts of the world, she knew this piece of history, just like every Indian did, and every tourist discovered through their visit. There was no denying the breathtaking beauty of the monument covered with exquisite engravings, painstakingly grooved, and inlaid with gemstones.

Ramu silently watched her, his head cocked sideways and his arms folded. He turned towards a section of the structure. He faced the left side wall of the inner mausoleum; it was darker, hardly noticeable. 'Look there,' he pointed to an oddly blank section. 'It is sealed. Don't you want to know what lies behind it?'

'Maybe it is sealed to protect it from the outside world. Why assume the worst?'

'You do live under illusions, don't you? The real world is a cesspool of secrets and lies, one faces it or hides, depending on who you are.'

Manzil smiled at the boy's street-smart attitude. He did have a point. His sharp mouth came with a sharper brain. Education would sculpt him to take a less morbid view of life, she hoped. Right now he was being rebellious.

She made her way through the arches. 'You are a strange young man.'

They walked around, like tourists, with Manzil, noticing the finer details with fresh eyes. On previous visits, she had viewed the Taj as a complete marble structure and its image was a ghostly glow of a dead love. Parag had turned it into a historical controversy. She wished she didn't know so much. It ruined its ethereal quality, its romance. She couldn't help but notice the segments of walls where the marble was white and areas where it was pink.

Why was it such a big deal? Over the centuries, the Taj must have been renovated to maintain it.

Ramu wasn't interested in the engravings or the tombs; he was busy watching for signs of danger. They had intentionally come early hoping to beat the crowds. But just as they had entered the complex, a busload of tourists approached, chattering excitedly as tour guides pedalled their limited knowledge and parroted the age-old story of the undying love of a husband for his wife.

The morning light cast a hazy glow on the Taj. The cool marble ground was cracked and the spaces were filled with concrete. Up close, the monument looked fragile, tired, as if the air around it was converting it to dust. But there was also a strength that seemed to emanate from the very core of the structure, it had withstood the test of time and now it had to withstand the test of its ode to love.

'I don't believe that we can classify this beautiful architecture as anything other than as a heritage to be proud of,' Manzil whispered, her eyes mesmerised by the beauty of the intricate work on the epitaphs.

I'm not going to the press.

From a distance, Mahesh Bhakti watched the woman with the young boy tagging along. Parag's wife. Quite a beauty, he thought. What a waste. In Indian social history, widows were ostracised and considered bearers of ill-luck. Mahesh didn't want to get close to her, she would cast a shadow of bad luck on him. But he had no choice. He had to talk to her, wean out any information she had gleaned from her dead husband. And more importantly, the scroll. He had to have it.

Mahesh knew the boy was supposed to be her protector. The kid was observant, he was keeping a lookout, watching out for danger. Mahesh didn't have anything to worry about, he would go to her, offer his condolences and help. After all, he had been in regular contact with her husband. That reason alone was enough. If she was smart, she would willingly return all the information he had passed on. The woman probably had no knowledge of its value. She would ruin all that he had planned. Now that the reporter was dead, the evidence was unlikely to reach the public. Manzil was a useless holder of such a deadly secret. Even if she went public, it wouldn't have any credibility. Who would believe the dead reporter's wife, a nobody, a weeping widow who could easily be accused of faking it? And he didn't need accusations that would lead to him, the IIA snitch.

Chapter 14

Mahesh noticed them taking the exit. He would have to work fast, he wasn't sure what Manzil's plan was, but he wanted to take all the incriminating evidence from this housewife and her emaciated bodyguard.

Mahesh approached her. They were done sightseeing and now had paused to buy some peanuts from a street vendor with a basket filled to the brim. Using a small clay pot of burning coal, the vendor roasted the nuts evenly, generating an aroma that attracted a number of tourists.

'Excuse me, madam?' Mahesh said.

Manzil looked at him apprehensively, 'Yes?' Ramu was close, by her side.

'I am Mahesh Bhakti,' he said, extending his hand. 'I am the archaeologist who met your husband.' She nodded and shook his hand. 'I was the one sharing ....certain information with him.'

Manzil withdrew her hand quickly. 'What do you want?'

'I wanted to pay my condolences. I wanted to tell you how sorry I am for your loss,' he whispered, softening his demeanour.

Manzil was wary. 'So, you are the snitch. You are the one who put Parag's life in danger.'

'Please don't say that,' he said looking around. 'I realise my mistake. I wish . . . I wish I could turn back the clock. Your husband was such a wonderful man, passionate about the Taj. I was just giving him proof of the information he had dug up.' He sighed, shook his head and took a step closer, 'Can we speak privately?'

Mahesh looked at Ramu.

'Say what you want in front of him. He's with me.'

Ramu, who had been silent all this while, spoke up. 'That bench, over there, let's go and sit under the shade. It's getting crowded here.' Without waiting for Mahesh to agree, Manzil followed his lead towards one of the stone benches under a mango tree.

The boy was purposely bringing Mahesh in view of the security guards nearby. It didn't matter. Manzil and Mahesh sat facing the Taj, looking like a couple, while Ramu hovered close by.

Manzil spoke first. 'Parag used to get carried away with every news story he came across. He knew it was dangerous. He knew he could get hurt, but he still pursued his lead...' Even to herself, her voice sounded hollow. 'You arranged for him to be here that night, didn't you? You knew the danger, and you led him to his death!' Manzil hissed.

'No! Please believe me. All I did was tell him about a suspicion. The possibility of seeing something that was hidden for centuries, with his own eyes. I wanted him to know the facts. During the repair work, the whole area was cordoned off. Someone noticed the crack in the wall, and the crumbling wet bricks. The worker removed a section of the brick wall and realised that there was empty space on the other side, it was a chamber.'

He stood up and pointed to the furthest part of the Taj, near the riverside.

'I was supervising another section, but by the time I got to that part, one of the workers had already shone his torch through that hole and shouted that there were idols inside. The man was trembling and seemed very disturbed. He said we were all cursed. We managed to calm him down. But I knew the rumours would spread. I had to tell Parag. He always wanted to be the first to know. I told him about the room. I didn't realise he would go there alone and that too in the middle of the night. If I had known, I would have been with him.' He paused, returned to his seat next to her. 'When I returned from Ahmedabad, I heard what happened. Parag was going to make this news big.'

He looked away from her, focussed on the monument. 'Parag and I met often. I liked him because he knew the public had a right to know, had a right to information. He was noble. I trusted him with photographs and various documents which belong to the Institute. This wasn't about treasure, it was about a theory... anyway, it doesn't matter anymore.' He turned to face her, 'Parag mentioned you were the only one who knew where he had kept his papers. I would like them returned to me.'

Mahesh hesitated. 'And also, I heard about a... a scroll. I know about this relic, it is an extremely useful discovery and I want to take it to the IIA, have it analysed.'

Manzil turned to look at him. 'What scroll?' she asked.

How could he know about it?

'Deva, a very well-known leader of the poor, arranged for you to receive it.' He smirked glancing at Ramu. 'Deva has this strange notion that as Parag's widow you will avenge his death by making the scroll public. But I know you are not interested. It's not your problem anyway. And it's risky business. I don't want you to get hurt. I'm sure your husband would want you to stay out of this mess.'

'I'll get in touch with you, when I'm ready.'

Mahesh looked at her with disappointment and was about to press further, the silent sidekick watched him like a hawk.

Mahesh stood up and gave her his card. 'I cannot force you to do anything against your will. But I know Parag would have wanted you to stay out of trouble. He knew the risks involved. You're better off giving me everything and washing your hands off the whole problem.'

'I told you that I'll get back to you.'

Mahesh's jaw worked in anger. 'You can call me anytime, day or night on my direct line. And one more thing, this information you possess is very, very sensitive. Please be careful. Another piece of advice...'

Manzil looked up. 'What!'

'This is between you and me. Please don't tell anyone I was

passing information to your husband. Not even the police. You do understand, don't you?'

She felt a chill.

'I will keep this confidential,' she replied, without hesitation.

Chapter 15

'There are more rumours about the Taj,' Rana whispered into the phone, as he manoeuvred his car, awaiting orders as to his destination.

'There is something brewing, and it is probably underground. Better to back off for now. Go to Puducherry. There is trouble at the church site. Keep me informed,' Dass said and hung up.

He felt suffocated with the pressure of being in-charge of one of the most underpaid, under resourced, and inadequate archaeological organisation in the world. To top it all, he had to be considerate of the sensitivities of every ethnic group in India. For him, every structure, every monument and ancient culture was to be studied and cherished as a prized heritage. But bigots turned ancient sites into issues to fight over.

Dass leaned back on his swivel chair, and stared at the ventilation slats just below the ceiling. His office space was even smaller than Rizvi's. His window faced a warehouse, a view of half-naked men lugging gunny bags of wheat on their backs and dumping them into trucks. It was a back-breaking job. Even from his fourth floor office, he could see the blood, sweat and toil written on their tired faces; they worked just for a few rupees to get through the day.

Delhi, the capital of India, was a city divided into two: The old consisting of mosques, monuments and forts reflecting the power and glory of India's Muslim history. And the new – a product of the British – spacious, wide roads, tall modern buildings; and constantly transforming itself to meet with the many challenges thrown at it.

No other city in India has such a rich history; going back three thousand years. Excavations at the site of the Old Fort or Purana Qila had revealed fine grey earthenware painted in black designs. Archaeologists called it the Painted Grey Ware and dated it to 1000 BC. The site revealed it to be associated with the story of the *Mahabharata* – one of the great Hindu epics. And even before that, earthenware from the Maurya period circa 300 BC was discovered, of the time of the the Great Mauryan Emperor Ashoka, who had embraced Buddhism.

The soil of India was complicated. Religions had survived on the same piece of land for thousands of years.

Today, Delhi was overcrowded and bustling between being traditional and striving to be modern. There was an overdose of information, too easily accessible, and too many conclusions drawn from it. Youngsters were looking westward. 'You fight your own battles, mum, dad. I'm through with living in the past,' Dass recalled his sister's fifteen-year-old daughter saying, when Dass had visited them on her birthday. He watched his sister's face crumble. At times like that, Dass was glad he was single. He had spent twenty years with the IIA and he had seen India live in the aftermath of four wars since independence. He didn't need to suffer another conflict at home.

Dass often wondered if secular democracy was good for India: A huge country, almost a continent within itself, so different and varied in culture, language, customs and people. Dass realised the enormity of managing such a nation of complex proportions. No wonder the government was always in a state of disharmony. Yet the country functioned, perhaps purely on the strength of its people, from all classes of society, striving to make ends meet, their willingness to accept their fate and live in their corner of hearth peacefully.

Dass was tired of the continuous hounding of the IIA. The sad truth was that whenever an ancient site was discovered, the IIA hoped it wasn't on religious grounds, or that it would not catch the eye of some hitherto unknown sect.

Dass stood up. He had an appointment. It was pointless to try and predict the future. Not even the most proficient of astrologers could say where India was headed and what lay in store for its more than a billion population. Theirs was a worldview that India was the next super power, but it stood on such shaky foundations. That one was always forced to wonder.

Dass took the rickety lift to the ground floor and exited the building. If they had the freedom, they would handle IIA differently – he would exert more control over the sites, get ethnic groups to join hands and sweet talk the government to allocate more funds and market India as a nation of peace-lovers.

Dass slipped a mint in his mouth and walked briskly towards the small tea shop at the end of the street. The meeting was at four pm. Glancing at his watch, he realised he was early. As he entered Ganpathi Tea House, the overweight owner with heavily oiled hair was sitting at the cash register, one leg neatly folded on the chair. He was counting his money with pudgy fingers and licking his thumb with regularity. He glanced at Dass and acknowledged him with a silent nod. With a jerk of his head, he indicated that someone was already in the corner booth waiting. Dass understood. Normally, Singh was late; but if he was early, then the news must be bad.

The tea stall was bustling. Employees from nearby office buildings came for a cheap quick snack of deep fried lentil cakes and brewed masala chai. The young waiters in stained t-shirts rushed from table to kitchen, shouting out orders. Further, towards the rear of the shop was an alcove consisting of four booths for those who needed privacy. The booths had thick curtains to keep out prying eyes. It was a popular spot for women in hijab; they could remove their veils without suffering the indignity of being seen. The service was slow and the area quiet compared to the front.

Dass found it useful for a different purpose. Meeting informants.

He entered the curtained booth, but didn't have time to react when a man grabbed his arm and twisted it behind him. Dass fell forward, his head banged the table, and his glasses fell to the floor. The man stepped on it.

'What . . .?'

The man pulled his head back and angled the sharp point of a knife at Dass's neck, 'One wrong move and you are dead.'

'What do you want?' Dass asked, calm.

The man pushed Dass into the corner. 'Sit down and be quiet,' he lisped.

A single lamp illumined their booth, and Dass caught a glimpse of his attacker's face. His hooded brows were knitted and cheeks were a criss-cross of scars. He still gripped the knife as if ready to strike. Dass wisely chose to keep quiet, but his mind raced. There must be something brewing that was far bitter than the tea served at Ganpathi's. He retrieved his glasses from the floor and put them on. The frame was twisted and the left lens cracked.

Two minutes later, a pockmark-faced man with henna-dyed wiry hair slid into the seat opposite them. He was wearing a policeman's uniform. 'Put down the knife, Raja. We don't treat intelligent people this way,' he said in fluent Urdu. His laughter a staccato beat of a drum. Just as abruptly, he stopped laughing. 'I am Anwar. And there is a storm coming. If you don't want the storm to break, then speak the truth here and now.'

'What do you want to know?' Dass asked. 'And, where is Singh?'

'Don't worry about Singh. He is a little bit tied up at the moment,' Anwar laughed again. Raja joined him, laughing harder.

Dass shuddered, wondering if they had killed his informant.

'What do you want?'

Anwar leaned forward, his eyes black marbles; Dass felt them boring in to his skull. 'We have been hearing things about the Taj, and we are not happy about what we are hearing.'

'Who is "we"?' Dass asked, his army instincts kicking in.

'You don't need to know. In fact, my friend, you don't *want* to know,' Anwar warned.

'There is nothing different about the Taj Mahal today than it was four hundred years ago.

'This guy is smart,' Anwar said, pointing at Dass.

Dass felt Raja's breath on his neck. He reeked of onions. 'Then what is this rubbish about idols being found inside?' Raja shot back, playing with the sharp edge of the knife.

'There are people who want to cause trouble. I am telling you that there is nothing inside.'

'I don't believe you!' Anwar slapped the table hard causing the flies to buzz angrily. 'You have a snitch in your organisation and he is spreading rumours. We know the reporter died because he took something from inside a sealed room in the Taj. That something is now in someone's hands and when I find out who, that person will be dead. Do you understand?'

There was a pause.

'I understand. I will find out who this person spreading rumours is. But what have they found?' Dass asked.

'You are truly ignorant. What do you do? Stick your head in the soil you dig up?' His laughter was harsh again. Then he stopped. His face was dark with emotion. 'They have found a letter written by a king. There are also some photos. Pictures can be fabricated, but the letter – that is something of concern. Make it disappear. Or, give it to me. The Taj Mahal is our heritage, our pride. We don't want anyone, anyone taking that away from us.'

Dass was tempted to tell him that the Taj was India's pride and did not just belong to 'him'. But he didn't think Anwar would take the patriotism kindly.

Dass nodded silently, his forehead throbbing. He touched it and felt an egg-shaped bump.

'I give you till next week to find out who has that cursed thing, you hear me? Or else, it could become very ugly,' Anwar leaned into Dass's face. 'Very bloody.'

Chapter 16

Puducherry

Puducherry is the most beautifully confused city one can ever find in India. In ancient times, it was invaded by the Greeks who called it Poduke, and then destroyed by Aurangzeb, a great grandson of Emperor Akbar, then rebuilt by the Portuguese and finally colonised by the French. Temples, mosques and churches have been destroyed and rebuilt on its soil several times. A particularly beautiful Catholic church built from the ruins of a temple had the inscription to prove its existence long, long ago.

Mahesh Bhakti was assigned to supervise the excavation of idols from one such church site. The dozens of buried artifacts covered with layers of sand and soil were being painstakingly removed with the aid of a small brush. Twenty men worked on different sections of the backyard of the cathedral. The earth was the colour of rich coffee and the deeper they dug the soil took on a dark reddish hue. It was a good discovery – worth alerting the press to show that the IIA was working hard at discovering and protecting ancient sites.

Recently, the IIA had received a lot of bad press due to the desecration of an ancient religious structure. Issues were escalating and minor scuffles between religious groups were being publicised by the press. The harder the IIA worked, the harder it became to avoid the angry voices of various factions. They took to the streets and demanded the prime minister take immediate action – which meant imprison the fanatics of one particular sect. An then, Christian groups had taken to the streets demanding that the Institute stop invading the privacy of a three-hundred-year-old church.

Mahesh felt a nagging uneasiness, the meeting with Manzil didn't go well and he was hoping she would get in touch with him before he left for Puducherry. She hadn't and was holding on to IIA research material and the scroll. And it was his fault. His job was on the line now. He exhaled deeply trying to focus. There was an archaeological treasure trove of valuable objects being excavated. He needed to stay focussed.

Archaeologists had already uncovered four brass pots, ten idols and a crudely shaped trident. Despite the linen hat, the sun burned down mercilessly on Mahesh's back and sweat dripped down the sides of his face in the forty-two degree Celcius heat. His two colleagues, Gaurav and Farhan, were busy instructing the local construction workers how to excavate the relics.

Mahesh shook his head. Waste of time, he thought. These workers routinely carried and poured cement for buildings, and were not trained for such delicate work. Another ancient site would be destroyed by their haphazard methods, Mahesh reflected. He skimmed the surroundings; the workers were on their haunches digging with their bare hands. But their fingers pressed and crushed the earth. At this rate, dozens of ancient pieces would be lost.

'Gaurav, these men are not meant for this kind of job,' Mahesh said.

'So what do you want to do?' He retaliated, looking hot and bothered like the rest of them. 'Should we dig like dogs in this blistering heat? Or call the university and check if trainees would like to work on site? That takes weeks of paperwork.'

Gaurav wiped his forehead with his large kerchief for the third time. 'There aren't enough people to handle our jobs and India is a gold mine of artifacts. We need more trained people.'

Mahesh waited for his colleague to give vent to his frustration, but he was panting. 'We lost another archaeological site when the director arranged for labourers to d and d.' Mahesh said, using their code for 'dig and destroy' certain sensitive areas. He hated using those words.

'Well, we got to do our job in the best we can.'

Angry shouting distracted them. Mahesh looked at Gaurav, as if bad luck had befallen them.

They turned to see Farhan calling out and at the same time holding one of the construction workers by his collar. They hurried toward him, and heard Farhan cursing.

'These bloody ruffians! Look, he destroyed an idol and tried to steal these,' Farhan showed them the idol with sapphire eyes. Mahesh and Gaurav's eyes widened. This was a great discovery. The whole site was going to be completely cordoned off and the director-general would come personally.

This was good news – they had a thankless job that involved hours of careful analysis and recording of the excavation. This would give them a pat on the back and here was Farhan ruining the moment with his cursing.

'I'm sorry, sahib, it won't happen again. Please forgive me,' the elderly construction worker said as he cowered on his knees, clasping his hands together. He tried to disengage himself from Farhan's tight grip. The other workers sitting on their haunches continued to work, purposely ignoring them.

'I have half a mind to call the police and have you thrown in jail!' Farhan, a strong hefty man, shook the emaciated-looking thief. The old man seemed to rattle in his grip.

'Please, sahib, I promise you that I will not commit such a sinful act again,' he cried, pulling his ear lobes and shaking his head.

Mahesh nodded at him, indicating to let him go. Gaurav waited, drinking from his canister, and periodically wiped his forehead.

Farhan eased his grip, 'I have eyes of a hawk and I will be watching you.'

The worker, having noticed that Mahesh had helped, thanked him profusely as well. With renewed vigour, the old man hurried to his corner to work on the soil.

'This is a major find, congratulations, Farhan!' Mahesh whispered.

Gaurav looked apprehensively at the rest of the workers. 'We have to watch these people carefully from now on. Inform the director we need more people; and bloody well make sure they are trainees from a university.'

After half an hour of digging, while the three men watched the movements of each worker, one of the diggers came running, 'Sahebji, sahebji, come quick, we found the idol of Lord Shiva and his third eye is made of blue stone!'

Two weeks, and many agitations later, the archaeological work continued. About twenty-five diggers covered the whole area surrounding the church. Like ants, they worked uniformly transferring mounds of soil into baskets and depositing them on the back of a large truck. Their serious expressions were intensified by the ten men who watched over them. The Puducherry Cathedral was cordoned off and protected by police as curious bystanders, reporters, and photographers tried to take pictures. Everyday, a morcha of saffron-clad bearded men suddenly appeared from nowhere, and as they punched the air with their placards, supporters shouted that the church should be shut down.

The papers were full of details about the IIA's recent find and how the government was putting every effort to protect the area. The value of the idols was worth millions and more were being discovered everyday.

It wasn't easy –

This time there was too much publicity. Mahesh was sure he would be caught by a mad religious fanatic or an overzealous reporter. The street lights were dim and it was difficult to see if there was anyone lurking on the empty road. Mahesh checked his watch, midnight. The darkness was alive with the sounds of crickets chorusing in unison. The cathedral was sombre, as if it was reflecting on all the finds of another religion within its boundaries. There were no houses in the vicinity except for a school that was closed, and a playground across the road that was completely enveloped in darkness.

The man appeared out of no where. 'I'm here with the cash.' He said without greeting. Hidden under a hat, a shawl around his neck that folded over his mouth, he looked like a night watchman out on a stroll. Except for the briefcase he was carrying. It wasn't cold to be dressed in such warm clothing, and Mahesh guessed the man must be suffering under it. One thing was sure, he was elderly. He walked with a slight stoop and his hand holding the briefcase was wrinkled with age. Can't hide everything.

'Come this way,' Mahesh said, opening the cathedral gate and gesturing him towards a corner wall that blocked the view of the road. The man followed and then waited silently for Mahesh to show him what he came for.

Mahesh unzipped his knapsack, removed the package and uncovered the cotton cloth. Even in the dim light, the idol's sapphire eyes seemed to blaze at him and the intricately carved detail of the stone image was intact. The man's eyes widened, he took a sharp breath, and then touched the idol with tenderness.

Without another word, he took the idol and gave the briefcase to Mahesh. 'It's all there, you can check it if you want.'

Mahesh didn't want to waste time. 'I trust you.'

He checked all was clear. The old man left the cathedral grounds carrying a plastic grocery bag.

Mahesh's mind was back on the widow. Damn you Parag. He desperately wanted to get his hands on that scroll – by hook or by crook – he would have it. It was his by right.

Chapter 17

The last time Mahesh had been to a dance performance was during his college days, when he was studying at the Delhi University in the Department of Archaeology. He had been bored to tears. The dancers were overweight and seemed like they had come from a retirement home. Their painted faces had more versatility of movement than their feet. But they ended up looking like clowns. Even the two-hundred-year-old brass idol recently recovered from Tanjavoor in Tamil Nadu had more grace than those classical dancers in stiff outfits that seemed to constrict, rather than allow, fluidity of movement.

He knew enough about Bharatnatyam, and had great respect for the classical dance form. It was considered to be the oldest of all classical dance forms in the world. Centuries ago, devadasis or dancer-priestesses led very strict and celibate lives. After disciplined practice, they would perform in Hindu temples in the praise of the gods. The art form required hours of regular practice, for years, before a student was allowed to perform in public. Only the guru decided when the disciple was ready for the public graduation or arangetram.

Mahesh wondered if Kanyadevi was half as good. She was an attractive woman, not quite beautiful but there was an intensity about her. He searched for the right word: Passion, yes that's what it was. She exuded the emotion. She had a broad face to carry her sharp features, combined with a dusky complexion, the colour of the earth. A beautiful broad forehead with a widow's peak added a touch of elegance to her features. Earlier that day she had visited the site wearing a t-shirt and jeans. With no make-up, and her hair spread loosely down her back, she looked more like a university student. Mahesh had introduced himself. He had been assigned to give her a run down on the finds. 'She has a great love for ancient Indian architecture. A very charitable supporter of our Institute. Be nice,' instructed DG Rizvi.

Kanyadevi had confided that her favourite monument was the Taj Mahal. When Mahesh told her that he was from Delhi, and had studied the Taj for the most of his four years at university, she couldn't contain her enthusiasm. There was nothing else, besides dance, she wanted to do more, than be at the Taj and soak in its beauty, she had said, with stars in her eyes. Mahesh held back his smirk and a cynical comment that was at the tip of his tongue.

Mahesh wasn't looking forward to the evening. But it was a pure public relations exercise – Kanyadevi was their largest supporter after the government. At the moment, he didn't think much of the government.

Outdoors, by the Puducherry shore temple, a stage had been set up and chairs placed under a canopy tent. Colourful strings of lights and flowers added an atmosphere of festivity. The wind blew away the afternoon's humid air and freshness filled the atmosphere. A young girl, heavily made up, and dressed in traditional dance attire – a specially stitched outfit made of red and yellow silk, bordered with gold – greeted and guided the guests to their seats. Despite her youth, she was enchanting. Her welcoming smile reached her dark kohl-lined eyes. The nose-ring seemed a little too big for her pug nose, but it was part of the costume.

Mahesh introduced himself, 'I am with the IIA, Ms Kanyadevi invited me.'

'We are very happy to see you,' she said, bowing slightly as if he were the chief guest. She escorted him, and explained the programme for the evening. He followed her towards the front row, where she gracefully showed him his seat. Mahesh glanced around and before he sat down, he overheard the young dancer repeat the same eager greeting to another guest.

It was a hot day, and performing outdoors was not such a good idea, worst still for the dancers in their heavy attire. He fanned himself with the flyer placed on every seat. He read the profile of the dancers. It was going to be a long evening, two hours at least. If it hadn't been for Kanyadevi he wouldn't have bothered. When he had met her that afternoon, she had mentioned there was some information he would be interested in. She said it was to do with the the Taj. Yes, that was the perfect hook. He sighed, he had to be patient she would only tell him after the performance. He would have to stay till the end.

A short, plain-looking man with his oiled hair parted neatly to the side, occupied the seat next to him. He introduced himself.

'Hello sir, myself Raghu and you?' He shook hands with Mahesh.

'Mahesh Bhakti.'

'Ah, the archaeologist? Kanyadevi told me about you. It is very nice to meet you. I am Kanyadevi's agent, organising the performances from south India to north India and across the Indian Ocean. That is what I do,' he smiled revealing brilliant white teeth. 'You are from the north, no?'

Mahesh shrugged, 'Yes.' He was used to friendly Pondi people introducing themselves and two sentences later, as if they were old pals, requesting a special visit to the restricted site that Mahesh and his colleagues were working on.

'I am hearing that you have found much ancient art in the cathedral area,' he winked at Mahesh. 'Kanyadevi madam has special liking for ancient Indian monuments. She is collector also, I will be arranging meeting with you and her later, after the performance.' He smiled again and headed backstage. 'Don't leave, wait for me here.'

The IIA had asked Mahesh to give Kanyadevi as much time as she wanted – she had money and they wanted her to keep sending more their way. He had to be nice and offer her a tour of any of the heritage sites she liked. She was a famous woman and it would be good publicity for the IIA, Rizvi had said. Mahesh could have said no and risked losing his job. Not that it paid much, but this was the best opportunity he had to gather information and feed the press with the secrets of the IIA. He had access to all kinds of information, including in restricted areas. That's how he managed to make photocopies of some of the Taj files and pass them on to Parag. He would have caused a sensation with the news.

Then an idea struck. Maybe Kanyadevi was a better medium to leak information to the press. It was an interesting idea... She was famous and he liked the way she could hold the attention of the people. He let the thought stew. And the more he thought, the more he felt she was the right person. But he had to be careful. The IIA bosses were closely connected to her. He would have to plan his strategy. As far as he knew she wasn't married, no boyfriends. She had taken a liking to him. Maybe...

When every seat was filled, the orchestra comprising a singer, mridangam player, violin player and the Natuvanga appeared and sat in the corner of the stage.

The dance academy chairwoman, bowed low facing the temple and then the audience. In a loud but pleasant voice, she welcomed her friends, the students, guests from out of town, looking at Mahesh. The performance commenced.

The dancers were spectacular but Mahesh was eager for Kanyadevi.

An hour and a half later, when Kanyadevi made her appearance on stage. There was a sudden but perceivable silence.

Mahesh's pulse quickened. She didn't look like the person he had met that afternoon. She looked like a goddess, straight out of the carving of an Indian temple. Strikingly beautiful, in the traditional Bharatnatyam outfit; heavily jewelled and made-up, she carried herself with grace. Kanyadevi's outfit was pink and green; it transformed her, highlighting the duskiness of her skin, making her glow. Every feature was enhanced, her face shone with an ethereal quality.

Mahesh leaned forward. Even the gods would be smitten by her, he reflected.

Her magnetic expression and the unique sparkle in her eyes seemed to blaze with her pose. With each movement, Kanyadevi stamped her bare feet on the wooden floor of the stage, in tune with the musicians' instruments. It was a hard rhythmic sound in rapport with the bells on her ankles. He could tell that she was completely absorbed in her dance. And so was the rest of the audience.

Mahesh was captivated; his heart thudded to her studied steps. He felt a strong sense of attraction. It was an odd feeling, something he had never experienced before. Was it love and that too so suddenly? He wasn't sure. But for that moment, in her presence, he let his emotions take over. Bharatnatyam was an artistic yoga, an expression of the spiritual through the corporeal. Kanya's rendition of the Bharatnatyam touched the core of his being. Through her abhinaya, her expression, he could read pain, pleasure, sadness, anger and ecstasy. This was the heavenly dance fit for the gods and goddesses of ancient India. Kanyadevi had the perfect face, and the curves of her body were meant for dance. He smiled, mesmerised by her grace, her elaborate footwork and movements of her body.

From the moment she started her varnam, the section of dance that tells a story of love and longing for a lover, with the positions of the hands and body, Mahesh was in awe. When she performed the finale, the nritta, pure dance, he wanted to kiss her feet.

It was brilliant and in time-honoured tradition, Kanya prostrated in front of the idol of the Nataraja, an avatara of Lord Shiva, recognised as the supreme dancer, who performed the Taandavam – the dance of the cosmos.

Mahesh felt tears sting his eyes. Never had he seen such purity and sensuality in any performance before. He wanted to get away from the maddening applause and congratulate her. She was a true goddess. He would make her every wish come true. He would take her to the Taj Mahal. Damn, he would build a Taj in her honour.

'You were absolutely brilliant,' Mahesh said when Raghu escorted him backstage to the cordoned tent. 'You are the perfect woman - a goddess.'

'Thank you very much,' Kanyadevi smiled, taken aback by his effervesent praise. That afternoon he had appeared bored. 'Please sit down.'

Mahesh sat on the makeshift stool. Kanyadevi, still dressed in her costume, drank from a tall bottle of water. He watched her surreptitiously: her head tilted upwards, the gentle curve of her luscious lower lip, her chest rising and falling beneath the embroidered blouse that modestly covered her bosom. He envied the broad gold necklace resting majestically around her neck, touching her skin. His eyes wandered below, and then he stopped himself. Such beauty was meant to be honoured, respected, deified from a distance, and not to be desecrated with lust.

'Tell me, when will your next performance be? I want to attend it,' Mahesh said.

Raghu looked at him happily. A whole institute of archaeologists would be a great audience. 'Sir, not to worry. I will inform you. Madam has no performance until next month in Khajuraho.'

'Raghu, thank you. Please give me a few moments alone with Mahesh,' Kanyadevi said.

Raghu nodded and before he exited, 'I will make some arrangements for drinks.'

'That would be nice.'

'Kanyadevi . . .'

'Call me KD, Mahesh,' she said, touching his wrist.

Mahesh took her palm in his, 'I know you will find this odd to believe, but I think I am in love with you.'

KD withdrew her hand, 'I'm not surprised. I get this reaction a lot. It is the effect of this nritya. Bharatnatyam is a sensuous dance. Tomorrow, you will be sorry you said this.'

'Don't trivialise my feelings. I mean what I say,' Mahesh moved closer, looking intensely at her. 'I've never felt so much emotion, such pleasure.'

'I'm flattered by your compliments. I'm a fan of your profession. Mahesh, you are doing a great job for our country – unearthing and protecting the precious treasures of our lost heritage. Please understand, that I am your friend. I'm not sure if I want to be more than that.' She turned away from him and looked at her reflection in the mirror. 'My passion, my love, my life, is my art. I have spent years learning and practising. For me, it is a form of penance. When I'm lost in the movements and expression of the dance, I feel like I'm up in the Himalayas, away from the complexities of modern life... in bliss. No other feeling can even come close.'

'You are as poetic as you are beautiful. KD, I'm sorry I came on too strong. You are right. I was probably carried away by the sheer intensity of your performance.' He smoothed his hair with the palm of his hand, looking at her sheepishly. 'I've been working too hard. The excavation site was full of ancient artifacts compact in just one area. It takes a lot out of me. I'm very precise, careful about the process of retrieving these pieces. I've become a little obsessive about everything.' He sat down in front of her.

'You had some important piece of news you wanted to share with me. What is it?'

KD looked relieved. 'I've heard that someone in your organisation is leaking information to the press. Sensitive information?'

He paused, eyes narrowed. 'Who told you that?'

'That does not matter. The fact that I know is bad enough. And some confidential information was released to the press recently in Ahmedabad.'

'There is nothing going on. The press is making up stories.'

'I don't think they would unless they have evidence. There's no smoke without fire.'

He stood up and paced. 'What is it to you, anyway?' Mahesh asked, a little too sharply. 'I mean, it's odd that you would be interested in what the press has to say.'

The woman had an interesting side to her. A Bharatnatyam dancer should focus on her self, her art, not politics.

'I have my reasons, Mahesh.' KD turned to look at him, her eyes soft and magnetic. 'Maybe it's because you and I share a passion.'

Mahesh felt a warm flood of emotion. It tugged at his heart making him feel flush with love. He leaned closer, 'I feel the passion as you do. There is so much I want to tell you. . . but it must wait.'

Mahesh couldn't tell her the truth.

An only child, Mahesh Bhakti's father was a scientist, his mother a professor. And both were Brahmins – the highest caste of the Hindu hierarchy. Mahesh's mother had taught him about being honourable and respectful to all, despite the constant display of discrimination amongst the different castes. He knew about the misfortune suffered by the lowest of castes – the Dalits. They were destined to clean toilets and skin cows for leather and make shoes. It wasn't their fault; it was due to their karma that they had to bear the injustices of society. While other Brahmins treated the lower castes badly, Mahesh's parents were different. They wanted him to learn the importance of treating every human with equal dignity and respect. When Mahatma Gandhi came along and shook the very foundations of the caste system of India, his parents were treated badly.

The untouchables were children of god, the Mahatma claimed. Mahesh's parents, also children of God, were classified as bad. Very soon, when the confused government chose to play god and help the 'scheduled castes' uplift from their shitty existence, Mahesh's parents were removed from their senior positions in their respective universities, through no fault of theirs. The university did nothing to stop the injustice. His parents were thrown out without their pensions or any other benefits, even without commendations.

Mahesh believed they suffered the indignity because other Brahmins had created a bad image of themselves. He was angry at the unfair treatment meted out at those who were innocent. And this is the thanks they got for being good.

It was forty years after the partition, 1987 in Mumbai. Mahesh's aged parents died in the mass communal killings. He survived, hiding in a bullock cart carrying a load of hay. He was only nine.

God had let him live for a reason and he, a Brahmin, would avenge his parents' death. The government was going to pay.

Kanyadevi was his devi; god had sent her to him. He just knew it, felt the connection deep in his soul. She would be the spokeswoman and make public all the information that was hidden because the government was afraid of the repercussions. Well, why didn't the politicians think about that when his parents were killed?

Chapter 18

Inspector Yadav had an appointment with Director-General Rizvi of the IIA. A very busy man, Yadav had to threaten him before he agreed to the meeting. It had taken a threat of arriving unannounced with five policemen in tow to persuade Rizvi to meet him that very day.

Without wasting time, Rizvi spoke, 'What can I do for you?'

Yadav noticed the dark circles around the man's eyes. He slouched in his chair as if the weight of the world was on his shoulders. 'We have heard the Taj could be a cause for concern,' Yadav said.

Rizvi stopped playing with the glass paper weight. 'Why?'

'Rumours,' Yadav responded with a half smile. 'You know how they start. One spark and we will be dealing with a massive fire and death of innocent people.'

Rizvi looked gravely at him. 'I'll be honest with you, Inspector. I'm just fed up.' He sighed and then stood up. 'You are right, there is a small problem. Someone has sensitive information that could lead to violence. That spark is out there and someone is holding it like a time bomb. Not only is that person's life in danger, but if this leaks, our Institute may be shut down.'

'That extreme, huh?' Yadav asked. 'Why don't you ask the police for help?'

Rizvi snorted and turned to the window, his gaze drifting out to the crowd of humanity that surged back and forth at the trafficlight with a never ending purpose. 'You guys deal with crimes happening every day. Burglary, kidnappings, murders. I cannot come running to you every time we are on an excavation site, and bother you about a potential problem that may or may not erupt. Frankly, it is our responsibility to handle our agency professionally, to ensure the survival of archaeological evidence.'

Yadav nodded sympathetically. 'Yes, but if you have a potentially dangerous element working within your organisation, it is our job to deal with such people.'

'Mine is to answer to the government. You think this is bad? If we do not control the situation, the enemy sitting on the borders will be waiting like vultures, to feed on the remains.' Rizvi returned to his swivel chair, his one comfort, and sat down heavily.

'You have quite a fatalistic attitude.'

'Developed over the years,' he said, smiling sadly. 'When I graduated, armed with a degree in archaeology and history. I spent many hours admiring the ancient art. Recovering such treasures was my passion. I researched and kept logs of the elegant, intricate carvings of the idols we found from different parts of India. Nowadays, I check the religious background of the art work before I study its age and significance.'

Yadav took out the little piece of evidence he found on Parag's body, 'We found a small note with MB and a partial phone number on it. I want a list of the people who work here.'

Rizvi shook his head. 'Sir, we have a staff of three hundred. And then we have part-time students who come in to get some experience and follow-up on research. Also, we hire some diggers on site. I'm not sure how quickly I can give you the information or how it will help you.'

'Just give me the list of your full-timers. How it will help me, director, is my problem.'

Rizvi nodded. 'It will take about an hour. If you prefer, I'll have it faxed to you.'

'No. I'll wait'. Yadav's mobile buzzed. He answered it immediately when he saw who was calling.

Police commissioner Akash Sinha was not one to ever mince his words. But this time there was a distinct hesitation in his voice when he spoke to Yadav. 'Where are you, Yadav? There is something we need to discuss . . . You can say that it is a delicate matter . . . I know your hands are full at the moment. But I need to see you. It is important.'

He was not making sense. 'Sir, if it is about the recent prostitute killings, I've got a team combing the area. We haven't a clue yet, but they will report back to me before the end of the day,' Yadav said.

Rizvi overheard and looked sharply at Yadav. Silently, Rizvi stood up and left his office, miming he would check if the lists were ready.

Yadav nodded. He continued to listen to his boss. 'No, no. It's... It is of national importance. Come to my office ASAP,' Sinha said.

'Sir, can you at least tell me what this is about?'

There was a pause. 'It's about the widow. You have met her – the reporter's wife, right?'

'Yes sir. The circumstances surrounding her husband's death were suspicious. And she is hiding some vital piece of information from me which could potentially help solve the case. But I will continue to monitor her.'

'Yadav, you will need to do more than that. You need to pass her a message. Come to my office and I will explain everything.'

Chapter 19

'What happened to you?' Rizvi asked, noticing the bump on Dass's forehead.

'Just a bad fall, that's all,' he replied, avoiding the question. Luckily Rizvi didn't push for details.

Rizvi picked up a list of names from a file on his desk. One name was highlighted in red. 'The police inspector investigating the reporter's death was here. He has found some connection to the IIA. Looks like we have a mole in our organisation, the recent morchas are the result of our man sharing our secrets with the press.'

He pushed his chair back in frustration. 'Damn it, I hate it when the police gets involved. This inspector has taken a list of our employees. He will quite easily put two and two together and come up with Mahesh Bhakti.'

'Why?' Dass glanced at the list.

'The inspector found MB written on a crumpled piece of paper on the dead reporter. Obviously the first place they will investigate is here.'

The last place that Rizvi and Dass wanted searched was the large locked room at the end of the corridor. It contained rows and rows of boxes filled with artifacts and idols unearthed from different parts of India. They were coded red. Only Rizvi and Dass were aware that it meant danger – a possibility of inciting violence by affecting the sensibilities of certain religious groups.

'We have a room full of hidden evidence – what are we going to do about it?' Dass asked. He was quite sure Mahesh had entered the room and stolen certain sensitive material. 'It's not like it is under special surveillance, anyone can break the lock and gain easy access.'

'I'm not sure which way to look – at the political implications or the scientific ones. We have some valuable relics in there and I think they would have been better off in their original location, below the ground, instead of our Institute.' Dass sighed. He sent a text message to Rana.

Rana paid the fee and entered the archaeological museum located inside the Purana Qila fort, to the right of the main entrance. Museums were his favourite place. He felt a surge of pride as he passed the exhibition from 1000 BC. Dass was waiting for him, staring at the pottery from the Mauryan era. He seemed quite lost.

'This is one of our greatest finds,' Dass said, pointing to the excavations carried out by the IIA. Objects and antiquities adorned the glass stands, the walls and deep alcoves representing a continuous cultural sequence from Mauryan to Mughal through Sunga, Kushana, Gupta, Rajput and Sultanate periods.

They walked slowly admiring the history represented in the unearthed artifacts. 'I've been with the archaeological teams at some of these excavations and dug with my bare hands,' Rana said proudly.

The Museum was open to the public but there were only a handful of people, and a class of primary school students with their frazzled teacher who kept parroting, 'Stay together.'

Dass fell silent when a group of tourists entered. They wandered ahead after a few pictures.

'These objects of the past are ancient history. Dead. Yet they have the power to affect our future,' he said softly.

Dass told him about his encounter with Anwar.

'How would Anwar know that someone was two-timing the IIA?' Rana was shocked at the bold confrontation. This was getting dangerous. Rana doubted if Dass understood the extent the dons would go to find the artifact.

They entered another room where the walls were dotted with paintings.

'I just heard, from the boss, the police have been investigating, and they have some proof,' Dass said. 'Mahesh Bhakti is responsible. He is the snitch in the IIA. He steals information and leaks it or worse still, sells it. He was the one who gave the Taj pictures to that reporter who was found dead. I'm not sure about the relics that he has excavated. I wonder how many have disappeared before they even reached the IIA. You have worked with him. What do you think?' Dass asked. They paused in front of a huge painting of Jhansi ki Rani, the brave warrior queen of Jhansi, of the Rajput clan, who led an army to fight the British.

Rana wasn't surprised at the revelation. The IIA's position was being compromised by an insider. In the past there had been burglaries, and who else but a person familiar with the layout of the Institute would know where the rare artifacts were stored.

'Mahesh seems like a dedicated archaeologist, very professional. But he is religiously inclined, often talking about Hindu heritage being the greatest.' He shook his head and asked Dass, 'What do you want me to do?'

'I think best thing for now is to keep an eye on him.' They moved towards the next exhibit. 'Find out what he's upto. I suspect the whole Taj Mahal issue is going to escalate out of proportion. Apparently, there is some proof, a document discovered inside.'

Rana stared into the distance. The sunlight sparkled through the dusty uneven Venetian blinds of the large windows.

'You have to be careful, these thugs like to create a mountain out of a molehill. The evidence is a scientific, historic discovery but they will twist it into something worse. Anwar's name is well-known. He is a cold-blooded killer. And he works for a man who likes to cause trouble. Khanbaba is financed by overseas money. He is a notorious extortionist. He has his fingers in every millionaire's pot – property, hotels, travelling, jewellers, clothing, cement - you name it, and the tycoons pay a so-to-speak commission so that their family members are not abducted, or slaughtered.'

'He seems more of a gangster, why would he want to get his hands on the Taj relic?' Dass said.

'He likes to get involved in big issues – religious or political, it doesn't matter,' Rana explained.

'The Taj is huge,' Dass frowned. 'Somebody out there has photos and proof that if released, would result in unnecessary agitation and fights.'

Dass headed out. Rana followed.

'Yes sir, and that is why we have to try and find the evidence and hide it,' Rana said.

Dass paused, deep in thought. The elusive relic preyed on his mind. As he reflected on the problem, a group of students entered. And the childrens' exuberant chatter lightened the mood in the room. He smiled. 'The Onyx is going to bring about the change our country needs. They have the enthusiasm of the youth – creative and idealistic. If the government can't create stability then the passion of Onyx will,' Dass said with optimism.

Rana wasn't convinced. He merely nodded.

Chapter 20

Chandni Chowk, Delhi

The beer bar was crowded as usual. And dark, as if the owner wanted to hide from the eyes of the gods. But, in actual fact, Govind Swami, the owner, was just saving on electricity bills. The sins that went on behind the smoky hall and the curtained rooms were pure indulgence of the flesh. Anyone was available to satisfy the cravings of the customers, available to perform for their whims for a few hundred rupees. In the hall, the girls danced provocatively in long satin skirts and tight fitting short blouses, exposing a generous portion of their midriff. Some women had curves that were as perfect as the ancient stone idols embedded in the Khajuraho temples, others not so. The overweight women distracted attention from their sagging bodies by exhibiting a deeper cleavage. Since the customer was king, the dance bar was appropriately named Raja Mahal Bar.

Mahesh Bhakti, on days when the past sat heavy on his heart like a ton of bricks, joined the ranks of the other frustrated businessmen, drinking beer and ogled the six or seven young women on the floor. The music was regular rehashed Himesh Reshammiya hit numbers of long lost love.

He found the woman he was looking for; she serviced him and knew how to satisfy his kinky desires. He liked them to be dressed up as innocent brides. Mahesh nodded at her and she came over to sit with him. Out of habit, the waiter rapped a glass filled with cola in front of Pushpa and Mahesh paid for it. It cost him twice the beer.

'I can meet you outside in fifteen minutes or we can use the backroom over there,' she said, smiling at him with bright red lips. Pushpa looked twenty-five but Mahesh guessed she was eighteen. The make-up was trashy and loud, concealing her real age, and her innocence.

'So soon?' Mahesh asked, as he sipped his beer and watched the other women. Pushpa was by far the fairest of them all, at least in his opinion. She had wide hips, and the perfect face of a devi; and a tongue that could make any man go wild. He wouldn't tell her that or she would up her rate. 'Not enough business tonight, Pushpa?'

'I knew you were coming, jaan. I kept myself free for you,' she laughed throatily, leaning back, highlighting her perky bosom.

'Aren't you going to drink that? I paid a king's ransom for it.'

'Jaan, I don't drink when I drive. Upsets the system. I will make up for it later,' she winked at Mahesh with her heavily kohled eyes.

She had told him her story – village girl from a Brahmin family. Father married her off to a man working in the city. He offered the family two thousand rupees as a wedding gift, and promised to keep their daughter well and happy. The husband was a pimp and sold her to his first customer: an overweight, middle-aged, unmarried jeweller. When she resisted, he thrashed her a few times, locked her in a room and raped her repeatedly. She was only seventeen.

Pushpa had laughed at the end of her story. 'I am well – I haven't got AIDS and I am happy – dancing all evening, who wouldn't be happy,' she had said, turning away.

'You talk too much,' was all he could say. Deep down he felt her pain as if it were his own.

The bar was noisy and smokier at two a.m. The owner had no intention of closing down at the curfew hour. He had paid off the night policeman in the neighbourhood and the man conveniently turned a blind eye.

'Do you know you look like Aftab Khanna, the film hero? The serious intense expression suits you,' Pushpa said watching him with bright eyes.

'You say that to all your customers?' Mahesh swallowed his drink. He dropped some notes on the table. 'I'll see you at the hotel in half an hour. Wear your red dupatta.'

'My jaan, I don't say that to all my customers. Only those who can get me out of this hell-hole.' With a generous sway of her hip, she went into a room that had a huge sign saying 'no entry'.

Two hours later, Pushpa took out a small black and white photograph from her bag.

'Who is that in the picture?' Mahesh asked, studying the photograph. Then he sat up and held the dog-eared picture under the bedside lamp.

'My parents. A photographer from a magazine came to our village. He took some pictures and gave this one to us, as thanks.'

'Your parents are... not Brahmin?' Mahesh's voice was a seething whisper. Mahesh felt as if cockroaches were crawling all over his body. He jerked away from her. 'You said they were Brahmins!'

'What's the difference nowadays, yaar. In the city, no one cares where you are from, only where you are going,' she laughed.

'You bitch! You lied to me!' Mahesh's eyes were burning, he gripped the pillow fiercely.

'No big deal. I like you. You were the only guy who showed me some decency and some respect, that's why I shared with you. If it makes any difference, my parents are dead.' Saying this Pushpa attempted to caress his face.

He pushed her hand away. 'It will take a lot of penance to get your dirty skin off my body.'

'You educated ones are the most hypocritical!' she shouted. 'What's wrong with you? You think you are superior than me?' she said pulling away. Instead she tripped on her red dupatta and landed on the floor. Mahesh didn't help her, instead he edged away from her 'I don't want to see you again. Ever.' Sitting there, she laughed, 'There are plenty more men like you. All they need is my body, and their satisfaction, just like you. No one cares about your background. The world has changed. A piece of advice – you had better change too.'

Mahesh slammed the door, her words ringing in his ears – 'you better change too'. He covered his ears, running out of the building, but the words lingered. Mahesh planned what he had to do; he had to take a hot shower, and then he would sprinkle gomutra on his body to purify himself. The next twelve days he would fast with just a few tulsi leaves to remove impurities. He was a pure soul, and he needed a pure body.

Chapter 21

Anwar glanced around. He tucked the knife deeper in the belt of his jeans, under the loose shirt he wore like a jacket. His t-shirt hugged his body like a glove, revealing the indents of strong chest muscles. He wasn't conspicuous, but he wanted to make sure no one noticed the plastic bag he had left at the corner, next to the bookshop. His boss had told him about the activities taking place within the bookshop – an illegal newspaper promoting a cause. 'We don't want to pollute the minds of our youth with such extremist viewpoints. Burn the place down,' Khanbaba had said.

Anwar nodded. His heart surged with pride, he wanted to please Khanbaba. These fundamentalists deserved to die – brainwashing the young ones with their ideologies.

The blast was small, just four deaths - the shopkeeper, and some customers. The main idea was the destruction of the shop and that was successful. Also, it created the desired effect. Fear had taken a grip on the people in the neighbourhood.

Anwar enjoyed the feel of power – the way a small act could result in a rippling effect and a larger tear in the fabric of the underground network of dons and their politics. Above ground, there was plenty of ruckus created by thugs, but if the aftereffects sunk lower, then it was worth his while to stay with Khanbaba, a ruthless cold-blooded soft-spoken mastermind. His boss wanted to take over the network eventually and Anwar was going to be his second-in-command.

Anwar grinned at no one in particular as he moved with ease through the bustling crowd in the vicinity of the IIA building. He had given the bosses of the diggers a good scare. And if they tried to pull a crazy stunt like announce the reporter's findings to the press, he would be the first to destroy them.

The widow was a slippery woman, he couldn't put a finger on that one – she was scared shitless. Yet there was something wilful about her. He had seen her at the Taj, looking pretty vulnerable. But he also saw Deva's puppydog with her. And the meeting between her and the IIA digger. He wondered what they were upto, but he guessed that with Deva's cronies hovering close she might be 'encouraged' to release the information. He couldn't wait to get his hands on her and shut her up. It would shake Deva's pedestal. Problem was that after he had taken care of the reporter, Khanbaba had warned Anwar to back off for the time being. But the woman, there was something not right. Instinctively he knew she was trouble, the sooner she was dead the better. And he would enjoy it, killing women was a favourite pastime.

He reeled back to the past. It was destiny that brought him to Delhi. After the horrific death of Uncle in Chennai, an icepick in his eye, and his body was found in a gutter, Anwar needed to find a new vocation, and keep a distance from the Chennai police. Uncle was his partner, the name stuck because that's what he referred to himself when he went to scout for girls in villages. Anwar knew the police would do nothing about Uncle's death, but it was better to be safe and he had left the city. Anwar had lost his easy commissions. In Chennai, he was the middleman, offering young fresh skin to rich city men, while 'Uncle' canvassed the villages for easy prey, he found the moneyed men. There were many desperate poverty-stricken families who would sell their daughters. As much as the supply, there was also a greater demand. It was a simple economic system that worked for all concerned. But Uncle had to go get himself killed. Must be one of those village girls, one of them must have escaped and mad with rage had killed the man who had duped her. Takes guts to do that.

When he moved to Delhi, Anwar worked as a shopkeeper's assistant. But it didn't last long. The man accused him of stealing, and when Anwar beat him up to a pulp, he was arrested and jailed.

Khanbaba heard about the man who was capable of such violence and paid for his release. The police pretended they didn't know who had paid his bail. The next day, the shopkeeper died. The police couldn't file a case. According to their records, Anwar wasn't responsible for his death. An intruder had entered the shop and beat up the owner. The case was closed.

Anwar had been with Khanbaba for ten years, initially as a hired assassin but later as a permanent part of Khan's network. They were fighting for control of the underground business, and Anwar believed that destiny had brought him to Khanbaba. He would have continued with the business of providing young girls to rich men, but Khan told him Delhi wasn't Chennai. He was better off working for him, in other areas.

Still, Anwar missed the entertaining side of his old business in Chennai. Before sending village girls to the rich men, they had to be trained and Anwar knew how to do it. The families of the girls were willing to give them up for a few thousand rupees. It was a good investment since they made money in lakhs. But these girls were ignorant and unaware of the ways of city life and what was expected of them.

Anwar and uncle would 'test drive' the girls and teach them how to be willing to do anything. It took time to bring these girls to the standards they had set but it was worth the investment. Anwar took to branding some of them. He used his knife to carve his initial on their bodies. The girls cursed, cried and willed him dead and he had laughed. Anwar guessed one of the girls' curses must have come true.

Anwar had gone into hiding when the police raided the Chennai dance bar. It was much later he heard Uncle was found dead in a gutter with an icepick in his eye.

Chapter 22

Mahesh Bhakti lived alone in a small but well-furnished apartment, fifteen minutes from the IIA. He prided himself on the neat and immaculate condition of his home, made even more antiseptic with white washed walls and stone-tiled floors. Before entering his home, Mahesh removed his shoes at the door and washed his feet before treading barefoot into his pristine hallway. The large shrine dedicated to the Hindu trinity was located in a small enclosure by the living room, and Mahesh lit an udhbatti to honour the deities.

The kitchen was just an extension of his living room, a small burner and three shelves to accommodate his meagre requirements. His home was his sanctuary, a place to think and meditate.

At the IIA, Mahesh's desk was covered with research papers, but he was too distracted to sort or file anything. Certain areas of the IIA offices were being secured and cordoned off from everyone. Trouble was brewing and he knew why. But he dare not approach Rizvi, or risk being the fall guy if the IIA was accused of mismanagement. There was no independence or control by the director general. Mahesh had been approached by rich businessmen, willing to pay a high price for valuable ancient Artifacts at sites, before it reached the IIA. Mahesh couldn't resist it; he succumbed to the obscene amounts of money offered. He had a sole purpose and it was to make sure that Artifacts reached the world. The country would realise the value of its own heritage when it was exhibited abroad.

And Mahesh's parents would rest in peace. He sensed their restlessness even now and it bothered him that they should suffer even in death.

He was upset with Manzil's cool reaction. He did not like her attitude and she should have agreed to return all the evidence immediately. What use did she have for it? KD was his perfect choice, she would show the world the ultimate evidence of the Taj, but first he needed the scroll to analyse it.

Mahesh reached for the switch on the right side of the inside wall, the hallway flooded with light. Mahesh turned and was about to reach for the water bottle, when a man dressed in black burst through. Mahesh felt the full effect of the power punch before he could react. His head whipped back and he stumbled against the wall. The bulk in the black t-shirt snickered. Mahesh grit his teeth and rammed full speed into his assailant. The impact made the attacker lose his balance and he fell back.

Before he knew it, two more men gripped Mahesh's arms and dragged him into the living room. The third delivered the hammering blows, sadistically drilling Mahesh at his already bleeding lip. Eyes squeezed shut, Mahesh hung his head after each blow. The throbbing of his bloodied face seemed to spread to the rest of his body, his legs buckled. The man stopped, he held a mound of white crystals in his claw-like hand.

'Salt. You want salt in your wounds?'

'Wait,' the voice said. It was only then that Mahesh realised there was a fourth man in his house. In the shadows, the man sat on his sofa watching silently.

The guy in the black shirt pulled Mahesh's head up by his hair. A thread of blood leaked from his chin and fell on the clean floor. Mahesh tried to focus on the man, his eyes were blurred. His head felt like it would topple over and roll away.

'How dare you go behind my back and approach that widow?' The man said in a soft voice. 'You do not mess with Deva, and with people I protect.' The don said leaning forward into the light. 'That woman, the dead reporter's wife is useful to us. I had already warned you. Do not talk to her, do not approach her and do not ask her for anything. Do you not understand me?'

Mahesh understood. He nodded. His assailants let go of him and he fell to the floor. Mahesh felt bile rise through his throat, he dry-heaved and coughed up blood.

'I have done nothing wrong. I said that I will keep my promise to you,' Mahesh croaked as he rose to his knees, he tried to focus, everything was a blur. 'I want the world to know what her husband found inside the Taj that night. She has no idea of its importance.'

'Do you really think you can do a better job?'

Mahesh nodded. His head reeled with pain. 'I have access to the right people and information.' He whispered weakly.

'You are only talk – no action,' Deva shouted. 'That scroll is going to make Khanbaba lose the faith of his men. I held that precious piece of writing in my hands. It was a scroll – proof of some sort, much more valuable than pictures.'

'That's why I must have it.' Mahesh said.

'Why you? She is the one who will tell all to the papers, just like her husband was going to do.'

Mahesh shook his head, and winced. 'I approached her because she will not do justice to this information.' His throat hurt as if someone had forced him to swallow steel wool. 'Who will trust an ordinary housewife? A widow?'

Deva's eyes glittered with interest, 'What do you mean?'

'There is another person who will make this news believable, not just by the masses but the educated lot as well. I have already made contact with her.'

'Who is this woman?'

'Kanyadevi – the famous Bharatnatyam dancer.'

Deva was curious. He came closer. 'Why do you think she will do a better job?'

'She is well-respected, well-known and when she holds a press conference, the publicity through her will make every single Indian sit up and listen,' Mahesh rasped.

Deva stared in silence for a few minutes. He grunted. 'I don't trust you but I will give you this chance to make sure this news reaches the entire country. Only then will we act.'

Mahesh looked up at the large man towering above him. 'I will make this happen. Give me everything the widow has,' Mahesh gritted his teeth. The pain was shooting through his lips as he felt warm blood slide down the side of his mouth. 'The scroll, I need to see it. I must check its authenticity. This is more valuable than anything we have discovered till today.'

'Come and see me in two days,' Deva said, indicating to his men to leave.

'Deva,' Mahesh said, kneeling down, as if praying. 'Please make sure no one steals that scroll – it is too valuable to lose.'

'It is safe with the widow. And I have my eyes on her. And you as well, don't let me down,' he said and walked past Mahesh, his sandals squeaking on the linoleum. The door slammed shut behind them.

Mahesh crumbled to the floor breathing heavily. Despite the searing pain, he felt a surge of joy, he couldn't wait to analyse the writing on the scroll. This could be the ultimate proof. The scroll must be the letter from the Sewai of Jaipur – Jai Singh to Shah Jahan. This was the elusive piece of evidence that he had been searching for in all the sites surrounding the Taj. He had heard rumours about treasure. What if this was some secret that revealed its location? Mahesh was keen to know the facts. The Taj had fascinated him all his life. It was the reason the revenge would be sweet. And now, there was writing in black and white. Who would have ever thought that it was lying inside a sealed room! But it made sense; Shah Jahan might not have read it, the messenger may have been killed and the scroll thrown inside the walled up rooms.

Mahesh couldn't contain his excitement. He tried to stand up, but before he could, he lost consciousness.

When he awoke, he didn't know how long he had been like that, but he could hear the crows announcing day break. Then as if drunk he stood up, swaying and leaning against the wall, he made his way to the bathroom. 'I must wash my feet,' he murmured.

He noticed the floor was streaked with the intruders' shoe prints and his own blood. It would take a lot of scrubbing to get the stains out. He was in so much pain. Gritting his teeth as he dragged his body to the bathroom. 'I will take my revenge,' he said as he checked his face in the mirror, his teeth stained red.

Chapter 23

Ramu wanted the filmroll. 'I must get it developed today, *didi.* You have done nothing so far. Deva is getting upset. You were supposed to go to the newspapers. Let me get the photographs for you. The sooner we have all the information, the sooner you can go to the press,' the teenager insisted.

Manzil was at home, reviewing the documents. She was carrying out her own research since Parag's death. And Ramu's constant presence in her life bugged her. She had told him to leave, but he insisted that her life was in danger and he could protect her. He just wanted to do Deva's bidding, which was to have all the information in the public domain. But she wasn't ready until she had verified the facts. And Ramu's suffocating behaviour was getting in the way. She didn't have the energy to argue with him. And damn it, she wouldn't be influenced by this indirect pressure from Deva.

Information wasn't something one just accepted at face value – just like numerical data, it required a more analytical approach. She needed an expert to look at these damning pictures and the scroll. The scroll! That's what scared her the most. It looked real. It possessed a latent energy and she could sense it would be trouble if its contents were translated and made public. There was a huge responsibility.

She had changed her mind about showing it to Parag's editor. Apart from a short announcement in the newspaper about Parag's death, he had expressed no sorrow. He had called Manzil, and wanted to meet for coffee. She had agreed and planned to show him the information. When they met, he didn't waste much time. He questioned her, as if it were an interview, hardly a condolence. Instead the man was fishing for information about Parag's death. Offered her some money for what he had discovered in the Taj. She had politely brushed him off. The next day he had a column on how he had spent the afternoon consoling the widow of Parag as she broken into tears. The liar! The gall of that man. She felt like she was surrounded by people with hidden agendas, and she wasn't going to get conned into doing anything that wasn't what she believed was right. Even if it meant keeping all the information in a locker and throwing away the key.

Staring at the computer screen for long hours was a bad idea, she was already exhausted from all the hullbaloo around her. And late nights were taking their toll on her – physically and mentally. A dull ache throbbed at the back of her neck. Ramu had been on his mobile, clearly talking to his goonda-boss, who was ordering him around.

The daylight streamed through the living room window, and highlighted the framed photograph. She glanced at her wedding picture, it was collecting dust, she observed at the back of her mind. Parag smiled at her, she turned away.

'I'm not ready to go public with this yet, Ramu. The press will release the information and then all hell will break lose,' Manzil said 'Why don't I get it checked and then maybe just give it back to that Mahesh Bhakti. He works for the IIA; he seems to know what he is talking about. Parag trusted him.' She stalled, trying to buy some time.

'Your husband's cause is your duty. How can you even think of passing it back to that man? What if he hides it and denies it ever existed. Your husband's death will be in vain. That sneaky fellow might even destroy it.'

'But . . .'

'Listen, how about you give me the roll. I get it developed. If it is nothing new but photos like the one you have then there is no problem.' He held out his hand.

Manzil clutched the back of her stiff neck. *God, help me.* 'I give it to you on the condition that you promise to bring back the photos to me first. I will make the decision about what to do with them Okay?' She shook his hand as if it were a pact between them. Ramu nodded, impatient.

'Good. I will keep the scroll in a safe place. And then decide what to do next.'

'I will inform Deva.'

'Do you *have* to inform Deva about everything? The scroll is my responsibility – tell him to back off or I won't do anything. And make sure you don't take the photos to him first.'

He turned away from her. 'I will do as he says.'

'Your boss will insist it goes public. *I* want to make that decision. Not him. Do you understand?' She said a little too harshly. People were trying to control her decisions, her life. She wasn't going to let them.

'Don't worry, he is a fair man, he will do the right thing.'

'Ramu, remember, you have made a promise to me.'

He swirled to leave.

'A piece of free advice, Ramu,' she added, before he raced out. He turned back, with a mulish look. 'Someday you will have to take responsibility for your own actions. You have to learn to think for yourself. Stop being a slave. Deva is a cunning man, a don, as you say. Hasn't he killed before, or been responsible for inciting violence?'

Ramu looked viciously at her, shook his head, as if it could shake away the bite of her words. 'Don't ever talk about Deva like that. He is a god-fearing man. I trust him.'

Pocketing the roll, he practically ran out of the door.

Ramu had a suppressed energy about him, ready to spring any second. If she helped him to school, get an education, all that pent-up energy would be channelised, she thought. But he didn't want that. She shook her head in frustration.

A short nap, two crocins and the coffee helped. Manzil was ready to face the day again. Ramu's behaviour nagged at her – she shouldn't have given him the roll, she could have got it developed herself.

She took a deep breath and then wrinkled her nose – the kitchen was a mess. The part-time maids had skipped work after they heard a policeman had come to visit. They didn't want to be involved with people who were in trouble with the police. Manzil didn't care. The mundane work of scrubbing, cleaning, mopping and sweeping would numb her constantly active mind and exercise her stiff limbs. She rolled up her sleeves and was about to start when the phone rang.

Manzil answered quickly, expecting Inspector Yadav, or Ramu, checking on her.

It was her father. She sank into her seat.

'I heard about Parag. I'm sorry,' he said in measured tones. The first time he had taken Parag's name. Her father had previously referred to him as 'that reporter'.

Manzil murmured a response and waited. Her father had a reason for calling, and it wasn't just to offer condolences. He would have sent an e-mail.

'Manzil, why don't you come to London? Stay here for a while, get away from it all.'

'No, thank you. And thank you for calling. Very kind of you to think of me.'

'Stop being so formal! I'm your father, for God's sake. Of course, I think of you all the time!'

'Temper, temper, Pa.' She used to cower in fear when he had his outbursts. But not anymore. Her mother was dead and Manzil didn't have to worry that her father would unleash his anger on his wife.

There was a long pause. She heard him take a deep breath. 'Sorry, my dear. I was just . . . worried about you.'

'Nice way of showing concern. You've been away for years.'

'You know I was tied up with a multinational merger and I couldn't just leave. There was a lot at stake.' His voice softened again. 'Just take the first flight out, I'll make the arrangements, you know I always provide the best for you. You will live with me comfortably. I would come for you but I can't leave yet. There's one final part of the deal we have to work out.'

'I can't leave either. This is my home, my country. I belong here…and so do you, Papa.'

'You will never change, will you,' he sounded disgusted.

'Pa, why don't you come back to India? You've made enough money. Why not live here and enjoy your money? With your own people?'

'We did once have a life India, remember...Then one day I had an offer to move overseas, great job, wonderful pay with all the perks. I wanted to make a better life for you two. But no, your mother was stubborn, and so were you.'

He paused. Manzil waited for him to finish the story he had been repeating for the last few years.

'We remained in India at your mother's insistence. It was the worst mistake I made.' She could hear the pain in his voice. 'They hurt your mother. She died and it was no fault of hers. Those monsters had no respect, they were just blind with rage, blinded by their anger to prove that they own the place...'

'Enough Papa,' she whispered, interrupting his tirade. 'It wasn't like that. Mama was at the wrong place at the wrong time. That's it. Don't blame it on something bigger. It was destiny.'

He created such negativity, spread so much anger. Manzil felt drained. 'I just lost my husband.'

There was silence. His wounds had had time to heal, hers was still fresh.

'Sorry.' He said, and cleared his throat. 'But it's time to move on. You need to get out of the country or it will destroy you and your spirit. In my opinion, that reporter got what was coming to him.'

How dare he talk about her husband like that. 'At least Parag was brave enough to face the injustices. Not like some people who run away and then denigrate their country. Is this how you talk to your

British friends? What do they do? Do you join them for a drink and talk about your bitter experiences? Do you complain about the corruption and the poverty and the religious squabbles? They probably think India was better off under colonial rule. Is that what you think too?'

She heard a click. The line was dead. Anger turned to frustration. She pressed her head against the wall as she tasted salt on her lips.

Chapter 24

The sprawling university grounds were a welcome diversion from the bustling city. The air seemed fresher; there was no rush of commuters, pedestrians and sidewalk vendors. It almost seemed a world unto itself. Students were moving around in clusters; some sat on the grass, under wide banyan trees, others made their way to one of the red brick blocks that housed the departments and classes. Life seemed to have slowed down.

Manzil wasn't in a rush as she made her way towards the main building. She recalled her university days when everyone looked forward to their lives and hoped to make a difference. Parag had been the livewire editor of the student's press. He knew how to psyche up people to further his cause. He wanted unity. United Indians, not divided by religions, was his motto. Many challenged his beliefs, threatened him. Once there was a scuffle, and then more students joined in, throwing stones. The police had to be called in. He suffered a few bruises, and a cut on his forehead. The scar remained, a beacon of his convictions. Manzil had begged him to stop being so vocal. Religion, unlike politics, was a sensitive topic. That's when he had asked her to marry him.

He was always out to prove a point.

Manzil guessed that when he viewed the evidence inside the Taj, all he would have thought about was revealing the truth. Only he was capable of doing justice with the information and the scroll. He would have stated the facts and avoided any coloured opinions in his story.

Now he was dead and the onus was on her.

Oddly enough, Yadav had given her a message, from Onyx. He was surprised when she said she knew about the organisation. Of course she knew, Parag had been invited to be part of the group. If the Onyx were involved she could trust him. 'Contact Professor Gupta at the university if you want to know more about your husband's research, he is a translator.' Inspector Yadav said and didn't question her further. He told her to be careful. 'And please keep Deva's man out of it.'

Yadav knew about Ramu. She shouldn't be surprised, he was a policeman after all. And seemed to be the rare good one. For the first time, Manzil felt safe, someone was watching over her. Someone she could trust. Maybe she would tell him everything.

Manzil asked one of the students for directions to the Department of History. The young man with thick glasses, spiked hair, and a heavy shoulder bag pointed to a red brick building which was slightly apart from the other three blocks that made up the university.

Manzil headed in that direction. She climbed the three steps to the porch and pushed one of the double doors inwards. The entrance was quiet. No one was around. She could hear a muffled sound of someone speaking over a microphone. It came from above. The staircase was to her left, she climbed up and an old man's voice was distinctly audible … '*It is you, the new generation, our future, that has the power to erase this fire of hatred, to replace anger with respect, to build a classless society tolerant of others, for the progress of our great nation. An India that shows the world that despite its diversity, it survives and grows and is great because of one common love of our country. I ask you, our hope for the future, will you make it happen? Do you have the courage, the compassion and the creativity to build a new India? Make a promise that you will start today. Start building a nation united in one common purpose.*'

The applause thundered like rain on concrete. It grew louder and more intense as Manzil neared the large auditorium where the orator stood on a raised podium. She entered through the back of the theatre, and joined the packed audience offering a standing ovation. A sturdy-looking old man, leaning on a wooden walking stick, thanked the audience. His snow-coloured hair contrasted with his black framed glasses.

A young woman approached the mic and thanked Professor Gupta for his inspiring speech and led him off the stage. Yes, that was the professor she had to meet. Manzil felt a renewed sense of hope.

Chapter 25

'Interesting…' Professor Gupta said, his frames perched low on the bridge of his nose as he studied the scroll. 'I now understand why you called to speak to me personally. This is not any ordinary piece of paper that you would flaunt in public.' His rheumy eyes focussed on his guest questioningly.

'Yes,' Manzil said, her pulse racing, eager to hear more.

'Tell me how it has come to be in your possession,' Professor Gupta said leaning back, as if he had all the time in the world. He seemed to blend in comfortably with his surroundings. His office was a large square space. The walls were lined with neat rows of books. It wasn't surprising that his office had a musty smell of old paper. She wondered if he ever got time to read those tomes. Besides teaching, he had written several books, she had checked his background. His wooden desk was spartan and she noticed a small brushed metallic sculpture placed distinctly on the right side of his table. It was intertwined ropes, in the shape of an 'O'. He wore a ring of a similar design. The Onyx.

'My husband . . .' she started. Then she thought it was better to keep Parag out of it. 'I happened to get it from someone. I would like to have a translation of the scroll.'

Professor Gupta grimaced and sniffed. He was obviously unhappy with her answer, but Manzil pretended not to notice.

'My dear, this kind of ancient script and writing is not easy to analyse. I will need more time. Give me a week or two. I will call you,' he said in a kind voice.

'I am in a hurry. I must take the scroll back with me. You can make a copy,' she replied.

Professor Gupta cocked his head to the side. He gave her a warm fatherly smile, '*Beti*, I need to keep this original – a photocopy might ruin it. I can see this is a very ancient document and I need to look at it more carefully. We don't want the words to get destroyed by the artificial light of a machine, now do we? We must protect it from the external environment – away from the humid air and the harsh light.'

'Professor sa'ab, I have the responsibility to take care of this scroll and I'm not letting it out of my sight. I'm running out of time – I need to decide what to do with this. There are people out there... who want it for their own reasons. So please just give me the gist of it. I have not asked you to analyse it, just read and tell me what it says.' Manzil said.

She stood and picked up the scroll from his desk, rolled it up and returned it to its holder.

Gupta watched her carefully. 'Sit down, young lady. You don't know what you are dealing with here. This is a very dangerous piece of evidence you are holding,' he said sombrely. 'It could cause trouble, serious trouble if it was leaked. It has to be handled responsibly or it could cost lives.'

'Then explain it to me, professor. You can be frank and honest with me.'

Gupta took a few minutes to study the script. He opened his notebook and began copying the distinctly curly calligraphy. As he wrote, he explained its contents. 'I can tell you, but there are some words, phrases that I do not understand. I need more time to check the details. It says here that this is an official *farman* from Raja Jai Singh to Shah Jahan. . .'

She gasped in disbelief. 'Does this means that the Taj was...,' Manzil gasped.

'Don't jump to conclusions, please,' Gupta said sternly. He removed his glasses and sighed. 'According to this, there is some implication that Shah Jahan may not have built it from ground up. Says here something about marble and jewels, but it could be, Shah Jahan asked the Raja to arrange these items for constructing the Taj. It did take more than two decades to build the monument. But...this piece of paper,' he tapped gently, 'I must warn you that it could very well be a fake.'

Manzil didn't care about his last comment. She leaned forward wide-eyed. 'No wonder… Parag, my husband…' Manzil stared at the ancient relic in the professor's hands.

This was too great a responsibility to handle alone. Fake or no fake, conspiracy theorists would have a field day with it. The press would feed on it, leading to street gangs adding fuel to the simmering fire... anything could happen.

The professor watched her, the strain visible on his face. 'Don't get carried away. Like I said this could quite easily be an elaborate fabrication. I need to authenticate this relic.' His hands trembled as he spoke. 'But you must also consider that even if it is a fake, this is a time bomb. In the wrong hands, it could explode. Let me help you.'

'I understand and that's the reason, I'm sorry professor, I cannot let you take the responsibility. I will deal with this myself.' Manzil carefully replaced the scroll inside the holder, into a plastic pouch and put it in her oversized bag.

'I know about you and your husband, Parag. He was the one who found this, isn't it? Please, he would have wanted us to help you,' he said, touching the Onyx symbol on his desk. 'He was a good man, had great dreams for our country. Helped the Onyx in so many ways.'

'That's why it cost him his life, professor. I need time to think and decide. I cannot put anyone else at risk.' She zipped her bag and placed it on her shoulder, clutched it tight. 'I will contact you when I'm ready. Thank you for your time, professor.'

Chapter 26

Yadav knew Manzil was in danger the moment Ramu left her side. He had already pieced together that Mahesh Bhakti was the link between Parag and the IIA. If he was leaking secrets then he must be committing other unscrupulous acts. Yadav would have preferred to monitor Mahesh. But, he couldn't be in two places at one time. The woman had more to hide and more to lose if she was caught.

He trailed her to the university and then to the bus stop. She was alert, but he was quick enough to stay out of her sight. A tall athletic man with henna-dyed hair, clearly conspicuous in a policeman's uniform, was tailing Manzil. It didn't look good. But Yadav couldn't attack yet. The man had done nothing wrong, except follow the woman.

Yadav felt the piece in his pocket, he was a good shot, if the situation required he could aim perfectly at a man's heart from twenty feet away, and shoot.

It was only when she was on the bus that she realised she was being followed. Manzil noticed the narrow-faced, red-haired man twice; once when she left the university grounds; and second now when she boarded the bus. He kept an even distance behind. But she could sense his presence. He looked like a policeman, but why would he be following her? Had Yadav assigned him? She wondered.

Her life had turned into a spectator sport. Parag used to say that – life was a spectator sport – you only get one chance. She wasn't sure what to think anymore. She had no handy weapon to defend herself. The policeman either wasn't very good at his job or wanted to intimidate her.

As she made her way, weaving through the crowded street towards the bus-stop Manzil had glanced over her shoulder, the red-haired man pretended to be interested in an English magazine at a news-stand.

He couldn't fool her. Of late, Manzil had developed a heightened sense of awareness. The scroll had turned her life topsy turvy. Crazy things were happening around her and it had tuned her to be alert and pre-empt the possibilities of danger. The professor was a kind old man, and she didn't want to dump her problem on him. The scroll landed in her life for a reason. And damn it, she would take responsibility, even if it meant facing risks.

Manzil clutched her bag closer to her body, quickened her pace, pulse racing, distinctly aware of being followed. She guessed the man wasn't really from the police or even paid to protect her. Manzil was an ordinary woman, one amongst millions of Indians. She wasn't a cause for concern. Yet. The scroll was supposed to have remained buried, she mused. All these centuries, the silent monument had kept it hidden. Now that Parag had retrieved it, there were some people who wanted to make sure the truth stayed buried. They would kill to ensure that it remained so. And yet there were others who wanted the secret revealed, to unravel an age-old story and its shaky foundations. These people too, would kill to reveal the truth.

Either way she faced death.

Manzil was in a quandary. The more she thought the more she realised that she should be under the government's protective custody. She had heard these words many times on television programmes about patriots and terrorists. But the Indian government didn't know about her. And she didn't know which minister would give her the time of day.

At the bus stop, Manzil waited in queue. As soon as the bus

arrived, she and dozens of others crowded quickly to hop on. For once she was glad about the push and shove. The man wouldn't attack in a public place, or on the bus.

Shouldn't, she amended.

Manzil found a seat, clutched her bag tight and stared out of the window. A mother sitting next to her played with her toddler. The child clapped and bounced energetically. Manzil smiled. Ordinarily, she would have played with the cute little thing, but now she was so tense she gripped the seat railing tight with one hand and held her bag close with the other. She was beginning to feel claustrophobic. The bus was emptying out too quickly at every stop.

Yadav was the last one to board and had chosen a seat at the back. He watched the man take the seat diagonally across Manzil. She chose a window seat. That was bad, she would be cornered easily.

Manzil's home was still five stops away, maybe she should have taken a taxi instead, or got lost in the crowded streets, taking a long circuitous route until the man got tired and gave up. That was not going to happen, she realised in panic. As stubborn and resilient as she was, he would be twice as worse and threatening. Her only hope was to stay one step ahead.

At the stop, the young woman next to her got up. Manzil would move to another seat after she left. The baby waved with a drooling toothless grin, drawing a warm response from the passengers. Some waved at the child grinning. All was normal in an ordinary day, an ordinary life. Manzil wished she had that luxury too.

Before the bus lurched forward, Manzil stood up to look for another seat. Too late! The stranger slipped into the vacant seat beside her. He pressed a button on his switchblade knife and a six-inch sharp blade jumped out. He aimed it low, at her stomach.

'Not a sound,' he said in a menacing whisper.

Manzil nodded.

There were two kinds of people in this world, Yadav mused as he chewed on a toothpick. One that thrived on information, using it as a powerful instrument to benefit mankind; and the other that manipulated information, using it to benefit himself. The second lot was sneaky and slippery as snakes and lived amongst the first lot as if harmless do-gooders.

Sitting at the back, nondescript, wearing a plain white shirt over beige pants, Yadav looked like any one of the thousands of working class thronging the city. He didn't react when he saw the red-haired man sit next to Manzil, but he felt an instinctive urge to jump up and aim his gun at his head. He was insulting the uniform. Yadav held back and watched carefully.

Manzil waited for the man to claim his needs. Her heart palpitated as if it was pushing itself out of her chest. She was sure everyone could see it thumping. Still, she tried to breathe calmly. No one seemed interested, after all it was only a policeman sitting next to her. One, two, three, breathe in and one, two, out. That was all she managed before she jumped at the sound of his gritty voice.

'Give me the scroll, I will let you go. Or else...' The stranger pressed the sharp point of the knife against her. If the bus driver went over a pothole, she knew she would be dead, bleeding all over the floor of the bus. She whimpered. With trembling hands, she removed the rolled up tube from her large bag. 'Here it is.'

The man took hold of it. Swiftly, he made his way towards the exit. At the traffic light, he hopped off.

Yadav smiled as he followed the red-haired man. He had to admit, the woman was brave. The man weaved his way through the throng of people. He turned into an alley.

Yadav kept his distance, he didn't follow the man into the alley, but waited across the road. Then he saw the man emerge, his hands formed fists and he trashed the tube that Manzil had given him. Then stamp on it in a rage.

The widow was not only brave, but smart. But what she had done was infuriate the man. She was in deep shit, this guy wasn't about to let her off easy now.

His phone buzzed. Yadav answered. When he heard what his boss had to say, still on the phone, he flagged a taxi. And indicated to the driver to hit the accelerator, Yadav had to show him his ID to get the cabbie to step on it. The dons were about to spring into action, he thought darkly. Yadav would know only after he checked the reports. The grapevine mentioned a bomb. He will question Manzil, she had to know something, something that would deter a catastrophe.

He swallowed the bitter taste in his mouth.

Chapter 27

'He's busy entertaining the Bharatnatyam dancer,' Dass said. 'He was with Farhan and Gaurav at the Pondi site. Now he has followed her to Khajuraho – he sent a message that he has discovered a Chandela artifact and needs more time to explore the area.'

'He was a reliable fellow, good at his job, very careful onsite with the artifacts. He is the one who discovered the carvings inside the Ajmer mosque,' Rizvi said.

'Yes, but that information was classified, yet oddly the press got wind of it and it was news the following day.'

'The police inspector will know right away that he is responsible. We need to get him back here and find out what he knows. Check his table, his workspace for anything that could prove disruptive.' Rizvi looked up from his desk.

'Rana has been keeping an eye on him. He is worse than we thought. He has been in touch with the reporter's wife. He must have been leaking information to the reporter. The man is tainted by his own views, out to cause trouble.'

Rizvi paused before he spoke. 'Reel him in. We'll give him a desk job for a while. There is plenty of research and information to sort through.' His lips set in a grim line.

'I think we should ask him to leave the IIA. He will be the death of us if he stays. The Taj incident is definitely his doing,' Dass said. 'It is time to get rid of the bad apple.'

Rizvi shook his head. 'He is a lose cannon and could go ballistic, doing our reputation more harm. We have to be careful. If he has leaked some official documents or IIA papers, we need to get them back. If they are with the reporter's wife, then she might use them against us. This is serious, Dass. It has to be handled delicately.'

'We also have a problem with the dons, they are tracking our movements and if they know Mahesh is the culprit, we are going to be targeted as well.' Dass seemed to have lost his stiff army stance. For the first time, Rizvi's assistant looked stooped, the situation had made him weary. 'This might explode in our faces any day now.'

Rizvi felt a sinking sensation in his stomach. 'What is Mahesh Bakti's hidden agenda? He is acting out. We have to find that reason, Dass, and we might be able to stall his next move.'

Chapter 28

Deva sat on a rope bed, in his airy living room on the first floor of his house. There were two doorways from the ground floor that led into his home; one was the main entrance that faced the road, meant only for close friends and family members. And the other, on the right, was a stairway from the exterior of the house that led straight to the veranda of the first floor. This was where Deva held his court with associates managing his various businesses.

Ramu raced up the short flight of wooden steps, two at a time, ignoring the two guards who stood on the veranda. They knew him and patted his back at his enthusiasm.

'Deva, Deva I have the pictures,' he called out.

As soon as Ramu saw Deva, he bowed quickly and handed over the envelope containing the photos taken by Parag. Breathing heavily, he sat cross-legged on the floor.

Deva's eyes widened as he glanced at the pictures, flipping quickly through the thirty-six photos and then spread them out. Ramu saw his face turn red with anger and he murmured fiercely, as he stared at each picture repeatedly.

Then, Deva reached out viciously and slapped Ramu hard. 'You idiot, you were sent to protect the widow. Where is she? And, the scroll? These photos . . . my god, these photos will change our country forever. How could I have bestowed such a huge responsibility on you? We need to get the woman and the scroll here.'

Ramu looked shell-shocked. He recovered quickly, he didn't

argue, nor even try to defend himself. 'I'm sorry Deva. Manzildidi is at the university. She said it was better to go alone. The professor might not meet her if I tagged along. She wanted to get the scroll translated to understand what it was. I will go now to make sure she is alright.' He was kneeling. Blood was oozing from a small cut on his cheek. There were no tears.

Four men were in the room. Two stood ominously with arms folded across their broad chests. They kept a watch at the entrance, another barked orders on the phone, and the fourth, with a deep scar on his left cheek, watched the proceedings. None of them batted an eyelid when Deva whacked Ramu.

'You better stick to her like glue. That man, Mahesh, is useful to us.' He turned to scar-face. 'Contact that digger now. I want to talk to him.'

'Make sure no one speaks to the woman. I need the scroll before anyone gets it,' he said to the boy.

'But Deva . . . the pictures, I must show them to...'

Another slap, and everyone turned. No one ever challenged Deva.

Deva fixed Ramu with a dagger stare.

Ramu held his gaze and then lowered his eyes. 'I will do as you say,' Ramu ran out the door towards the veranda and then down the staircase that led him straight to the gate, away from his God's den, where different rules applied.

'Don't try anything stupid,' one of Deva's men said, blocking his path. His skin was as black as a cobra's. And his eyes were coal. 'I see how you talk about that woman. Manzildidi, Manzildidi, didi my foot! Remember, she is not your sister, and don't expect that these people who live in these big concrete homes will ever take you in. We take care of our own; the street is our palace and is our death bed. Keep your distance from her.'

Ramu nodded without glancing at him. Wiping away the blood from his face, Ramu raced out as if his mission had taken on a new urgency. There were bloody streaks across his face.

Deva turned to scarface. 'Keep an eye on that boy, he is capable of making mistakes. Give these pictures to the newspaperwallahs. Start a stir on the streets and make sure there is a large morcha of protestors two days from now. Find out what the professor has told this widow. I want some passion on the streets, the police should be involved, you understand?'

The man grinned broadly, 'I know what to do, Deva.'

Chapter 29

Standing outside her apartment door, Yadav gave Manzil a slight nod as greeting before he pushed her door wide open to let himself in. She moved back and let him pass.

'You are not being honest with me,' he said, without breaking stride. Ignoring her sour expression, he looked inside every room and found no one. 'I need you to come clean or else I will have to take action against you for abetting and aiding a known criminal.'

Manzil's red-rimmed eyes turned bright with anger, 'How dare you come into my house and talk to me like that? I don't know any criminals.'

Yadav leaned against the dining table, where Manzil's bag lay. 'You mean you don't know Deva's man Ramu? How about the man on the bus, didn't you pass some information to him?'

'You've been following me? Spying? How dare you?'

'It's my job,' he responded calmly.

He gave her a questioning look.

'That man threatened to kill me.' She turned away. 'Ramu is... is helping me, actually protecting me. He knew my husband and was just trying to...'

He gripped her arm. 'Trying to what? Steal secrets and plant them in places that could cause havoc? You think I don't know what's going on. Or are you so stupid that you don't know what's going on. Stop this charade!' He said, shaking her. His voice had taken a steely edge. 'What is with the Onyx and you? Why are they trying to protect you? What is in the scroll?'

'Let go of me,' she said simply. Yadav saw the anger in her eyes. He felt a twinge of guilt at harassing her. He let go.

Manzil took a step back. 'I've done nothing wrong. Parag found the scroll inside one of the Taj chambers. I have the scroll with me. It is safe.'

'Where is the filmroll?'

'With Ramu, he promised to get it developed and bring it straight back to me,' Manzil said as she picked up her bag and clutched it. 'Please understand, I'm just as concerned about what Parag found, it can cause...major problems.'

He took a deep breath and gritted. 'You did what? You *gave* the film to Ramu. You actually think he will bring it back to you before Deva gets his hands on it? For a smart woman, you do have your stupid moments.'

She looked at him enraged. 'Get out of here! You have no right to speak to me that way.'

He had to protect her. She didn't understand. She was in danger. 'Look, I'm sorry,' Yadav ran his hand through his short crewcut. 'It's just that the commissioner is not giving me any details. Just gave me a message to pass on to you to visit the professor. You don't want to tell me what's going on. How can I do my job if I'm not kept in the loop. What did you find out? What did the professor say?'

Her cheeks were flushed. He could see that she was agitated. There was a part of her that wanted to trust him and another that feared him.

Yadav wanted her to realise the extent of danger. 'Look, that weirdo knows you gave him a fake scroll. He is majorly pissed and I won't be surprised if he is heading here right this minute. Give me the scroll. I will keep it safe.'

'No!'

Yadav wanted her to trust him, but wasn't handling the situation correctly. He should have approached her with kid gloves. She was being obstinate. God, why are women like this! This one is ready to crumble, yet she holds back, she won't unburden herself.

He decided to take a different tack. 'Look, I'm not the enemy. I followed you, because you are in trouble. Deva's man is not going to guard someone unless he can benefit. You have to be careful. That red-haired man maybe working for another don but they are both out to cause violence. They will kill without thinking twice. Bloodshed is what excites them. The police are familiar with them, but we are also powerless many a times. They train and brainwash illiterate street kids and form an army. These kids' lives are disposable. And so is Ramu, your so-to-speak protector.'

'Please leave,' Manzil said quietly.

'Mrs Saxena, I will leave, but first you need to give me your passport.' He took out a sheet of paper from his pocket. 'This is a court order.'

'You cannot do this.'

'I can and will if you do not cooperate with the police. We can confiscate travel documents of any person or persons that have suspicious links to extremist or terrorist groups.'

Manzil gave him her passport and told him to get lost. The scroll would remain with her.

Chapter 30

Khajuraho

Kanyadevi couldn't concentrate. She had received disturbing information from the professor. Her thoughts revolved around the dilemma that the Onyx faced. Manzil had made contact with Professor Gupta but refused to part with the scroll. The contents were explosive.

'We have to face the fact that this is a very big responsibility. By now, the various factions must be aware of its existence and spreading their own rumours about its contents,' Gupta had said. And if he said an issue was serious, then there were no two ways about it.

Kanyadevi was worried that his life might be in danger. Even Inspector Yadav had contacted the professor to make sure he was alright. And also asked about the contents of the scroll. The professor had told him the gist but also added that he didn't have the exact details as he needed time as some of the words were not easy to understand.

The message to KD had come wrapped in a gift box, marked with a large 'O'. Kanyadevi knew the moment she unwrapped her gift that the news would be bad.

'Raghu, please let me know as soon as Mahesh arrives,' she had said as she had unwrapped the gift.

'I will keep a look out for him. Madamji, you are looking worried, is everything alright? Your performance is six hours from now. If you want, I can postpone it.'

'No, I'm fine Raghu. It's just…' looking at his concerned expression, she realised it would be unfair to burden him with her worries, 'it's just some trivial matter. I can handle it. How is the stage set up? How many other dancers will be performing tonight?'

'Four young dancers; very eager to meet you. You will be performing at the end, the grand finale. The outdoor stage is beautiful with floodlit temples in the background. We have a good response – it will be a full house.'

She smiled her thanks. 'I will meet the girls before the performance. It is good to see so many youngsters taking an interest in classical dance. It is our culture. We should make sure it doesn't die out.'

'Madam, you are an inspiration to many.'

'You are a good man, Raghu. I think you work too hard organising all my performances; seeing to every detail. After this, why not take a break? Go on a holiday, with your family. My gift to you.'

He looked at her, horrified. For the first time his smile lost its lustre. 'Madamji, have I offended you? Why do you want to fire me? Have I committed some wrong?'

'No, no, Raghu you misunderstand me. I just want you take a month's holiday, switch off for a while. I need a break too. Not getting any younger, you know. And when you come back, we can start the tours again. Raghu, without you, I'm nothing, how can I fire you?' She laughed.

Raghu nodded, his head swung from side to side, yet his expression of doubt betrayed his smile. 'No problem. We can discuss after this performance, Madamji.'

The audience comprised mostly tourists who were distracted by the spectacular backdrop of the Indo-Aryan architecture. Khajuraho was famous for the exterior stonework of its Hindu temples. The sculptures that drew most attention were the figures of women and depiction of poses from the Kamasutra. The tourists fanning themselves with the paper flyers whispered and snickered amongst themselves. Once the performance began, they were mesmerised.

After the four young dancers had performed, Kanyadevi walked seductively on stage.

Mahesh was at the back, in the shadows. She was captivating, as usual. As if a stone apsara had come to life to entice the audience. When she looked towards him, her eyes smouldered with an intensity that gave him goosebumps. He wished desperately he could hold her in his arms . . . he wanted her, like he never wanted anyone before. She would give him salvation; she was the one who would soothe the wounds that scarred his heart more than his body.

He could not understand why he was so attracted to her, maybe she was just the perfect embodiment of Indian beauty. It was definitely love he felt. The feeling washed over him, renewing him, filling him with joy. KD brought heaven to earth and he would move mountains to fulfil her every desire. He would give her the scroll and tell her everything. She would believe him and love and respect him for his ideals. She was a strong, disciplined woman. Her dance had a magnetic quality and the energy that flowed from her, felt as ancient and pure as the Sanskrit mantras.

He had wanted to visit Manzil again and demand the scroll, but he had to wait. The police were expanding their investigation of the killings of three prostitutes. The press had made a big deal about it, blaming the police for not taking the situation seriously because the murdered were low-caste women, and prostitutes. Mahesh knew that there were some men out there who thought they were doing a good deed by killing off these women. Twisted beliefs resulted in twisted acts. He may have had his issues but murder was never his way.

Mahesh couldn't hurt a fly, but he was worried when he heard that Pushpa was one of the murdered women. He had visited the dance bar often, and someone might recognise him and he could be suspected.

Mahesh's bruised lip still ached from Deva's beating. But he ignored the pain, losing himself in the thudding sounds of KD's feet and the ankle bells that resonated like the sounds of the doorway to Indra's court in the skies.

Mahesh closed his eyes and let the tears wash their way down his face. The salt burned his split skin. His hands tightened into a white-knuckled fist.

Fifteen minutes later, when the magic was over, he looked at his hands. Little moon-shaped cuts welded his palms. He found a washroom nearby and cleaned up before he went backstage to meet his love.

'You are hurt, what happened?' KD asked, concerned. Mahesh smiled, resulting in stabbing pain where his lip stretched. He winced. KD looked at him with such compassion, he wanted to smile again. She touched his face tenderly.

'I was in an accident . . . a motorcyclist. But not to worry, I'll be fine. Just being here, close to you, makes me feel better,' Mahesh said with a stutter. He kneeled in front of her, drinking in her beauty. 'God should never have created such temptation for man. You will not be able to understand how deep my feelings are for you. Just saying, I love you, trivialises the emotion.' He took her hands in his and started kissing them.

'Love is the one emotion in life that brings most grief. With love comes attachment. With attachment there is desire and with desire there is suffering,' she said.

'You quote from ancient scriptures. And in the same thread, there is also moksha from love. I am a man of science and emotion is different from religion. I believe love is not to be identified with any system of philosophy, it is simply to be experienced. With each magnetic glance of your eye, I burn with desire to touch you, to feel you, to kiss you...'

'So I've turned you into a poet, eh?' she said to lighten the mood. Mahesh spoke with such seriousness; she didn't have the heart to hurt his feelings.

KD knew he wasn't in any accident. She studied him carefully. He was jittery, shifting nervously on his chair. Overly emotional. His hands shook as if he had hit them hard against the wall. He said he loved her. Deep in her heart it rang true. She felt sorry for him.

'No. You've turned me into a lover.'

'You give me more credit than is due,' she smiled gently retreating. 'Give me ten minutes to change. I will meet you outside and we will spend the whole evening together. Just you and I. Okay?'

'An evening I will cherish forever,' Mahesh said. 'Today I will show you the raw beauty of Khajuraho.'

KD relaxed. She liked Mahesh. He was such a complicated man. Yet, a good man deep down. He meant no harm. He was the snitch in the IIA, but there had to be a reason for it she was sure. Mahesh's love was finding its way into her heart. She shook her head wryly. She was defending his actions. She knew he wanted something from her. She wasn't sure what to expect but she needed to know if he had information about the scroll.

She changed quickly and informed Raghu she would be with Mahesh Bhakti. He gave her a knowing smile. 'Ahh, now I understand why you want to give me time off. It's okay; you take your time to know this good man, Madamji,' he said and walked away briskly, without giving her a chance to explain.

The evening was pregnant with hidden feelings. There was a warm breeze and the gentleness of its caress filled her with a sense of loneliness. Despite herself, KD enjoyed Mahesh's company. He was extremely knowledgeable about ancient history. They had dinner at Raja's Café, under a large shady tree in the courtyard. Later they walked slowly towards the cluster of ancient monuments on the western side of the town.

KD prided herself on her inner strength. She didn't fall into the emotional trap. If she liked Mahesh she still had a grip on her emotions, and if she wanted, she could go all the way with him. Physically.

Her insular world was focussed on dance. She was careful who she got close to, who her friends were and was almost totally self-reliant. Life had taught her to be independent. But with this man, there was more, she wanted to know more about him. She was strangely drawn; maybe it was the atmosphere of Khajuraho that steered her towards the baser pleasures of life.

They made their way through a narrow path. The moonlight providing a route and guiding their steps. 'So where were you born? Is Bharatnatyam a family tradition?' Mahesh asked.

'Born in Kanyakumari. Parents died in an auto accident and lived most of my life in Pondicherry, I mean Puducherry, with my uncle. There I developed a passion for Bharatnatyam. Luckily I had a very capable guru who instilled the discipline of the dance, and I fell in love with it,' Kanyadevi lied baldly.

'I see,' he murmured.

They strolled through the dusty street. The number of people strolling was getting smaller. And most were starry-eyed couples.

'What about you?'

'We share similar backgrounds,' he said, as they followed a clear path towards Kandariya Mahadev, the largest of the Khajuraho temples. 'I used to live in Mumbai. My parents died when I was young. My mother's sister and husband lived in Delhi, I moved in with them. They were childless. I guess I understood the meaning of their love when they asked me to cook and clean in return for food and boarding.' He looked at the stars that glittered, like oil lamps in a temple. 'My aunt was a very religious, she would wake up at five am everyday, prod me with a stick to get started with work – usually involved cleaning her prayer room, polishing the silverware, specially used only for the idols, and roll a dozen cotton wicks for the aarti. She used homemade pure ghee to light the aarti. Oddly enough, she died when she slipped on some ghee that had dripped to the ground. My uncle blamed me for the accident, but I didn't do it.' His eyes distant, sad, recalling the past. 'Anyway, it's all behind us. I managed to get a job, study and get a degree in field archaeology.'

They reached the western enclosure of the towering, most majestic temple she had ever seen. He took her hand in his and caressed her palm. She liked the way he made her feel.

'We seem to have a similar destiny: passion for ancient art,' KD said, unable to take her eyes off the exquisite statues dotting the temple walls.

They were quiet for a while, gazing at the thousand year old structure before them.

'KD, which caste do you belong to? Brahmin?' he asked suddenly.

Unaccustomed to such a question, she looked at him in surprise. The last time she was witness to the influence of the caste system was when a man she slept with asked her a similar question. The caste system had an ominous characteristic, and existed within the social hierarchy in a society that she hoped didn't exist in this day and age. But in one incident, KD recalled the arrest of a village priest. He had sex with the women of his choice, claiming to be the direct conduit to god, a Brahmin, a superior class. And thus offering the women a chance to achieve nirvana.

'I'm not sure, does it matter?' she asked.

'I would imagine you are a Brahmin.'

She shrugged and continued forward. His hand held hers lightly. They walked in silence for a while.

'Mahesh, you do realise that being a man of science the question of caste is odd coming from you. Why do you ask?' KD asked.

'Life's lessons are odd. I cannot explain why. But please don't judge me on this.'

She wasn't satisfied with his answer and she would find out what mysteries lay buried in that mind of his. For now, she let it go.

The path sandy and as they entered the ancient shrine, a strong wind blew in their direction whipping up a layer of dust. He let go of her and fell to the ground. 'Ahh,' Mahesh cried holding his face.

Kanyadevi knelt by his side and gently eased his hands away. She used a soft kerchief to wipe his wounds. He was such a strange contradiction.

'Thank you,' he whispered, looking at her with eyes that glimmered with desire. She felt a rush of emotion, and she let it wash over her, glazing her eyes, drawing her lips towards his. An owl hooted in the distance. Then the moment passed. KD stood up, and moved away.

'Why do you hold yourself back, KD?' he whispered, close behind her. She felt his breath on her neck. 'It is not a sin to love.' He grasped her hands, and gently brushed his lips on her shoulder.

'Look around you. Love is in all the art, in the air we breathe, even the gods are aware that love must be satiated to achieve nirvana.'

'I cannot....' she said breathlessly.

Mahesh loosened his grip. 'Whenever you are ready.'

She didn't respond, and moved ahead. There was a deep stirring within her, it had awakened a desire and she wanted to satisfy it.

They made their way to the smaller of the temples and sat on the steps. The largest one consisted of the famous erotic sculpture of a man and a woman in the throes of lovemaking. The entwined couple were emblazoned above the entrance to the main temple.

'Tell me about Khajuraho,' she said. KD tried to avoid staring at the vulgarly ecstatic expressions of the lovers.

Mahesh leaned back, resting on his elbows he stared up at the bands of sculptures. 'Khajuraho is derived from the word khajur or date palm, which grew freely in the area. The old name, however was *khajuravahaka* or scorpion bearer - the scorpion symbolising poisonous lust. These temples were built under the late Chandela kings in the early tenth century. They were followers of the Tantric cult that believes gratification of earthly desires is a step towards attaining the ultimate liberation. Tantrism is mostly misunderstood and the philosophical part of the Tantras has been totally forgotten. This is one of the reasons why Tantrics perished, while being the distinct path of spiritual practice, it has very few followers across the world.'

'I would have imagined that such philosophy would be taken advantage of, don't you think? Look at that sculpture,' she said pointing to the one that looked like a complicated Kamasutra pose.

'It's sculpted on a temple wall and it's as if the gods are willing participants.'

Mahesh shook his head. 'It is a misconception that the temples depict sex between deities. The Khajuraho temples do not contain any sexual art inside the temple or near the deity, only on external carvings. They are symbolic. To visit the deity one must leave sexual or material desires outside the temple. They also depict the inner deity of the temple as pure as the soul which is unaffected by sexual desires and other carnal urges.'

He stood up and held out his hand. 'Come with me,' he led her to the front of the temple. 'See, only ten per cent of the carvings have erotic themes, they are between humans, not deities. The rest depict the common man's life of those days. There are potters, musicians, farmers. All these are away from the temple dieties. They give the message that one should always have god as the focal point in one's life, even while engaged in worldly activities.'

'You are a staunch believer, aren't you?' Then it dawned on her why he had asked her which caste she belonged to – he was old world. 'You are a Brahmin, right?'

He nodded and she saw the pride in his eyes.

'Do you know the history of *nritya* or the dance form that you so beautifully perform?' Mahesh asked.

KD laughed. 'No. But tell me.'

Mahesh was trying to entice her, woo her. Love existed, she knew, in the deep dark corner of his heart. 'Lord Brahma, the creator, took the words from the *Rigveda*, the elements to communicate from the *Yajurveda*, music from the *Samaveda* and the emotional element from the *Atharvaveda* to form the fifth artistic yoga – the *Nrityaveda*, revealing spiritual through the corporeal.'

KD was genuinely impressed. 'You are amazing – a bottomless pit of information.'

'And a bottomless pit of passion for you, my love,' he said with lustful eyes.

KD nodded and smiled. She wanted to tell him what she thought of lust and desire. Suffering the pain of love, of longing, it enriched the beauty of her art. The need for sex existed, but as a need for food or drink or any other need. When the deepest physical desires had been quenched, her performance was even more intense, more focussed and energetic. The audience reacted differently, they looked at her as if she was an angel, that she performed magic and hypnotised them.

For her, dance was a discipline to control the mind and body. The men who wanted her were handsome, some of them powerful, and many of them in love with her, and her form. When they recovered from their trance, they moved on. And KD wasn't sorry.

Her art was her real lover, the true intoxicant, the one that completed her. It was permanent; the rest of the world and relationships was temporary.

Mahesh smiled the lop-sided smile. It had a warm effect on her.

Chapter 31

He wanted her to come back to his room. He asked her if she was okay with the idea. KD agreed.

Mahesh kissed her in the corridor, on the way to his room. Gently tasting her lips and then probing deeper. KD returned his kiss, hesitantly at first. Then she parted her lips.

There was pent-up heat building inside her body, her heart pumped and she felt the pulsating rhythm through his shirt. They heard voices and pulled away. He gave her the keys to his room, told her to go ahead; he needed to get something from the stallowner nearby and then winked.

KD could turn away and leave, the voice pushed at her that he was unstable. She hesitated, then determined with a now-or-never resilience, she pushed the key in the lock and turned.

The room was clean and functional, as it should be in an impersonal way. KD traced her finger along the smooth grooves of the wooden bedside table. She was going against the grain, she reflected. What if she fell in love with him? She was overreacting, she realised. Love wasn't happening here, it was lust. She was prepared. *What if you are hooked on him and want to spend the rest of your life with him?* That was impossible, and she knew how to control those feelings, just like before.

KD shut her mind. She looked at herself in the mirror; she applied some lipstick and neatened her hair. Then she lay down on the soft bed. This was an evening for the here and the now.

Her own desire was the focus of her attention. This was acceptable, because, after it was over, she would be able to face herself. Discipline and self-control were the cornerstones of her life. It was a fair balance. Everything in life was about balance: love and hate were just emotions that controlled the mind, and she had learned to control them. KD never fell in love, and never could.

That evening, in a nondescript hotel room, with a Brahmin man, Kanyadevi let herself go. Mahesh, the archaeologist with big dreams, was unbelievably sexy in the nude. His text-book broad shoulders tapered down to firm abdomen muscles that rippled to her touch and then lower down the tight rounded buttocks flexed.

The desire in his deep dark eyes matched hers and she savoured the moment. When he touched her she sizzled with pleasure, his large palms stroked her lower back, pushing her closer. Her body was on fire and she burned with the intensity of his touch. Mahesh was a skilled lover, an expert with his lips, tongue and hands. She let him take control, so she could lose control. He was a kamasutra expert, of course. She smiled. He didn't know that she was just as accomplished.

Much later as they lay spent. KD felt his hand linger on her thigh, where the sheet didn't quite cover her skin. Mahesh tenderly traced her curves with his fingers. 'You have a scar here?' he said quietly in the dark. Kanyadevi jerked her leg away. 'It was an accident,' she said quickly.

'A slight flaw in my beautiful goddess,' he whispered in her ear.

She turned on her side. He slid closer and he spooned her from behind.

'I always thought love was an emotion we could do without. But now that I feel the emotion with such intensity, I wonder how I survived all these years,' he whispered in her ear.

'Love is an emotion that can bring intense pain. Be careful,' she warned. Then changing the subject, 'Don't you have something important to tell me?'

He nodded. Then sitting up he began. 'Well, it is about the Taj Mahal.'

KD said, 'It is the greatest monument and built as a symbol of Shah Jahan's undying love for Mumtaz Mahal.'

Mahesh chuckled. The world believes the monument is a symbol of love. But what if it's not true.' He let his words linger, moving closer. 'Think about it. Does it make any sense to you that an emperor who had so many wives and God knows how many consorts and dancing girls, would waste twenty-two years of his life building a monument for one of his women, albeit the mother of fourteen of his sixteen children?'

'Why not?' KD retorted. 'In those days the rajas and emperors were all about building the most beautiful monuments and palaces for love or as a symbol of their strength.'

Mahesh laughed, brushing her suggestion aside. 'Think about it, what if there is something else Shah Jahan was hiding? A treasure or some dark secret.'

'That's far-fetched.' KD wondered where he was going with this. All she wanted to know was how much he knew about the scroll and what he planned.

Mahesh put on his tee, and paced as if excited with his find. The air was cooler, and KD pulled the sheet around her. 'Let me explain. Indian history only focuses on what was written by Shah Jahan's court historians. They were nothing more than sycophants. They obviously wrote stuff to make their king appear as worthy as a god. But what if it is possible that there is another truth about the Taj? That the Mughals had hidden some information about the monument?'

'I know what you are getting at. The rumours, I've heard them. You can't really believe that there's treasure, and idols and all sorts of stuff inside the Taj. I can't believe it. You are distorting everything we know about the monument,' she responded heatedly. He was exaggerating. His theories were unbelievable. 'You are making this up, aren't you? People are going to die because of your nonsense and thugs will start coming from all parts of the world to hunt for the rumoured treasure. Are you out of your mind?'

Mahesh sighed, as if tired of convincing people. He folded his arms across his chest and looked at her with cold eyes. 'Don't forget I'm a trained archaeologist, I've studied the monument. There is evidence about the Taj that not everyone is aware of. The decor displays symbols and even the most obvious: hexagonal features of the layout. It's all of a different architecture and orientation. It implies a deeper secret.'

'So what? It was well known that sculptors and artisans from various cultures, and religions were employed in building the monument.'

'Maybe, but then what about the hidden chambers, blocked up so no one knows what's inside?'

'That's the responsibility of the IIA. Why would the institute hide the truth?'

'That's the problem.' He sighed, turning away. He pushed the curtain aside, and stared out. 'They are afraid that our country will not be able to face the truth. They are afraid to antagonise certain sects. But the evidence is clear and more research needs to be done by opening up the hidden rooms. There is something buried in there and it needs to be revealed.'

KD got out of bed, clutching the sheet, and stood next to him. Outside, the area was dark and deserted. The sky was black, moonless, littered with white crystals. They were on the first floor of the small motel. No streetlights visible anywhere. The darkness was complete except for a tiny burning flame. From the window, KD could make out a small temple by the glow of a single diya. 'Mahesh, all this is in the past. The Taj is recognised as a world heritage site, an Indian pride. Why are you raking up the past and inciting chaos and controversy? Let it be,' KD said, she let the sheet fall and pressed against his body. 'Let it go.'

He took her in his arms. What he said next left her speechless.

'The widow, the dead reporter's wife, Manzil has the evidence. Not just photographs. There was something else, an artifact was discovered by her husband, Parag. It is proof, it is what I have been hunting – the evidence. It's a scroll. A royal document that reveals in writing the secrets of the Taj. Isn't that amazing?'

KD gaped at him wide-eyed. He had clearly become obsessed. What he said next, shocked her. 'I have chosen you to announce this fact to the world. Once I get my hands on the scroll, I will get the message analysed, give it to you. You are the perfect person to reveal the truth. The Ministry of Culture is organising a large reception to showcase the statues we discovered at the Puducherry church site. That's the perfect time to make your presentation. The world press will be there. It will be perfect…' he whispered, his eyes shining with a strange glow. He grinned devilishly at her and carried her back to bed.

KD was too shocked to react.

Much later, in the quiet of the dark night, KD sensed a change within her. She stared at the slowly rotating ceiling fan, focusing on its circular route. Round and round it went, squeaking at regular intervals. KD's thoughts rotated, there was a distinct shift in her perspective, and her stiff feelings were flaking away like dead skin.

KD reflected on the Taj. She had performed there once. It was an ethereal feeling, as if the great emperors were also part of the audience enjoying and applauding her. She never questioned its foundations, its secrets. She just basked in the glow of its beauty and was sure others felt the same. There was a magical quality about the romance surrounding the monument of love.

She thought of the possibility that what Mahesh said was true. In her mind, he was turning it into a monument of hate. She had to admit that he was good at what he did. He was an archaeologist, a trained professional in his field, but not an objective one.

She would try and talk him out of his ludicrous expectations. Tell the world the truth, and then what? Didn't he even want to think of the consequences? The riots, the embarrassment for the government, the IIA, and then the possibility of a full-fledged outbreak of violence between sects that might lead to destruction of the monument.

KD turned on to her side and let the stillness of the night penetrate her. The steady drip of the washbasin was now clearly audible.

Mahesh slept soundly next to her, the sheets still tangled between his legs. She pulled on the sheet to cover her nakedness. She lay there quietly trying to match her breathing to his calm sonorous ones. She couldn't. Her heart still pounded with the memory of his words and the intensity with which he expressed himself. She was afraid of what he was capable of doing. He wasn't an evil man, but his actions were leading him in that direction. His obsession with the scroll was distorting his ideology. The scroll wasn't just an artifact, KD realised. It was a ghost from the past, and it was haunting them. It had possessed Mahesh.

She got out of bed, put on her clothes and went into the bathroom to wash up and to turn off the irritating drip that was pounding its way into her brain. She looked in the mirror, stared at her face in open curiosity. 'Why do you care for him?' she whispered. Her eyes sparkled under the bare bulb.

'I love him, I think,' she whispered, and then smiled. 'He loves me. You are nothing but a hopeless romantic.' And then she laughed at her own image.

KD closed her eyes and then opened them again. She was determined to keep the scroll and its contents quiet. In his bedroom, she went through his bag, searching for any clue that would help the IIA and if possible get Mahesh fired. Then she went back to bed and woke him up.

'Mahesh, we need to talk.'

This was no small matter. This was the grandest monument in India - the Taj – the crowning glory of Indian heritage. And he was out to ruin it. Mahesh wasn't thinking straight. She had to try and convince him otherwise.

Chapter 32

New Delhi

Deva's guard, Naaga, was the most feared amongst his men. He carefully placed the black briefcase under the taxi, next to the drycleaners shop, and another by the bicycle-stand where the vegetable sellers would set up their carts.

It was dawn. The shops were still shuttered; a few people were going about their morning routine sleepily. Naaga never slept more than two hours a night. He hadn't since he witnessed his father crack open his mother's skull with the back of an iron pot. He was only four and he stood there as his mother's empty stare locked on to his and her blood spread quickly across the concrete floor. The metallic odour of his mother's blood stuck to his nostrils and impressed in his brain that even to this day, thirty years later he could smell it a mile away.

When he started to cry, his father had carried him like a sack of wheat and ran out of the slum towards the main street. At the temple, Naaga's father placed him soothingly by the entrance. He was going to go get a doctor for his mother, his father told him, and left him there to wait. Naaga waited and waited until the pandit took him in and he worked and lived inside the house of God. He still waited there every evening, hoping that one day his father might come back for him. Naaga had that faith.

In the mean time, he met Deva and became a part of his league. It allowed him to get on with his life. His future was mapped out. Deva was a good man, worthy of reverence. And Naaga would do anything for Deva. Through him he had learned to face street thugs, the ones who used to bully him all the time as he sat at the temple steps waiting for his father.

Naaga stood at the street corner until it was crowded with vendors and customers. Then he left. Crossing the road and then the railway tracks, Naaga sat at the platform and pressed a button. He heard the distant boom. Smiling, he withdrew the second device. After a few minutes, he pressed it and heard the second boom, louder than the first. It must have been the one under the taxi. He looked up into the distance and squinted, the clouds formed a mushroom in the sky. He smiled with glee. This was a sign that he had succeeded. He couldn't help himself; he laughed out loud. Deva would one day give him his throne. He prayed that day would come soon.

Chapter 33

The old woman had hobbled to the crowded south Delhi market, her saree tucked tightly around her stooped waist. One withered hand holding a small cloth bag and the other the plump fingers of her grandson.

It was 10.30 am. They were halfway to the vegetable seller when the explosion tore through Ali Provision store, bursting into orange flames, sending a whole cart of onions into the main street. The ground was black and burning in places as dark fumes rose, darkening the blue skies. People fled; several in flames and many bleeding as the force of the heat hit the already crowded market place.

The grandmother lay dead, in a twisted heap of bone and flesh. Her slipper, fitted neatly on her left foot, wasn't attached to her body. Fragments of debris, newspaper, vegetables, and shattered chunks of cement rained down on the charred street.

The little boy's eyes were wide with horror, his mouth open, no sound emerged; as if his voice was caught in his throat. Streaked with his grandmother's blood, and black smoke, the boy was lucky to be alive. Unsure of what to do, he wandered aimlessly amongst the blackened remains of dead bodies, and survivors crying for help. He breathed heavily, his chest rising and falling, and then the cry tore through his lungs.

Thirty seconds later a second explosion overturned a minivan in the corner, sending it careening towards the boy. It slammed into him, the sound drowning his cry.

For five minutes, nothing moved. The smell of barbecued flesh rose in the midst of clouds of black smoke. Then there was confusion as bystanders rushed towards and some away from the horrible scene. Two men darted frantically towards a Sarojini Nagar shopkeeper, their clothes on fire; they rolled themselves on the ground, screaming for help. The shopkeeper did nothing. In the distance the whining sounds of sirens echoed, as if in answer to the shrieking survivors.

It was later discovered that the bombs were made of rough plastic and filled with nails and razorblades. It was remote operated and set to detonate near a market place.The officials confirmed that more than fifty people had died; eighty were in hospital and at least ten were in critical condition.

'You are a butcher, you know that?' Manzil shouted at Ramu. The television was switched on and all that was visible were scenes of the carnage and confusion. Her lips trembled with emotion. Her eyes were red and puffy from the anger and sorrow that racked her.

Ramu watched her quietly. He didn't know how to convince her that Deva wasn't responsible. His boss wouldn't harm anyone unless they had caused a problem. Deva wasn't responsible for the deaths. Ramu knew she would call him a fool, and a mindless slave, if he even attempted to defend himself. She didn't know about the street gangs. And how they worked. Nor did he want to explain anything. He was there to protect her and that's what he intended to do. She was the target.

Eyes downcast, he listened silently. Unemotionally. The news reporter announced that the prime minister had cut short his visit to the north-east of India, to return to Delhi, urging people to stay calm.

'See that,' she cried, pointing to the repeated slides of the destruction. 'Don't you have anything to say about your precious God? Deva? He did it, didn't he? He sent out the pictures and caused the hungama, the bombings, the murderer!' Manzil felt like punching him. She hated herself for believing the boy. 'I told you not to give Deva those pictures. You, of all people, I trusted you. I don't know why I thought you were smart and strong and capable of seeing the power of this kind of information. How it could destroy lives, could generate more anger and hatred. Don't we have enough of this already that you had to be the cause of such terror? No, it's not your fault! I'm to blame for this!'

Weakly, she leaned against the wall, sliding to the floor, as if the strength had left her body. 'Parag please forgive me. It was not my doing.'

She sat there, and pointed to the door. 'Get out of my house, and don't ever come back again.'

Emotional. First thought that entered Ramu's head as he watched Manzil succumb to her feelings. Feelings. Why did she feel so much and care what happened? And for people she didn't know? She should have not made this her fight. It ended the minute her husband died. She should have let it all go and have forgotten about it and just let herself grieve for her husband.

Yet, despite the fear, the nervousness, there was a steely side to her. She wanted to fight, to fight for justice, for the right thing. Stubborn.

He wondered what would make someone want to help a stranger so much. She wanted to help him, to make him a 'good person' she had said.

People like her were stupid – because they always ended up dead due to their eagerness to do the 'right thing', to save the world. Ramu had not killed before but he had been involved in killings many times. If Deva said kill, maim, torture, beat if it was for a reason, and he supported his boss. Should he have asked himself why? Ramu couldn't think beyond pleasing his god who saved him from the streets. He had become immune to others' pain. He had seen too much and his heart did not reach out for anyone but himself.

And yet this woman wanted him to be her brother.

Brother – the word had a strange connotation, related to someone, feeling of kinship. A sense of responsibility and pride emerged in his heart; another person cared about him, besides himself. He wasn't used to it.

For the first time he felt a twinge of regret. '*Didi*,' he whispered. 'I'm sorry. I'll do as you say from now on.'

She ignored him.

'I will leave,' Ramu said softly. 'But not tonight.'

'Do whatever you want,' Manzil said. She stood up, went to her room and slammed the door in his face.

Chapter 34

'You are needed in Delhi,' Rana said, studying the archaeologist's face carefully. Mahesh looked haggard. His hair was dishevelled and purple blue blotches marked his cheeks and forehead.

He smiled, 'It's not as bad as it looks, I was in an accident,' he leaned back and watched the waitress serve snacks at the neighbouring table. 'I cannot leave yet.'

Khajuraho had been a gruelling two days journey by bus and train. Rana had made his way towards Puducherry train station after Dass asked him to talk to Mahesh Bhakti. Dass wasn't sure what he had planned and was afraid that Rana would be too late. The dancer woman had caught his fancy and muddled his brain. Rana had to knock some sense into the fellow.

'Why?'

'None of your bloody business, Rana.'

Rana leaned forward. 'It is my bloody business. I know what you are up to.' He was tempted to give the archaeologist another purple shadow on his face. But they were in a public place. Mahesh was unstable, he was fidgety and his eyes shone like he had a fever.

'Dass sent me to bring you back. There is a … situation.' Rana said, stirring sugar in his coffee.

'I know. I read about it. It has nothing to do with me.'

'It has everything to do with you,' Rana snapped. His voice low in the crowded coffee shop.

'All I've done is unearth the truth.'

'And cause murder and mayhem in the bargain. Just pictures caused the bombing. And anything else can create utter devastation. Information that can cause violence needs to be discussed with the higher authorities. Don't forget, you work for the IIA, not as a freelancer. You've been leaking sensitive information to the press. Who are you to decide what the public should know? You have to check with Dass or Rizvi.' He took a large slurp of the milky coffee.

'You are spineless, Rana, and so is the IIA. We are just puppets. And the politicians, cowards. They don't want to antagonise this group, and that sect, and this caste. Bloody hell, are they running a country or what? That doesn't mean we have to hide the truth. My parents died in riots, because the government was trying to appease minorities. You think that will not anger me? I cannot hide a truth about the origins of our country. People should know facts. Not nonsense stories made by conquerors.'

'Again, who gives you the right? Don't you see? Innocents are dead. Your parents were innocents. I know it hurts but you are only escalating the violence. Because of those photos, and now that scroll. More innocents will die.'

'I am not a coward. I fight for my principles. If people cannot handle it, that's not my problem.'

'You are too far gone to understand what is right anymore, Mahesh. Stay away from trouble, for your own good.' He stood up. 'I will report back to Dass. One last chance – are you coming or not?'

'No.'

'The man has lost his marbles, sir, he is seeking revenge for his parents – they were killed in some communal violence twenty years ago. He is holding the government responsible and this is his way of getting back at them.' Rana said from an STD phone booth. The town was bustling with tourists in shorts and open-toed slippers, many white-skinned men and women had wrapped their heads in a traditional turban style. They looked out of place amongst the burnt copper skinned locals. The tourists would try anything to fit in.

'Inform Kanyadevi of the situation. Maybe, she can help,' Dass said. He surely was desperate if he was seeking help from her, Rana thought.

'Okay.'

He hung up.

The offices of the IIA were bustling with activity. Unlike the usual slow-paced movement of individuals who habitually took their time to get through the day, the frenzied search of a few documents in the basement of the institute was about buying time. And preparing a sensible press release to counter the effects of another outbreak of violence.

Rizvi and Dass searched Mahesh's desk for stolen records of the Taj. They had to isolate every shred of evidence, Artifacts and letters related to the Taj and hide it in such a place that no one would find it for at least another century.

They pried open Mahesh's locked drawer under his desk and found a list of contacts. Parag's name was on top. All the names on his list were linked to the press and local goons. Dass noticed an Englishman's name on the list. 'Mahesh could be selling Artifacts overseas,' he said in frustration, pointing to the names.

'And he is selling secrets to local thugs,' Rizvi said.

'I wonder...' Dass paused, drumming his fingers on Mahesh's table, and then he noticed the small black and white photograph of a couple under the plastic coating covering his table. The man and a woman were holding books and standing in front of a building. He studied the picture carefully. He saw the words University at the edge of the photo. 'What do we know about Mahesh's background?' Dass asked. 'Rana mentioned he had revenge on his mind because of his parents' death in some riots.'

Rizvi nodded, 'I checked his records. Born in Calcutta, moved to Delhi to live with his uncle and aunt, no record of any other family. He graduated from Delhi University with degrees in field archaeology and heritage management, impressive results.'

'Do you know anything more about his parents?' Dass asked.

'Nothing. It didn't seem relevant to hire him,' Rizvi said, then he realised what Dass was thinking: personal vendetta. 'I'll see what we can dig up about Calcutta. But it's useless now, the damage is done.'

'For now, I think we should call that inspector and get Mahesh arrested,' Dass said, concerned about what more damage he could cause.

'We can't. Not yet. He has had access to all areas of the IIA and the museums. We have to clean up house first, or you and I are both in serious trouble.'

Chapter 35

Rana watched the people board the buses at the bus station. It was crowded, hot and smelly. Beggars were scattered about, some sitting in groups, and others chasing a cluster of tourists.

Rana had received an anonymous phone call from a woman, claiming to have some news.

He thought it was a crank call, until the woman mentioned Mahesh's name. That man was trouble, ever since the murder of the reporter, things hadn't been the same, and he just knew Mahesh was going to be the reason something terrible would happen, if it hadn't happened already.

What more had he done? Rana wondered. He glanced at his watch, obviously the woman had no sense of time. She was already thirty minutes late. He would give her another five minutes, then leave. He paced restlessly and looked out at the main entrance. Three buses had already departed in a cloud of dust and smoke that had choked the small enclosure.

'Rana?' the female voice drifted from below. Rana turned in that direction. He noticed saw her sitting on the ground, leaning against the wall. She turned her back to him, but indicated he should come closer.

He wasn't sure, but she could have been there all this time and he hadn't noticed in the milieu of people sitting, standing or moving around the station.

'I am Rana. Who are you?'

She had covered half her face with her saree. 'I'm a nobody. But the man you talked to today is a murderer,' the woman said.

'A murderer?' Rana tried to get a good look at the woman, but she kept covering her face and looked suspiciously around her.

'Yes, he has killed two women. My friends.'

'I don't understand! Mahesh works for the government, why would he kill anyone?'

'We are nothing more than the scum of the earth to him, because we sell our bodies to survive,' she said, in a heavy voice.

'I don't believe you. You are trying to pin the blame on an innocent man,' Rana said sharply.

'Chandni Chowk. Go there to Raja Mahal dance bar. Ask the manager if he has seen this man there – he asks for certain type of women, acts all high class – as if he was some priest. The manager tells us to lie. That man wanted to satisfy his hunger, but did not want to be tainted by the lower castes, the bastard!' she muttered.

Rana was quiet. He knew a little about Mahesh's background, but not his fetish, or his leanings. This was a new problem and he had to bring it to Dass's attention. 'How do you know all this?'

'I've been following this man. Justice has to be done; he needs to be put in jail.' She shook her head, her eyes glazed with anger.

'There have been two other women who have died in that same place. It was definitely him.' She turned to him. 'You will make him pay, won't you? He is a murderer, he must pay for his sins.'

Rana stood up. The woman was crazy. He didn't want to take her seriously. She grabbed his hand and pulled him back down. 'I know you don't believe me but I took something from his pocket,' she snickered. 'I don't normally steal from my clients, but I suspected he was the one who murdered my friend, when she left to meet him that night. Nobody cares for our lot – all they say is one less to worry about. The police don't investigate. They use this opportunity to sell our organs to the hospitals, our bodies are used even after we are dead.'

She noticed Rana's impatience.

'I went with him the next time he came to the bar. I stole this.' She took out an identification tag from her saree blouse. 'I knew if I went to the police, they would throw me in jail instead and have their fun. I have been following this man, and let me warn you. That woman he is with is in great danger too.'

Rana stared at the ID card – it had Mahesh's name and other details. It was the IIA identity card. But he could have left it by mistake at the dance bar. This woman could have picked it up and now wanted to frame him. What would she get out of it? Money? She hadn't asked for anything, yet.

'I know what you are thinking. I am not making this up. I just know he is dangerous, you do what you want with this – I am out of here.' The woman moved at such a pace, that when Rana looked down at her, she was gone. He looked up and couldn't find her; she had melted in the crowd.

'Did he buy it?' Anwar asked. They were in an alley behind the bus station.

'Yes, I think so. The ID seemed to have convinced him. Give me my money – I did your job.' The woman said impatiently.

He scowled, looking at her angrily, and shoved a roll of rupees in her hand. 'Now disappear.'

Chapter 36

Manzil didn't expect her life to turn into a speeding truck ready to crash into a brick wall. Events of the last three weeks had eroded the years of wedded bliss with Parag. She felt like her emotions were unravelling like a ball of string falling from the tallest highrise in Delhi. It seemed like a lifetime ago when she talked about having children. Now, she was dealing with dangerous strangers, hidden agendas.

She watched the television almost as if she wanted to torture her mind with the visions of the carnage and how it all connected to her.

'India's long-term enemy Pakistan condemned the explosions,' the reporter said.

Manzil turned away from the scenes that were being re-run ad nauseum, the newscasters wanted to imprint the horror on the minds of the viewers. She stood by the window watching the sunset in the distance. In the building across the street, she noticed all the homes were watching some news channel or the other.

Ramu was an uneducated street kid; she had been stupid to rely on him. Mahesh Bhakti was behaving strangely when she met him. He tried to hide his desperation. She didn't trust him either. Yadav, the police officer, even though he had helped, suspected her, and was keeping one eye on her.

The professor at the university had totally shaken her. A goonda proved him right by almost slicing her on the bus. Luckily she gave him a useless lookalike.

The red-haired man had a stick wrapped in cloth. She had the presence of mind to keep a smiliar sized scroll in her bag. He was enraged, Yadav had said. She was in danger. Like she didn't know.

The Taj Mahal had turned her life upside down. Manzil wished she did not have the responsibility of keeping the scroll. But the deaths of innocent people weighed on her mind.

She returned her attention to the television.

The grim face of the prime minister appeared on screen. 'These are dastardly acts of hatred. We must leave behind communal anger and instil true patriotism in the minds of our youth.' Easier said then done, Manzil thought snidely.

What should her next step be? She wondered. Yadav seemed like the right person.

Manzil thought about what her father had said. Maybe it was a good idea to leave the country. Take the scroll and all the other evidence. Away from India, the evidence would not cause harm, or cost more lives.

The scroll.

She checked her bag, it was still there. She sighed in relief.

Manzil poured water into a glass from a jug by her bedside table, and sipped slowly. Leaving the country would be an act of cowardice. She loved her India.

And at the moment, she realised, she might not even be able to make her way to the airport in one piece. The photos had caused such anger and death, what would be the reaction if the inked details of the scroll, written by a prince of Jaipur, were made public. She looked at the looped handwriting. It was such an honour to hold the ancient parchment of a glorious past in her hands. She had half a mind to tear it up. But no, that wasn't right; instead she inserted it in its gold holder, wrapped it up carefully in cotton cloth, then sealed it in a plastic pouch and hid the scroll.

Manzil was in a dilemma as her hand hovered over the phone. She could call Yadav, but fear made her fingers tremble. Or contact her father. No. Never. He would destroy everything; ruin all her efforts and Parag's.

Manzil had the power to decide, to choose what she would do. No one would influence her.

'I have your strength, Parag. I will decide how to end this,' Manzil said to herself firmly.

Then she heard a muffled shout and a crash of glass outside her door.

Chapter 37

Tell the world the truth about the Taj. KD thought again of Mahesh's intentions.

The archaeologist was lost in a world of his own – one of revenge. He had told her his story; then about Brahminism, the new world order and the importance to return to a class society. He talked about completely changing India's landscape of democracy to autocracy.

He must be mad!

Didn't he realise the origins of Hinduism weren't about divisions. It was about seeing the soul as god in each individual. Valmiki was a *shudra*, a low caste, and he had written the story of Rama, who's existence was proven to be around 7000 BC according to recent discoveries by the IIA. Even she knew that.

Dance had become secondary; she couldn't focus. Raghu had called her about another schedule. She had asked him to cancel everything. She was taking a sabbatical. KD heard the disappointment in his voice. He would get over it.

Most important, she had to find Manzil. Guide her to do the right thing – give the scroll to the Onyx for safekeeping.

Rana saw the woman from a distance. Kanyadevi was at the Holiday Inn, a few kilometres from Mahesh's three-star Hotel Payal. The woman obviously had made good money from her dancing. She looked beautiful, wearing a silk kurta with a trendy pair of jeans. She was sitting in the lobby, sipping a glass of orange juice, waiting for someone. She looked around a few times. Then someone arrived, gave her a message. The man left and she continued to sit there fiddling with her mobile phone.

Rana approached her cautiously. 'Madam, I need to talk you,' he said, bowing. 'I'm with the IIA. The matter is sensitive and I need to discuss it before you meet Mahesh.'

Kanyadevi paused. She surveyed him coolly then pointed to the seat across her. 'Sit down. Tell me how I can help.'

Chapter 38

Heart pounding, pulse racing, Manzil opened her room door slightly. An intruder was holding Ramu in an elbow squeeze. His knife glinted in the darkness.

'Run away, run away, *didi*,' Ramu managed to say, before the man squeezed harder.

'Shut up,' the man shouted and split Ramu's cheek with one flick of his wrist. Blood spilled easily.

'Stop it. Stop it!' Manzil screamed, as she came closer. Then she realised her mistake; it was the man from the bus – the red-haired man. He was back for the scroll, and looked deadlier. Fear clenched her stomach. Manzil wanted to run back to her room and hide. But no; she had to save Ramu. He held the lanky teenager in a vicious grip and moved backward slowly, dragging the boy with him. The knife was now at Ramu's ear.

'You bitch! You gave me some crap on the bus. Give me the *badshahnamah* or I stick the knife in his brain,' he warned, the sharp point was touching Ramu's earlobe.

'I left it with the professor,' Manzil said calmly.

Ramu struggled, pulling at the man's muscled arm. 'Don't…' then he screamed, as the knife cut a section of his ear.

'No lies or I will kill you as well, woman!' The intruder said, pointing the knife at her. Sweat spilled down the sides of his temples, running rivulets down his face, his eyes glowing with rage.

Manzil watched as if through a lens, fear was draining her, she tried to ignore the paralysing sensation. *Focus*, she said to herself. There was a buzzing in her ears and then she felt strong with every heartbeat; no fear, no hatred, no anger. 'I already told you. I do not have what you seek,' she said. 'I was afraid, so I left it at the university. You want it? Go get it from the professor. I don't want to be involved in this mess.'

Manzil folded her arms and stood still, staring at him with unflinching eyes.

The murderer paused, watched her with a narrowed gaze. Ramu was still bleeding; his breathing in deep rasps. Manzil waited for him to give up his fight, her heart was going to burst through her chest, she felt. Manzil maintained a straight face.

The red-haired man waved his knife at her. 'I don't believe you.'

'Then, search my house,' she said, opening her arm in a wide arc. 'Just let him go. He will not run away in this condition. I have nothing to hide. So what are you afraid of?'

The intruder loosened his grip slightly. Ramu regained his balance and stamped his foot hard on the man's toe. The man let out a yelp and let go of Ramu. He slipped out of his reach. 'Run, *didi,* run!' Ramu yelled, as he rolled away. But the man was too smart for him; he grabbed him by his collar.

'You are nothing but a cockroach,' he said and plunged the dagger into the boy's heart.

'No.' Manzil rushed to his side. The boy coughed and tears streamed down the sides of his face. 'I'm sorry, *didi*,' he managed to whisper before he went limp in her arms.

Manzil looked at the man with hatred. 'You bloody heartless murderer! You are cursed to suffer the same fate.'

'Shut up!' He waved the bloody knife in her face. 'Anyway what was he to you – nothing but a useless street rat. A dime a dozen in this country, they just come pouring in from the villages with their big dreams and small ideas.' He laughed. 'Only the tough ones like me survive.'

Ignoring him, she held Ramu in her arms, and muttered a prayer under her breath, 'He was my little brother, you idiot.'

He laughed at her. 'That's a good one,' he said wiping the sweat from his forehead with his sleeve.

He pulled her by her arm, 'Show me your place of prayer.'

'Let me go,' she slapped his hands away.

'Give me what I have come for, you bitch. Where is your prayer room?' He grabbed a handful of her hair and pulled. She winced in pain. 'I don't have one.'

Noticing the brass vase within her reach on the nearby table, she grabbed it and slammed it blindly, hitting him square in his face. She heard the sound of bone crack.

Blood spurted from the man's nose and she saw his eyes widen with shock. He let go of her hair and lurched backward. Taking the opportunity to get away, she rushed towards the front door and ran out. Manzil heard the man cursing behind her. He was stumbling in her direction. She knew if he caught her, he would kill, scroll or no scroll. But she had to find a way to give someone the information about the scroll. She had hidden it so carefully that no one would find it. What if she died, who would find it? And if it ended up in the wrong hands that would be worse.

Instead of descending the staircase, Manzil ran upwards, towards the top floor of the apartment building. She was buying time. The red-haired man must have expected her to run down.

From the top floor, Manzil hoped to take the lift down to the ground floor and escape his clutches. She kept going, her heart pounded and breathing heavier. The thought of Ramu and the brutal slaying by his attacker made her nauseous. The poor boy, he did care for her, and had stayed to protect her. She wished she hadn't spoken so harshly to him. Tears threatened to choke her. She paused, then doubled over. Clutching her stomach she dry retched in the corner of the fifteenth floor landing. Exhaustion slowly took over her body. Manzil sat down on the stairway and wept for Ramu.

Then she stopped. Why did the murderer ask her about a prayer room? She wondered. Strange. Then it dawned on her. Parag had told her that in the old days the Hindus hid their wealth inside temples. When invaders entered India, the first place they looted were the temples, not because they wanted to desecrate the Hindu religious places, but because they knew that was where the valuables were hidden. This man obviously thought she would hide the scroll similarly.

The idiot.

Manzil smiled. Suddenly she felt strong, she could win this; she might be able to outwit the murderer. She started to climb up slowly.

The twentieth floor was quiet; she noticed the panel of numbers above the lift. The indicator lights showed the lift had stopped on the eighth floor, her floor. She pressed the call button.

The lift climbed slowly. Manzil waited restlessly, her heart pounding. What if the murderer was in the lift? No. He wouldn't risk it and the liftman must be operating the lift manually. The murderer must have gone back to her house to search for the scroll. The bastard won't find it. Or he might have guessed her plan and started climbing upwards. She had to act fast. The lift approached. It was on fourteen, fifteen. She paced restlessly, looked down the stairwell and heard nothing. Nineteen lit up on the panel. Manzil's instinct kicked in and she hid behind the exit door that led to the staircase. The lift door slid open. She waited, breathing slowly. She heard the liftman call out if anyone was there. Manzil rushed into the lift and jabbed at the close door button.

'Memsaab, are you okay?' the short stocky liftman who normally looked half-asleep, was wide-eyed with concern. Manzil shook her head.

Suddenly she realised if she took the lift down, it might stop on the eighth floor. 'Teku, don't let the lift open on my floor,' she said, in a trembling voice.

'Memsaab, has there been a robbery? Shall I call the police?' He noticed the bloodied t-shirt, her dishevelled appearance.

'No, no not yet, just operate the lift manually and make sure it doesn't stop on any floor. And another thing, Teku,' he turned to her. 'I want you to do something for me. This is very important – it's a matter of life and death. Here, take this paper. There is a message on it. Call Inspector Yadav, give this message to him, only to him, you understand?' She gave him the folded piece of paper and Yadav's card with his direct line on it.

He nodded furiously and placed the note and the card in his pocket.

'Also, if anyone other than Inspector Yadav asks for me, say you don't know where I am, okay?'

Again he nodded furiously.

The doors slid open on the ground floor. 'Teku, you are a good man. I trust you will help me,' Manzil said, giving his arm a gentle squeeze of thanks and ran out into the darkness.

As soon as she left the building gate, a man grabbed her arm and shoved her into a waiting van. Before Manzil could shout for help, the door had slid shut and the van turned the corner, its wheels screeched in the night as the night watchman yelled after them.

Chapter 39

'The man is a threat,' Rana said. 'I wouldn't be surprised if the bombings in Delhi were the result of his actions.'

'What Mahesh has done is simply the job of an archaeologist – dig, retrieve, and expose the truth,' Kanyadevi said. 'You cannot accuse him of anything else.'

'Madam... that may be true, madam. But there are some truths that can be twisted to suit certain ...how shall I say this...extreme views.'

'So are you saying he is making up stories and feeding them to the press?' Kanyadevi retorted.

'Possibly,' he responded. The woman was being difficult. 'I'm just saying that he is not to be trusted. Please be careful.'

'I'm always careful. Unless you don't tell me the real reason, I cannot do anything for you.'

'Then contact Mr Rizvi. He will tell you. The police are investigating the IIA, and it is possible that a certain piece of evidence has gone missing.' He saw the sudden interest. 'Yes. He has stolen from the IIA.'

Kanyadevi handed him her phone. 'Call him. I will speak with Rizvi now.'

'Yes, madam.'

Chapter 40

Professor Gupta paced restlessly in his office. He had called Manzil a few times but she hadn't answered. He was beginning to worry.

'Saraswati, I have some news. It's worse than we can imagine. Can you come to my office now?' The professor left a message on her voice mail. He knew she was teaching that evening and hoped that he could share the information with her before she left for the day.

Professor Gupta felt old and tired. He couldn't handle this anymore. All these years the Onyx had worked to protect the youth from the resentment of their past and it just never seemed to end.

Junaid, Suresh and even the commissioner had recruited train loads of young illiterate men and women who came to the big cities with their dreams of making big money, only to fall in the hands of goondas and forced to work for them – and follow their crusade.

Besides money, what did these bigots want anyway? Why did they have to brainwash the children, the new generation with their stories of war and hate. He was tired of teaching about the importance of unity and peace for progress. He sat down and waited.

Professor Sen was an intelligent and strong woman. She had an optimistic outlook and as she taught anthropology she also included the viewpoint relevant to the country. Very cleverly, she included the Onyx's message of peace and unity in her course. He admired her spirit. His was flagging.

Kanyadevi sensed his reluctance to get involved. But he was the senior-most member of the group. He had seen so much violence wrapped in the garb of education, and felt the pain and suffering just as much. All he could do was write and lecture.

His phone beeped twice. 'I'll be there in an hour. Just one more class,' she messaged back.

He began to write. There was no point waiting, he must keep the information ready for her, in case something happened to him. Lately, his left shoulder ached dully. He could easily drop dead from a heart attack and his spirit would wander if he couldn't give her the important piece of information.

'Professor? Professor Gupta?' Saraswati called out. The secretary and other research assistants had left for the day. She entered his office. Gupta had a habit of staying late in his office, his sanctuary. His den. Often she would visit him after class and share a cup of coffee and news on their cause.

Onyx was the glue that held them together. The convictions they shared were so strong that sometimes she wanted to go up to the minister of education and physically shake him, to knock some sense into him. To make him realise the urgency of the situation. The illiteracy rate was so high she cringed every time the government released new Census data.

Saraswati noticed that the professor was resting his head on his desk. He must have fallen asleep. But there was something about the odd stillness in the room that bothered her.

She rushed towards him, 'Professor? Gupta are you alright?' she nudged him. He didn't move. Saraswati raised his head gently. 'Professor?' Then she noticed the blood.

'No!' she whispered. There was a small but circular hole in his chest. He was dead, but his body was still warm. Looked like a gunshot wound straight to the heart. Wouldn't someone have heard it?

Quickly, Saraswati called for help from his desk. The window behind was ajar, the curtain fluttered slightly in the evening breeze. The professor liked fresh air to circulate in his muggy office, and often left the window open. Clearly the intruder had used this as a point of entry. But, it didn't make sense; the professor would have noticed a man entering. Unless the intruder was already hiding in here.

Saraswati suddenly felt conscious of her surroundings; maybe someone was watching her from the dark recesses of the professor's room. She felt the hair rise on back of her neck. She grabbed the letter opener from the table and held it up as if ready to face the murderer. She checked the room carefully. No one. The murderer had left, probably just before she had entered. She wished she had come sooner, the professor would be alive.

Enough, she told herself. Saraswati focused on the urgency of the message she had received before he died.

He wanted to meet her – he had some information. Where would he keep it? Saraswati knew the professor well; he had a habit of pre-empting situations. Expect the worst, he would say. Gupta always had the last word; he must have left a message for her.

She searched his table. Nothing seemed out of place. The murderer had taken what they wanted? She wasn't sure. Then she picked up the Onyx metal ring. Saraswati knew where to look. She turned it over and opened the base. She took out the folded piece of paper and read.

I may not be alive when you get this. The scroll is genuine. I had snipped a corner of it and sent it for carbon-dating. The information came back today from America, 85% positive on authenticity. Find it between Mahatma Gandhi's lifestory and Gandhian Philosophy. This one will test the spirit of India. With peace for O.

Saraswati kept the message inside her handbag and picked out the book from the shelf, just in time before the staff and police came in.

Chapter 41

Yadav answered his mobile on the first ring. Ever since the bombings, there were calls coming in about other sporadic outbreaks of violence. He, with his team of *hawaldars*, was all over the city investigating and arresting suspicious characters. But the night wasn't over yet.

When he heard the voice on the other side, and the man's voice whispered Manzil's name, that he needed to meet him in person, Yadav knew that the bombings were somehow connected to her. The widow was a magnet for trouble. This time he would get the truth out of her.

Yadav was there within the hour. Where the hell was Manzil?

'Sahib, my name is Teku. I am the lift man. Madam Manzil asked me to call you. She gave me a very important message to give you,' he whispered conspiratorially and took the policeman aside.

'What is it? And where is she?' Yadav asked, trying not to appear irritated at the short stocky man. He was wide-eyed and spoke as if he was a hero in a Hindi movie. He stressed and intoned each word.

'She was taken in a van just outside this building,'

'What?!'

'You didn't call the police?'

'We did, they said they are on the way.' Teku said looking concerned.

'Make sure all of you stay for questioning.'

The police were busy responding to other calls, Yadav realised. Shit! He would have to handle this on his own.

'This message,' Teku looked around to see no one was watching.

'Hurry up!'

Teku handed the folded piece of paper to Yadav. It was a receipt for a supermarket. When he turned it over, he saw the scrawled four lines of writing.

'What does it mean?' Teku asked, raising his eyebrows. 'Madam sounded very serious, I think someone was chasing her.'

Yadav curbed the urge to smack the fellow. 'Who was chasing her, did you see? Did you see the van? What colour was it?' he folded the paper and placed it in his pocket, trying not to panic. Manzil could be dead by now.

'The one that took Manzil *memsaab*?'

Yadav nodded impatiently.

Teku ran towards the gate, Yadav was right behind. 'As soon as she left the building, the night watchman said he saw some people holding guns in a moving car. These thugs caught her and pushed her inside.'

Teku's pitch seemed to increase as he explained the dramatic abduction.

Yadav shut his eyes. 'Didn't the watchman see anything else? How many men were there? Number plate? The colour of the car?'

'No, sahib. He can't see very well at night,' the liftman replied sheepishly. 'He is my cousin brother, from my village. I got him this job.'

'He must have at least seen the colour of the car?'

'No sahib, it was too dark, but he said it was big, like a van. And everything happened very fast.'

'Take me to her flat,' Yadav said, returning briskly towards the building lobby. Teku hurried behind him. He then rushed ahead of Yadav into the lift and waited dutifully by the bank of buttons. He didn't press them.

Yadav continued his line of questions. 'Anyone noticed anything, neighbours? The first floor residents?'

'No, sahib. No one came out of the building.' Teku stood erect as he answered. The lift was still stationary.

'What are you waiting for? Let's go,' Yadav said in frustration.

'Yes, sahib, that's what I thought you would say.' The liftman smiled and salaamed enthusiastically before he pressed the manual button. The lift lurched upwards. Yadav noticed droplets of blood on the floor. He bent down.

'Its okay, sahib, I will clean it up later.'

Yadav grunted under his breath. And then suddenly, he moved. Roughly he pushed the liftman against his stool. Teku fell heavily. 'You will do no such thing until the policemen, and investigators arrive. Do you understand me?'

'Yes, sahib,' Teku said, open-mouthed, shaking his head from side to side, confused by the policeman's reaction.

Yadav couldn't hold back. 'A resident of this building has been attacked and kidnapped. Her home probably ransacked. Don't you care at all what is happening around you?'

Teku offered a meek expression. 'Sahib, I care.' He put his hand to his heart and sniffed. 'That is why I called you and gave you memsaab's message.'

Yadav took a deep breath. 'Stand up. You did a good thing by calling me.'

'Yes sahib. I understand you are angry. The police is always fighting crime. Manzil memsaab said I was doing an important job if I called you. I understand your tension,' Teku said magnanimously, his eyes wide with pleasure. He pressed the lift button. The lift doors glided open on the eighth floor.

The door to Manzil's apartment was wide open. There was one other apartment on the floor, but it was padlocked from the outside. The neighbours must be out.

As soon as they entered Manzil's home Yadav noticed the extent of damage. He made his way inside. 'Walk carefully. Don't step on or touch anything,' Yadav said to Teku.

The corridor was covered with broken glass, it crunched underfoot. In the living room, the sofas were slit open and the stuffing pulled out, the television set was bashed in. He turned to the left, towards the main bedroom, and noticed the pool of blood.

The liftman suddenly went pale at the sight and smell of death. 'Sahib, I have done my duty, I have to go.' Teku rushed out as if a curse might fall on him.

Yadav approached cautiously. Closer towards the entrance to the room, he saw Ramu's body. The dead boy was lying on his side. One side of his face was cut and swollen. The blood had dried up but not completely. Yadav noticed the streaks that wet his cheeks. Flies buzzed and settled around Ramu's nose and eyes. Yadav shooed them away. He felt a tightening in his chest. This was bad, this was worse than bad, Yadav thought, as he waved away the flies when they tried to settle on him.

Yadav's mind raced. This was the work of a brutal killer – a man who would stop at nothing. Manzil couldn't have escaped his clutches – yet, she had the presence of mind to hide the scroll, and run. She must have witnessed the boy's death. He saw the brass vase lying in the corner. Manzil escaped, and the killer returned to look for the scroll. Someone else was responsible for abducting her.

Yadav stared at Ramu's face; in death he looked almost child-like. Deva's boy. The cuts on his face were deep, almost to the bone. The boy had suffered.

For Deva, Ramu was nothing more than a pawn and Yadav knew that once Deva found out Ramu was killed, he would move heaven and earth to take revenge. An excuse to cause more violence.

Yadav stood up. He stepped carefully noticing that all the rooms were similarly ransacked. Even the cupboards had been broken into and the clothes strewn all over the floor.

The anger and viciousness with which the intruder had attacked the place was evident in the kitchen. Every single drawer was pulled out and overturned. The refrigerator had been emptied out, the vegetables lying in a pool of milk, the bread scattered on the floor. A segment of the tiles on the wall was bashed in; the murderer had used the marble pestle to vent his frustrations. The flies were having a field day. Soon cockroaches would find their way in here.

Obviously, whatever the killer was looking for, he didn't find it.

Yadav retrieved the note from his pocket and read it again: *Like the gushing Yamuna river, where the elixir of life flows, look at yourself and beyond, you will find the truth in a scroll.*

Why didn't she just say where she had hidden it. Then he realised. The liftman might understand the contents and search for the object himself or he might not have called him.

Yadav stood silently, closed his eyes and imagined what Manzil would do. The words rolled around his head and he waited, collecting his thoughts. He knew the answer would come to him. She had trusted him to find it.

The jarring sound of the phone interrupted him. Surprisingly the intruder hadn't bothered to cut the phone lines. Yadav looked around for the phone. He found it under one of the overturned armchairs. He picked up the handset but didn't speak.

'Hello, hello, Manzil? Is everything alright? I heard about the bombings? Hello? Can you hear me?' The anxious voice of a man echoed through the lines.

It was long-distance. 'Hello, this is Inspector Yadav, Crime Branch. To whom am I speaking?'

'Police? What is the police doing in my daughter's home?'

Ah, of course a concerned father. But where was he? Why wasn't he there for his son-in-law's funeral?

'Sir, I am investigating a case. What is your name? And where are you calling from?'

'My name is Zaheer Akhtar, I live in London. Manzil is my daughter,' he said in clipped tones. 'Now please tell me where my daughter is? I want to speak to her.'

Manzil was a Muslim.

Yadav closed his eyes as the seriousness of the situation dawned on him. He better act fast. Or his daughter would be dead before dawn.

'Sir, Manzil is not here. She is staying with a friend of hers.' Better to give him vague answers instead of telling him that she was being hunted by two don, that she held a national secret, and that there was a dead boy in her home.

'What are you doing in my daughter's home?'

Looking for her?

'I am investigating the death of your son-in-law and got an emergency call that someone had broken into her home.'

'Oh god! Please protect that obstinate girl. Ever since she married that reporter, her life has been a rollercoaster, I told her a million times to leave and come and live with me in England but no, she had to be in her beloved country, and now look what has happened.. Stubborn girl,' he muttered. 'I've been trying to get flights to India but since the bombings, nothing is available.'

'Sir, I have been in touch with her. Staying with a friend is good for her. I would suggest that you don't come yet. Sir?'

'I will keep trying anyway,' Zaheer said, concerned.

'Sir, please do not come yet. It is chaotic at the airport. Better wait till things cool down. I will inform Manzil you called.'

The voice sounded relieved. 'Yes, tell her to call. I'm not done giving her a dressing down.'

'Sir the phone lines are not very reliable. It's better that I give you my cell number and request you to call me directly.'

'Yes, yes. Thank you. You are a good man.'

Yadav gave him his contact and mentioned his name again, and hung up.

Suddenly he felt as if a huge boulder had risen in front of him. He had to hurry to find the scroll and then Manzil.

Would this night ever end, he wondered.

Chapter 42

It was pitch black when Manzil opened her eyes. Bile rose in her throat as she struggled to sit up. The aftertaste of vomit was still in her mouth. It was worse in the suffocating darkness. The last thing she remembered was being dragged into a van and then a very strong smell of a doctor's office before she had passed out. Her throat felt as if she had been forced to swallow a cup of sand. She licked her lips and felt the cracks where she had bled.

Manzil wished she could see where she was being taken. It would also help with the nausea. The smell of the sack and the speeding van was making her dizzy. Her hands were tied behind her, and her shoulders ached from the pressure.

This was no time to fall apart. She hoped that Yadav had found the scroll and it was safe. Now whatever happened to her didn't matter.

The van screeched to a halt. She heard the voices. The door slid open and a man pulled her out. 'Let me go,' she managed to say, as she fell to the ground.

She heard a man's wild laughter. 'Let you go?' he laughed even louder.

'Shut up, idiot. We have a job to do. Throw her in that storage room. Deva will attend to her in the morning.'

So Deva's men had kidnapped her. The red-haired murderer wasn't involved in her abduction. She was wanted by two opposing bloodthirsty men – what a way to be popular!

'I want to talk to Deva *now,*' she squeezed out. Her throat hurt with every word. 'Ramu is dead. A man entered my house and killed him. I think Deva needs to know this right now.'

Silence.

'Take this damn sack off of me. I'm not running away. I need to talk to Deva, you idiots.'

Manzil struggled to sit up. It was claustrophobic. She would faint any second if they didn't let her breathe some fresh air.

A pair of feet shuffled towards her and she felt the tug of the rope. Someone pulled the sack off. She blinked and drank in the cool air in large gasps. She felt slightly better now that she could see her surroundings.

Three armed men stood over her. 'Untie me,' she said in a stronger voice as the fresh air helped the adrenalin pump the fear out of her mind. She looked around. They were in an open courtyard and she could see the stars in the sky. 'What is this place?'

'Shut up,' said the man with the bushy eyebrows. He pulled her up and led her to the inner courtyard.

She noticed a water tap. 'I need some water, please,' she coughed.

Bushy brows filled a brass pot of water. Her hands were still tied. She squirmed. He held the pot to her lips and she sipped the cool water. Most of it spilled over. Her parched throat burned as the liquid slid down. She coughed and retched a few times.

The man waited until she had her fill and then led her to a small shed. Without saying a word to her, he untied her, opened the wooden door, pushed her inside and slammed it shut. She heard the snap of a padlock and knew that there was no way out from that route.

Manzil surveyed the dusty surroundings as she massaged the soreness from her arms. There were cartons stacked up in one corner, a wooden stool, a bench and some rope on the other side. No windows were visible, but light entered the shed through the slats of wood strips on the roof. Manzil sat down, knees drawn in, leaning against the cartons. Slowly exhaustion took over her body and her head sank to the ground. She fell asleep instantly.

The morning air was cool. The sunlight cast squares of warmth on the dusty ground. Manzil felt a patch of heat on her forehead; she opened her eyes and squinted against the brightness.

Every movement reminded her of the torturous journey the night before. Her limbs ached as if she had climbed a mountain. She shifted slightly and turned on her side, hoping the throbbing ache would subside. The thought of Ramu brought fresh pain. She felt guilty.

Manzil heard voices outside her door. She wiped her eyes and waited for them.

'I need to use the toilet,' she said, as soon as one of them opened the door. This time it wasn't bushy brows; this man was tall and stick thin.

'Come, I show you,' he replied, amused. 'Don't try anything stupid,' he added.

Manzil glared at him; as if she had any chance with the men standing around the walled area. She followed him to the back of the large airy house. It looked like it belonged to the British era in India. The dilapidated staircase creaked when she climbed slowly behind him.

'Here,' he said, pushing open a door that led to a bathroom with a toilet and basin. 'Deva will see you shortly.'

Manzil entered tentatively. The single bulb illumined the dirt tiles and the black water marks on the ceiling. She shut the door on the man's face. 'Don't waste time. I'm waiting outside,' stick man said.

There was one window above the toilet. It was sealed shut.

Deva reclined on the rope bed on the porch sipping tea. A young boy massaged his feet and three men stood guard three feet from him.

Stick man pushed Manzil forward. 'The woman,' he said, shoving her like a piece of garbage they had found on the street.

Deva flicked his hand dismissing the young masseur. The boy took the empty glass from Deva's hand and ran indoors. Deva squinted against the sun. His oiled hair glistened and his kohl-lined eyes watched her carefully as if she was an insect.

'What do you want from me?'

'What does any man want from a woman?' Deva asked, and his eyes gleamed at her. He saw the fear in her eyes and the gut reaction as her hands glided to her chest. He smiled without humour. 'You do have a dirty mind, don't you?'

He picked up a long metal trishul leaning against the wall. 'I have no interest in your body, widow.' He spat.

'Wha- what do you want?' Manzil repeated, ignoring his rhetorical comment.

'I heard from the grapevine that my boy, Ramu, was killed in your house,' he drawled. Then in anger, he pointed the trishul at her chest. 'I want revenge.' He pressed. The three sharp points drew blood.

Manzil showed no emotion. 'You should be proud of your boy, he died protecting me,' she said. Deva pressed the trishul until the spots of blood were visible on her already stained t-shirt. The pain made her focus. She didn't flinch.

'I can finish you off, here and now and make you disappear. As if you never existed,' he said.

'So do it,' she said without blinking. Anger made her dizzy. 'What are you waiting for? Christmas?'

It was foolish of her to provoke him. But she was fed up. She was sick and tired of all this hiding information and the risks involved. Ramu was dead, bombs had claimed innocent lives, how much worse could it get. She didn't care anymore, made her reckless.

Deva turned to his man. 'You! Get this woman a cup of tea and bread. I don't want her to die on an empty stomach,' he laughed and put down the trishul.

Manzil felt her breathing slow and her pounding heart eased. She felt drained, and her legs gave way as she sank to the ground.

'We have a lot to talk about, widow. And you have something that I want. The archaeologist was supposed to take it from you?'

'I don't know what you are talking about.'

'You are one of those who don't like to see others suffer, right?' he asked. 'That boy will die unless you tell me the truth.'

The masseur seemed to freeze, but for a split second only. He returned to the kitchen.

'It's with the inspector,' she murmured.

The sun burned her face. She shut her eyes. Then she devoured the tea and bread as the men watched her.

Chapter 43

Delhi

The news of the professor's death reached the senior Onyx members, and then filtered down the ranks until every single member knew. Saraswati Sen informed them that Yuva, the youth group, were on standby for orders.

Recruited by the Onyx, the small army consisted of farmers, cobblers, sweepers, woodcutters and any villager who wanted to be a part of the 'programme'. Just like the city dons recruited young impressionable illiterates from villages to do their killings, the Onyx, using the Yuva Bank as a front, offered money and security to those who wanted to join the 'programme'.

All they had to do was attend a weekly meeting and they would receive loans for food and education. Healthcare was provided for family members. Another condition was that they had to keep what ever they learnt confidential. It was a costly affair. But they had used this technique for a few years, and the army that fought the religious bigots was only too eager to pay back their loans.

They knew that a time would come when the favour would be called in. The police and politicians turned a blind eye, pretending no such organisation existed. Onyx was the shadow, and the insurance that the country did not fall apart.

Khajuraho

They were drinking coffee in the hotel lobby. It was teeming with tourists excited about starting their tour.

'I have to leave,' Kanyadevi said, stirring her coffee. Her eyes were elsewhere.

'So soon?' Mahesh faced her. He sipped his tea.

'Yes, I have to return to Delhi. A good friend of mine has died,' she said cautiously. She observed him for any reaction. He seemed ignorant of what was happening elsewhere.

'I'm sorry to hear that,' he whispered. 'Are you alright?'

'I am fine.'

He smiled. 'I will return with you. There is no where else for me to go.'

'You are a hypocrite,' Kanyadevi whispered. This wasn't the right moment, but she wanted to gauge his reaction to her.

He looked at her hurt. 'Why do you say that?'

It was a long shot but she couldn't think of any other way to counteract his insane desire to reveal the contents of the scroll. 'Because in our nation, there is illiteracy, exploitation of children, poverty, and the lack of basic necessities, and all you can think of is for me to talk about the dead, about the past – about the Taj Mahal - when I'm more concerned about the future?'

'I don't understand . . .'

'You want me to talk about a dead historical fact that could have a devastating impact but does not help anyone. What we need to work on is the here and now. Change the attitudes of people. The Indian society has some fractured areas. We need to heal, not wound. If you love me, you will work for *my* cause. And forget the past.'

Mahesh Bhakti felt his anger stir. It clouded his senses and he felt a crushing sensation in his heart. What the hell did she know about oppression? He had seen it with his parents – killed because they were not wanted. She only wanted to talk about the masses, if she was affected personally she would understand.

He gave her a pained smile, acknowledging her ideals. Mahesh didn't know what else to say. If she didn't want to talk about the evidence, he had no back up plan. Except if the press 'accidentally' got wind of it. That wasn't as strong and powerful as a Brahmin woman, like KD, talking about it.

He couldn't bring himself to hate her. He loved her so much. It was a new experience for him – to care so much for a woman. She was his soulmate – he felt it in the very core of his being. He dropped his gaze. 'I am talking about a different matter and you are talking about an unrelated issue. They are two diverse issues. I don't see your viewpoint.'

'I want to be the one to decide whether the world should know about the Taj evidence,' Kanyadevi said. She folded her arms. 'It could cause trouble. You know for a fact that this will happen, and yet you want me to announce it officially?'

'You don't have a choice. If we don't, Deva will. Or I will send it to the press myself.' He threatened.

A new group of tourists entered the lobby. KD noticed from the glass wall of the coffee shop. It was getting busier as the day progressed. KD returned her attention to Mahesh.

'You assume too much, Mahesh. I don't share your noncommittal attitude to the consequences of your actions. We have to take responsibility.'

He shook his head. 'I was giving you a great honour, asking you to be the bearer of such great news. I didn't give you the option whether or not to reveal it. That wasn't my intention, KD.'

'Then why do you need me? You go do it yourself.'

'I cannot. I will lose my job and never be able to work as an archaeologist again. There are dozens of hidden artifacts that contradict existing stories and legends in history books. My intention is to bring it to light. India needs to know its past to pave a path in its future. Besides, a great Bharatnatyam dancer, a beautiful intelligent woman like you has more power than an ordinary man like me.'

He leaned forward and took her hands in his. Mahesh looked at her with eyes brimming with love. 'Promise you will think about it.'

Kanyadevi glanced at her watch. 'It's time for me to go.'

Mahesh would tell Deva the good news. 'Yes, it's time for me to go as well.'

Chapter 44

Like the gushing Yamuna River
Where the elixir of life flows
Look at yourself and beyond
You will find the truth in a scroll

Yadav wandered around the house repeating the words. The kitchen had been viciously destroyed. There was no place, the sink or the ceiling, that a scroll would have remained hidden. It was completely ruined. He hoped the murderer hadn't found it yet.

Then he paused in front of the bathroom. The murderer obviously hadn't ventured inside. The tiles were intact, the floor pristine and even the shower curtain had not been ripped to shreds like the drapes in the living room.

Like the gushing Yamuna River. Of course. Water gushed in the bathroom. He went inside. It was like any other bathroom in an apartment – compact, tiled and functional. He scrutinised the white square tiles on the walls, there were no visible loose edges. The ceiling was whitewashed, nothing there. He had to search quickly, before the team of police officers, crime scene investigators, and forensics arrived.

Think, Yadav, think, he told himself. The woman was obviously in a rush, she wouldn't have had much time to hide anything.

Where the elixir of life flows – water. He looked at the shower, the head was fixed in the wall. It was sealed, there was no way the woman could have opened it. Okay, that meant it was the washbasin. He turned on the tap. He looked under the basin, at the curved waste pipe, it was tight. He twisted other smaller pipes, none of them were easy to unscrew without any tools.

Yadav stood up and stared at his face in the cabinet mirror. *Look at yourself and beyond.* He was looking at himself. He opened the cabinet doors and looked inside. The usual bottles and creams haphazardly crowded the slim shelves.

Beyond, he repeated, beyond. He shut the door. Then he noticed the cabinet was slightly crooked. The edges didn't align with the tiles. Placing his hands on either side of the cabinet, he moved it, expecting it to be heavy. It shifted easily. He lifted the cabinet and it came of the hook. He saw the hole in the wall. It was stuffed with newspapers.

Yadav could hear the distant siren sounds as they grew louder. He quickly removed the newspapers and there wrapped in plastic was an object. It was heavy and made of metal. He would examine it later; he removed it from the plastic and placed it inside his jacket pocket. Before exiting, he replaced the bathroom cabinet on the wall to its original position, made sure it was straight.

Yadav dialled the police commissioner's direct line.

Chapter 45

It's all my fault,' Rizvi said, hands holding his head.

'Will you stop it? This is not the time,' Dass said, tapping the table. 'We need a plan and we need to act now, before this gets out of hand.' Dass paused. Then he clicked his fingers. 'I will call Kanyadevi.'

'Call that dancer woman? Why?'

'She's part of Onyx – I spoke to her about Mahesh and she is willing to help. We need to keep her updated. She has connections.'

The demonstrators carried placards and flung their fists in the air. Parag's pictures had been released to the press. His story was one of sacrifice, that of a worthy journalist who lost his life in the search for truth. Those who wanted to hide the truth, murdered him. Deva laughed when he heard the story. It had had the desired effect.

The anger was palpable. The angry crowd cried in one voice, bad-mouthing the killers. They weaved their way through the maze of streets that had recently been the scene of the bomb blasts. Their words rang like a mantra. People inside homes, offices and shops stayed indoors, but the words were hard to ignore.

Aslam's tailoring shop was damaged and all the clothes stained with red ink. He paced restlessly while his family huddled together. They heard someone throwing stones at their home. 'What did we do?' he murmured in fear.

In the midst of the furious demonstrators, a group of white khadi-clad men approached, turned and faced their counterparts from across the road. They lifted their placards. *'United we stand, Hindustan ki jai ho'*, they called out. 'Hindu-Muslim *bhai - bhai*', their voices rose. *'Hum sab ek hai'* - we are one, they waved their message in the air with equal verve.

While their opponents watched with open-mouthed surprise, the peace-lovers moved towards them collectively. Holding their placards higher, they drowned the voices of the mob.

For a few moments there was stunned silence, as the agitators considered their position. Then the volume rose as the demonstrators began abusing the peaceful march.

'Useless cowards!' they yelled. 'That's why our country has gone to the dogs.'

The khadi-clad group ignored them, and continued their peaceful march.

In the distance, the police watched anxious. 'We have a situation,' the sub-inspector whispered into the walkie-talkie. 'There seems to be some other group – protesting as well.'

'What are they protesting for?'

'Peace, sir. And unity,' he said with a heavy voice.

Chapter 46

'You must pray with me,' Deva said, studying his captive carefully. 'Today is Monday; Lord Shiva's day.'

'I need to go home. '

'Why? Who is waiting for you, widow?' Deva said sarcastically. 'No husband, no family, not even a pet.'

Manzil ignored him. Deva picked up his phone, 'What is the inspector's number?'

Manzil had memorised it. She rattled it. He dialled and spoke almost immediately. 'We have the woman. You want her? Bring the scroll.'

Deva paused listening to Yadav. 'I don't have time for your nonsense. Come with the scroll or we kill the woman. You have five hours.'

Deva disconnected and turned to Manzil.

'This inspector seems very concerned, very worried about your wellbeing.' Deva's laugh was a booming echo. 'I'm sure he has more use for you alive than dead.'

Manzil knew he was toying with her. She tried to look indifferent.

'Prepare the temple for my pooja,' Deva called out to the young boy who was massaging him earlier. 'Today we have a guest who prays with me. She will worship the lingam as I do.'

Deva turned to Manzil. 'So which idol do you worship? Is it Krishna? Women love Krishna, the naughty playful lover. Or is he Rama – the righteous, disciplined hero. Or, like me, you pray to Shiva – the ultimate and the most powerful.'

The sun beat down on Manzil. She was parched. 'I don't need to tell you – it's personal.'

Deva smiled coldly. 'God is not personal – he is meant to be shared, to be idolised and respected by one and all,' Deva's voice was soft, yet there was an icy edge to it. He raised his hands in the air as if preaching to a large group of people instead of an audience of one.

The lanky guard who showed Manzil the bathroom came forward and whispered in Deva's ear.

'Yes, yes, call that digger from the IIA – what is his name?'

Deva sat cross-legged on his rope cot, massaging his toes.

Manzil moved closer to the stone steps that led to the shaded part of the courtyard, 'I need some water,' she whispered, resting her head on the cool stone floor.

The boy noticed from the grille window of the house. He brought out a glass of water in a tall steel glass. 'Deva, shall I give it to her?' he asked, spilling some water on her.

Deva waved his hand indicating that he didn't care.

Manzil took the glass and saw the concern in his eyes. 'Be careful or your fate might be like Ramu's. Leave this violent man and start your own life. Use your commonsense,' she whispered, took the glass and slurped thirstily.

Deva's back was towards them. He heard the whispers. 'What did she say?'

The boy paused for a moment before he spoke. 'She is mad, Deva. She says you act as if you are God,' the boy replied without taking his eyes off her face.

'How dare she say such a thing?' Deva's voice rose as he stood up from his reclining pose. He turned to her with the trishul in his hand. 'Apologise!'

'Only if you let the boy walk out that gate,' she responded defiantly. The water had strengthened her. She felt its coolness dissipating the exhaustion from her body.

'You are just a woman, a useless woman,' he said, pressing the trishul in the same place on her chest. Manzil felt the pain in her already sore muscle. Gritting her teeth, she glared.

'Kill me, Deva. Do it in front of these men and forever lose your respect,' she whispered.

Manzil saw the doubt fleeting across his face. 'You are not worth the effort,' he said moving away.

Manzil was tired, her mouth felt dry again. Her body ached with each heartbeat. There was no way out of here. The main entrance was guarded by three of the toughest and meanest men. Along the outer walls of the courtyard were four or five men. Deva was at the centre, and intermittently called one or the other guard to give them instructions on tasks to be done outside. Many were for extortion.

Did Deva really have the conscience to face god, she wondered.

Manzil hoped Yadav had found the scroll. She shut her eyes.

It seemed like only two minutes had passed, when someone prodded her. 'Wake up, it's *puja* time.'

Deva stood over her; he held the trishul in one hand and a steel tray in another. 'Come with me and honour the lingam.'

'I will not do anything you say anymore,' Manzil replied.

Chapter 47

KD's home was filled with the babble of several voices in simultaneous debate. The news about Manzil's abduction had the commissioner of police pacing restlessly. Saraswati Sen was voicing her bleak visions on the future of India.

Now the editor had started his comment on how the story had slipped out and he didn't know about it until it was in print. The film director jumped in to contradict him. He blamed Pritam for not keeping an eye on the print media.

Onyx was falling apart. This had never happened before. Previous cases of sensitive conflicts had been handled with a single-minded approach towards solving the problem – which meant no street killings and no attacks on monuments. But now the group was stuck, blaming each other. Professor Gupta's murder had weakened their spirit.

'Please, everyone, enough opinions and blame. Let's focus on the issue,' KD said, trying to silence her colleagues. 'We have to save this woman from Deva. He is using her as bait to get the scroll. Inspector Yadav is on his way there. The commissioner has briefed him and we had no choice but to let him know about our group, and the importance of keeping the scroll a secret. Any other policeman would use this as opportunity to make money. But it will be blood money and we do not want another bomb explosion. Mahesh is a lose canon. I believe he is resolving a past issue, had nothing to do with the release of the information to the press or the death of the professor.'

'What is our next step?' asked Junaid, the specialist on Islam.

'Call in the army.' Lavina, the investment banker responded, smoking in her corner by the window.

'That's a bit drastic, don't you think?'

'Yes, but one of our honoured and respected members of Onyx has been killed. He has died for his country – protecting a powerful secret. We owe him this much.'

'If the army comes in, it creates fear, and could cost innocent lives,' Junaid countered.

'Deva has started the war. Mahesh, despite his personal agenda, has provided the ammunition. We have to end it. They need to know that there is one army that is not afraid of him, or cannot be bribed,' the police commissioner replied.

'Are they skilled enough?' KD asked.

'Yes, the hills of Ambala have been used wisely. Ex-military men and CID have provided the disciplined training.' Satish said.

'We do have a slight problem, though.'

'What?'

'We just discovered the woman is Muslim.'

'But her husband was Hindu.'

'Yes, that's why they kept their religion a closely guarded secret. Society can be cruel.'

'She seems to be level-headed. So far she has protected the scroll with her life. I think she is on our side.' Saraswati said. 'The professor got the information from her and she didn't let the scroll out of her sight.'

'The only way to find out if she is worthy, is if we save her, isn't it?' Junaid said sarcastically.

Chapter 48

When Yadav arrived at Deva's den, it was still daylight. The sun was white hot. He put on his shades. He had to admit the security was as good as the Yeravada Prison in Pune. The area was surrounded by high brick walls spiked with nails and shards of broken glass to discourage intruders. He stood at one of the side entrances.

Wordlessly, a guard approached, opened the gate and let him in. He was unarmed, or seemed to be. But the man was built like a boxer; one knuckle fist to his chin and Yadav knew he would see stars. He followed.

In the middle of a large dusty courtyard, Yadav stood facing the porch of the house. There was a table and a few plastic chairs, giving it a friendly ambience, as if visitors were regularly entertained with tea and snacks. Despite the slowly sinking afternoon sun, the heat was sharp and he felt the trickle of sweat running down the back of his neck, turning his khaki uniform a deeper shade of brown. Yadav scanned the area but could find no sign of the woman.

'Wait here,' the boxer said and went inside. Yadav noticed a string of dried chillies and lime hanging above the front door, believed to ward off the evil eye.

There were three men standing by the gate, watching him. Two more on each side of the two storey building. Yadav was impressed. Deva must be popular guy with street kids. What was his interest in the woman anyway? What would he gain from her? The whole case was getting too complicated, it was like a hydra; it wasn't about the dead reporter anymore. It was more than that.

The police commissioner had mentioned the non-governmental organisation with support ranging from former secret police, army officers to business tycoons, professors and the top echelon of the entertainment industry. An odd bunch. A group that was beyond religion and had one goal: unity of India. It was unbelievable that such an organisation existed, or even survived under the circumstances.

No one in India was ever free of religion. The ritualistic worship, births, deaths, marriages, festivals, even start of a new business, purchasing a new car, all involved invoking the god. And it wasn't just one God, it was a multitude, and then the many religions. How could anyone not be influenced. But the commissioner said they were focussed. Heavily financed by Indian tycoons, the Onyx had survived changes in government; terrorist attacks, and over the years formed an army of like-minded Indians. Many were able to sleep at night aware that they were part of a group protecting India's integrity.

Yadav was sceptical. No one did anything for nothing. Even though patriotism still lurked in the deepest corners of the hearts of Indians, there had to be an ulterior motive.

Yadav wasn't the only one fighting a losing battle. These Onyx guys were facing thugs – who have seen murder and mayhem from a very young age. Violence was deeply ingrained in them.

Yadav wondered about Manzil: a Muslim. Logically, like any other Muslim, she would want the scroll destroyed, yet she had taken the trouble of keeping it safe. If the information were released that a Muslim was protecting an artifact, that might disprove the origins of the Taj, or reveal secrets of the hidden chamber, it would escalate the violence. Religious issues would come into play.

In all this, no matter which side protested, Manzil would be the first one dead.

He had a duty, Yadav realised. He had a duty to save her life and that was all he would focus on. The next step would be dealt with later.

Deva wasn't alone when he emerged from his domain. Mahesh was with him. 'Give me the scroll,' Mahesh said, snarling like a mongrel.

'Where is the woman? We had a deal,' Yadav approached cautiously. Via his earpiece the commissioner heard every word a few hundred metres away.

Deva seemed extremely agitated. His eyes glowed like embers. 'Your woman is an atheist,' he spat. 'If it wasn't for the scroll, you would be looking at her dead body.'

Yadav sighed relieved. Deva would have definitely struck down the woman with his trishul, if he discovered she was a Muslim. 'What have you done to her?'

'Nothing.'

'Then where is she?'

Mahesh slowly removed a gun from the back of his pocket. 'Give me the scroll,' he said, shifting from one foot to the other.

Yadav lifted his hands. 'What's the matter, Mahesh? Ants in your pants? The scroll, the scroll? What is your problem? You have brought shame to the IIA with your double dealing ways. After we are done here, you will be arrested.'

Deva raised his hand. 'Stop your nonsense and put down that gun, Mahesh.'

Deva nodded and a tall thin man opened the door to a shed. Yadav noticed Manzil as she stepped out into the sunlight. Her hands were tied behind her back. Gaunt and weary, she looked like she had survived a famine and an earthquake. Her t-shirt was torn in places, dark maroon spots had dried around her chest area. Blood. Her long hair, usually in a neat ponytail, was in disarray around her shoulders and her face streaked with dirt. Hunched over, she blinked a few times. When she saw Yadav, she gave him a small smile of recognition.

'She seems to like you,' Deva laughed.

'Are you alright?' Yadav asked cautiously.

Mahesh blocked his path. 'The scroll,' he said, raising the gun.

'Take the slut,' Deva responded with a grunt, approaching them, 'She is damn stubborn, even refused to enter my temple.'

'The scroll,' Deva said.

Yadav reached into his back pocket.

'Wait,' Manzil shouted. 'Are you crazy?'

Deva turned to her, his eyes ablaze and gave her a back-handed slap.

'Cowards!' she yelled, wiping the blood from her torn lip.

Deva pointed the trishul at her. You keep out of this.'

'Bloody murderer! You killed my husband.'

Mahesh pushed her back. Yadav lunged forward and punched Mahesh in the gut. He doubled over. The gun fell out of his back pocket.

'That's lesson number one: you never abuse a woman,' Yadav growled, grabbing the gun.

He gave Deva a hard look.

Deva held up his hand in warning: 'Don't shoot,' he shouted.

His men had trained their guns at them.

'Let's just end this here and now,' Deva said. 'Give me the scroll and you can go.'

Blood was oozing out of Manzil's mouth. She was on her knees, trying to stand up. Yadav felt she wouldn't survive another act of violence.

'Stay low,' Yadav whispered to Manzil, signalling with his hand.

Yadav took two steps forward, 'Here it is!' Removing the object from his back pocket, he flung it towards the house. Deva suddenly froze staring at the flying stick. He turned away. Despite his bulk, he was surprisingly agile as he jumped for cover, away from the stick.

'Come with me,' Yadav grabbed Manzil's hand and pulled her in the opposite direction. Mahesh was right behind.

'You bloody a-' before Mahesh could finish, there was a flash of light and the stick exploded as it hit the entry to Deva's house. Debris of glass and concrete rained down on them. Chaos.

Then Deva's voice bellowed through the sound of fire crackling and spreading through his house 'Grab them!'

Yadav heard the continuous staccato of AK-47s. The Onyx had surrounded the area. Mahesh had dropped to the ground, his eyes on Manzil. He inched towards her.

Deva jostled towards the house. Before he took a step into the doorway, a shot to his knee knocked him. 'You bloody idiots! Get the girl!'

Deva's men didn't respond. They were dropping like flies as gunshots continued to rock the air.

Yadav led Manzil away from the fire. They darted, head low towards the exit, away from Deva's den. Mahesh, right behind them, gripped the inspector's leg. He fell flat on his face. Yadav didn't waste a minute; he urged Manzil to keep going, and kicked Mahesh's face with his other foot. Mahesh howled in pain. Yadav would deal with this man later. He caught up with Manzil and guided her towards the exit. They raced along the boundary wall towards the main gate. The entrance was clustered with Onyx men. One of them led them away from the crossfire.

'Wait!' Manzil said. 'There's a little boy in there we have to get him.'

'We can't go back in. It's too dangerous,' Yadav said impatiently.

Dozens of Onyx men were inside scouring the grounds. The house was burning, while the area was covered with injured or dead men. Intermittent sounds of gunfire continued from all sides. Some of Deva's goons were inside the shed fighting a losing battle. They were surrounded but unwilling to give up and continued to fire at random.

'Then I'm going inside,' she said turning back. Her face was as gaunt as a refugee's, but there was strength in her eyes, a fire of hope.

Damn, she was stubborn.

'Wait. I'll go get him,' he said. He turned to the fighters, 'Take her outside. I'll go get the boy,'

'You will need assistance. I'll send some men with you.' Clad in riot gear, the two men were well-equipped to enter. Yadav followed them inside.

Only an army officer could have taught these men combat. Yadav had to admit, the Onyx seemed well-prepared.

'Stay close,' one of them addressed Yadav.

Manzil watched them go in, 'Be careful,' she whispered.

Deva's men were firing at them through the bullet-ridden shed. The black uniform responded with a rapid round.

Silence.

They moved stealthily, the fire from the first floor was rising in intensity, black smoke billowed from the windows. Everything was covered in black oily ash. The heat was fierce as Yadav leaned low and edged towards the porch. The steps had turned slippery from the soot.

The uniformed men directed him. As they entered the house, the heat shattered the glass windows on the ground floor. It rained down on them.

Deva was lying on the ground, barely conscious. Yadav dragged him away. The Onyx men were at an advantage, they wore night vision goggles, Yadav followed them deeper into the burning structure. The hair on his arm had singed. He felt his skin tighten from the heat. It was burning. He stayed focused and continued forward.

He saw the boy crouching, head down, hands on his ears. Quickly, Yadav got him up and noticed the men lead three other boys out of the burning house.

'Let's go. We are done.'

The fire had spread and it blocked the exit. The left side of the front room, wasn't affected yet, but there was no opening. The fighters fired a round and the wall caved. It was easy to pull away at the rest of the bricks and concrete. Quickly they scrabbled out as the fire began to eat at the floor boards and the ceiling looked like it would fall. They raced out towards the waiting ambulance and police vans.

'We'll get them to a doctor,' one of the men said. 'Better get as far away as possible before this place explodes.'

Deva was among the survivors. He looked old and weak holding his head and weeping.

Yadav checked the surrounding area but Mahesh was nowhere in sight. He must have escaped. Two men supported Deva, dragging him to a waiting van.

Manzil smiled her thanks when she saw the boys.

'Appreciate the vote.' Yadav said, guiding her to the commissioner's jeep.

The driver hit the pedal and the car sped away.

'We need that archaeologist alive,' Yadav whispered over his communicator.

'Don't worry, they will find him,' the commissioner responded. In the distance they could still hear the chaos, the gunshots were nothing more than popping sounds, like firecrackers on a Diwali night. And the blaze from Deva's house lit the night sky.

Chapter 49

KD studied the young woman as she slept in an exhausted heap in the back seat of the car. A grey blanket was wrapped around her, hiding her stained and torn clothes. Fair-skinned, slight freckles dotted her cheek, and lustrous brownish-black hair spread around her shoulders. Punjabi or Kashmiri even, Kanyadevi thought.

Manzil's face was innocent in sleep, untouched by the gruesome madness of the outside world. KD knew a little bit about her background. She had lived a sheltered life – her family doting on her. She was a chartered accountant, worked for one of the top firms in the city. Married to her college sweetheart, she lived in a small apartment and survived on a daily dose of love and security. Until her husband got caught in the wrong place at the wrong time and destroyed the perfect 'happily ever after'.

It must have been a terrible blow, but KD had to admit the young widow had an inner strength and courage. It stemmed from strong roots, and a generous dose of optimism.

KD felt a twinge of regret that she had never experienced such strong familial and cultural roots. It wasn't easy to forget the brutal physical attacks. Many times the nights suffocated her, bringing back torturous past images into focus. She had tried to blur them into non-existence, but they refused to leave her subconscious and resurfaced as if she had been violated recently. The bitter aftertaste stuck to her, leeching the strength, the happiness from her very core.

'She has been through a lot,' Yadav said, breaking the silence. He drove the van up the ghats of Lonavla, towards the safehouse. Just the three of them in the vehicle. The police commissioner had provided a four-car escort out of the city, and then the sturdy minivan.

'Yes, she has, hasn't she?' Sitting by the window, KD stared out at the inky sky as they sped towards one of Satish's holiday homes.

'Don't worry,' Yadav said, driving at a steady pace. 'We will protect her and keep her safe.'

KD saw the soft look in his eyes and smiled wistfully.

For the rest of the night, Yadav drove quietly.

A glimmer of dawn and then a bright orange orb appeared splashing the earth with its warm rays. Manzil stirred, opened her eyes to the sparkling light dancing against the rear window. She sat up and blinked a few times, trying to recall why she was in a car heading through vast empty fields. Her neck felt stiff as she moved it. Her mouth felt like she had been eating cotton wool. Her throat was raw and a dull throbbing remained in her chest. Her head hurt every time she moved. She lay still.

Manzil noticed the dusky woman sitting in the front seat, next to Yadav. She studied her profile. Nice face, strong chin and features. She looked familiar. Manzil couldn't recall where she had seen her before.

KD sensed her gaze. She turned to find Manzil awake. 'Hello Manzil, I'm Kanyadevi. KD for short.' She handed her a bottle of water.

Manzil returned a smile of thanks. She swallowed half a bottle before she attempted to speak. 'Nice to meet you,' she said softly, as she gathered her hair into a ponytail. Kanyadevi offered a clasp.

Manzil accepted it gratefully. She ran her fingers through her hair and then tied it back in a loose grip. 'What's happening? Where are we going?'

'We are taking you to a safe place.'

'Where is the scroll?'

'It's better that you don't know,' Yadav replied.

Manzil couldn't see his eyes behind his aviator glasses. 'For your own safety,' he added.

'I'm already marked. There are people who know I have this relic. You think they won't come after me, scroll or no scroll?'

'I understand, but we can discuss this later. We will find a rest stop. I'm sure you want to wash up and get something to eat,' Yadav said, changing the topic.

Silence.

'Stop the car!' Manzil said after awhile. 'I'm not going anywhere until I know what is going on. I've had enough of people taking over my life.'

KD nodded at Yadav. He hit the brakes and slowed the car to the shoulder of the road.

'Okay, here's the gist,' KD sighed. 'Mahesh Bhakti, Deva, and a hired assassin from an opposing gang...'

'Khanbaba's guy, Anwar,' Yadav explained. 'The guy who followed you on the bus.'

'He came back to my house demanding the scroll. He is the one who... who killed Ramu.'

'Yes, all these people are looking for you.' KD said. 'They want to see you dead and use the scroll for their own agendas. We just want to make sure that no one, I mean no one gets hurt. That's why we have to get you out. Things are going to be crazy, what with Deva's gang falling apart. We cannot protect you there. My friend has a farm house, where we will be safe for the time being. The scroll is safe with me. We will then decide the next course of action.'

'If you don't mind my asking, how can just the two of you fight off these murderers?'

KD smiled at Manzil. 'It's not just the two of us. We have guards. We have people monitoring the situation in the city and sending us updates. We also have the police informing us of the latest action in the underworld.'

'And there's Onyx.' Yadav added, giving her a sidelong glance.

'The Onyx is a network of likeminded people. We have spread our wings, with strong support in various areas, including trained army men you saw at Deva's hideout. There is Yuva, the peace protesters, and a large network of individuals in different professional fields. They are our eyes and ears. Your husband was one of us, you know?'

'So I discovered much later, after he died. He had written a letter, and mentioned Onyx. Parag seemed aware that danger lurked at every turn. But he didn't share it with me. Only after his death, did he share his life.'

Yadav looked at her through the rearview mirror. 'Your husband was a brave man, and I think he would have wanted the Onyx to help you.'

'Thank you, Yadav. For saving me too.'

He seemed embarrassed by her gratitude, KD noticed with interest. She turned to her.

'Manzil we have to be careful even though we are far away from the city. These thugs have snitches at every corner shop, petrol pump, restaurant and village well.'

With an impatient nod, Yadav started the engine and headed back on the dusty narrow road. He hit the accelerator as the sun smacked hard and the roads glistened as though they were wet. It was an illusion, Manzil noted surprised at the mundane nature of her thoughts. For she knew everything was not as it seemed.

She gazed out at the racing fields. 'A cup of strong tea and some breakfast would be nice,' she said softly. There was time. Manzil realised they were there to protect her. She needed to gather her strength – there was much to learn and this was just the beginning.

'Your father is worried about you,' Yadav said. His face was inscrutable. 'You can use my phone to speak to him.'

'He called you?'

'I answered your phone when I was at your house, looking for you.'

'Then you know,' Manzil felt a tightness in her chest. Oh my god, they knew. She panicked; the first thought that crossed her mind was escape. These two might be taking her to some isolated place to kill her. And would call it an accidental death. She had read enough newspaper reports.

'Yes, we know you are a Muslim,' KD replied.

Chapter 50

Dass wasn't happy. The news on the Mahesh Bhakti front was bad, not only was he a suspected murderer, he was in cohorts with an underworld don and looting the IIA. Rana had fed him the facts and it took a lot of strength to hold back the words, 'Get rid of him, Shoot the bastard.'

Dass barely suppressed his emotion as Rana continued his heated spiel about Mahesh's sudden amorous feelings for Kanyadevi. 'If that woman is next on his hit list, then we are in big trouble. It would reflect very badly on the IIA,' Rana stated the obvious.

The crowded shopping mall wasn't the ideal place to meet, but Dass had stopped going to the tea shop where he was attacked. His previous informant had disappeared, never to return his calls or contact him with information. Rana was his only source, the link to the outside world. He was a good man, a true and loyal Rajput.

The open food court in the basement was loud with American music that boomed from all directions. It was also the most visible area from all the floors above, tempting shoppers to come down for a few moments of respite. One had to speak at least an octave higher to be heard.

Jeans-clad teenagers sat in groups, some eating burgers, others sipping coffees from American-sized paper cups. He didn't think they were too bothered about how any of it tasted. They just wanted to look 'cool': the new word in the teenage lingo. It used to be 'hot' in the old days.

Rana and Dass sat in the corner, away from the waxing and waning energetic youngsters. The new generation couldn't care less if their country was in trouble, or divided, or suffered from dozens of social issues – they just wanted to be 'hip' like the heroes in Hollywood movies.

Rana was picking on his *aloo bhajiya*, deep fried battered potato balls. It was obviously not what he expected. He had chosen it from a range of other snacks under the glass showcase of a coffee bar. Dass could tell the food looked at least a day old.

'It's in all the papers – some thing or the other related to the Taj,' Rana said grimacing as he sipped his coffee.

'More information has leaked. Now the whole country suspects there actually is some evidence, and we are hiding it. They claim we know more than we are letting on and that it concerns with the Taj and its origins.' Dass sighed. He knew the Urdu-speaking goon would call and threaten him again. But what could he do. The situation was already out of his control when the bombings took place after Deva had made the pictures public.

'We have to do something. But what?'

Dass smiled sadly. 'I think it is out of our hands. We have been asked to keep quiet. The instructions are coming from the top.'

'Sir, if I can make a suggestion?'

'Go ahead.'

'Instead of denying it, why not face the facts? We haven't done anything wrong. Why is the blame falling on the IIA?'

'IIA has always been the scapegoat. Our government is not ready to face facts, Rana. Look around you. Do you think these kids care? We have no support from any one – the university, the schools, and even the intellectuals don't care about the IIA's work. We are fighting a loosing battle, and we can't afford to risk any more lives. We let the government handle it now.'

Dass suddenly felt exhausted. The world had changed so much – the wars were all forgotten, the soldiers who died for their country – nothing. He sighed and leaned back.

There was a single popping sound. When Rana turned to look at his boss, he noticed his stunned expression, then a hole in the assistant DG's shirt turning crimson. Dass stood up and then stared in shock at the growing red on his chest, his mouth widened in horror as the realisation sank in. Everything happened in slow motion. Dass lurched back in his chair and fell crashing to the floor, clutching his chest. Blood spread quickly.

On the balcony above, Dass caught a glimpse of the red-haired man; his arms folded together as he watched him die.

Rana darted to his boss' side. Leaning against the wall, Rana held the dying man in his lap, pressing the wound with his jacket, the blood flowed on to the floor forming a pool next to the coffee bar.

People were starting to notice and draw back. A woman screamed. And then pandemonium.

'It's no use, Rana. They had warned me already.'

Dass went still.

'Call the police. Get a damn ambulance, you stupid idiots,' Rana shouted into the crowd of laughter and American music.

'You have not done your job well, Rizvi,' the deep voice drawled over the phone.

'I have, sir. But there is too much that is beyond our control now,' Rizvi stuttered, gripping the handset tight. 'We are working on it. Give me another chance. I will make this go away.'

'We have received instructions. Listen very carefully.' The voice had taken on a harder tone.

'Sir, anything...'

'The wise thing to do is to wipe out all the evidence, and the people who have it,' the voice paused as if waiting for the director general to digest what he had been asked to do.

'Sir, I understand. But the information is out in the open. Who shall I hold responsible?'

'The widow, and the archaeologist working for you. They must be dealt with immediately, Rizvi.'

'Yes, sir. I understand,' Rizvi let the handset fall from his grip, sank in his seat and put his face in his hands, shaking. The only person he could talk to was Dass. Where the hell was he?

Rizvi dialled his number.

Rana answered. 'What's happened?' Rizvi asked.

Dass never allowed anyone to answer his phone.

'He's dead,' Rana whispered. 'Someone shot him through the heart. The police are here.'

Rana assumed Mahesh Bhakti was involved. He would get him – shoot *him* in the heart. Rana was upset with himself. He was a descendent of royal guards; he had failed in his task as protector. He should have guessed Mahesh would try something foolish. Now there was no other way but to hunt him down and drag him by the collar back to Delhi.

Chapter 51

Deva was jailed, convicted on charges of inciting violence and abducting an innocent woman. The police commissioner made sure the man was behind bars for as long as the scroll was out there.

Mahesh heard about the fire and the news on the radio. He was on a train to south India. Towards KD's city. He had tried to contact her but her phone was disconnected. Best to get away for a while, he realised. He thought of KD and relived the moments he had spent with her. They were a balm to his aching heart.

The train raced rhythmically, a hypnotic beat, through the night. Mahesh dozed off a few times but jerked awake when his neighbour's nodding head fell on his shoulder. He continued his interrupted sleep with one image in his heart.

As the train paused in the heart of the country after eight hours, the rusty window railings couldn't hide the beautiful dawn that broke through the darkness against the backdrop of a vast flatland.

India was such a beautiful country – Mahesh felt a surge of pride at the sight. He loved his country, the ancient forts and palaces, the villages with their unique characters, and sometimes, during his journeys, he came upon numerous dilapidated temples, a small clay idol in its midst, offering solace to the traveller. He wished KD was with him. He wanted to share his feelings with her, his experiences and his passion.

Mahesh blinked back fresh tears. For all these years he hadn't felt so alive. This new feeling of love was unusual, but it had turned him soft. He needed to be tough and focus on his goals, to find the widow and seize the scroll. There was work to do. This would be the ultimate effort to avenge his parents' death. The government needed to be shaken up, knocked out of their secular dreamland.

He would make sure the scroll was revealed to the world and then the world would realise that history was falsely reported. India was the greatest land ruined, desecrated and conquered by foreigners for centuries. Now the country was nothing more than a dominated nation – confused about its rich heritage, and confused about its identity. It was the hand of fate that the discovery of the most powerful evidence about the Taj would help build the nation to a stronger and more honest reality.

Mahesh closed his eyes to revel in the moment. He was being offered a perfect opportunity to show the country what he was capable of, once he got the scroll.

His mobile rang.

'What?' Mahesh snapped.

'Deva wants you to go to Mumbai.'

'Who is this?'

'Yama – god of death – what difference does it make to you. Go to Mumbai. The widow has been seen going in that direction.'

'Where in Mumbai?'

'Our contacts will inform us. You wait for instructions.'

The man hung up.

Damn! He so wanted to be with KD to convince her to take his side. But this was more important. The widow was as slippery as an eel. He would get the scroll from her by hook or by crook.

Chapter 52

Anwar walked away at a measured pace. He exited the building and sprinted towards the left. A white car waited for him, and it started moving as soon as the driver noticed him. Pulling the rear door open, Anwar jumped into the moving car. 'It's done,' he said to his boss.

Anwar had threatened the IIA boss but the man had done nothing. This would teach them a lesson – messing with the origins of great monuments. Who did they think they were, daring to change their proud history? All their evidence was fake and now the scroll was creating needless doubts. It must be the biggest fake of all. But Indians would believe anything. Make his boss and clan out to be the bad guys. The only way was to kill the rest. Deva's men were on to him. Deva and Khanbaba ran the two of the biggest underground webs in Agra and if they wanted to, they had the power to turn a street into a bloodbath.

'*Shabash*! Well done, Anwar,' Khanbaba said. His left wrist weighed down by a gold Rolex. It hung as if two sizes too big for him. The three rings on his pudgy fingers matched the metal band of the watch, and his neck weighed down by a thick chain of gold. He leaned back in pride as if he had accomplished the job himself.

Anwar smiled, revealing a gold tooth. 'Boss, I will get that woman next.' He slid into the back seat and rubbed his scalp as if it itched. His red wiry hair stood comically where he scratched.

Khanbaba nodded, watching the passing traffic through the tinted window. 'I have just heard from Dubai. They are giving us more support. They are providing the manpower and money we need. A source has told us the woman's route. She is not alone, there is another woman and a police officer. They are on the road. Easy to dispose.'

'Where to, Khanbaba?'

'Near Mumbai.'

Chapter 53

Manzil felt oddly calm. She knew she had to take charge again. There was no one she could trust. Yadav was slowing down at a rest stop. This would be the opportunity to make a run for it. KD was being nice, polite and friendly; but, Yadav? He was reserved, behaving coldly. They both had an agenda. Why did they need her now that they had the scroll? What use was she to them? It was obvious they were going to kill her.

'Where is the scroll?' she asked again.

'Why?' Yadav asked.

'I just want to take a look at it, to make sure it's the real one,' she lied.

'When we reach the safe house, you can look at it,' KD responded, giving her an odd look.

'No. I . . . I need to look at it now. There is something about the symbol, Professor Gupta told me about it. It's a clue. I might forget it later.'

KD leaned forward and opened the glove compartment. 'Here's pen and a notepad.Write down whatever you remember; then, when we get to the safe house, you can take a look at the scroll. It's a sad situation. Someone killed the professor after your visit to him.'

Manzil felt a chill. She felt as though KD was accusing her . This didn't look good.

Manzil sighed. 'The situation is worse than I thought. The professor warned me to be careful. I didn't mean for his life to be in danger. The Onyx has lost a great man.'

'The Onyx will never be the same again. But we will continue with our work,' KD said.

'Parag believed in their cause.'

Manzil was behaving oddly. It wasn't safe to remove the scroll from its location. Surely she understood that. KD wondered why she would want to look at it. They had to get to the safe house before nightfall. Satish Kumar had offered his residence in Pune, 200 kilometres north of Mumbai – a highly secured residence, he had said.

Word had spread about Deva and his encounter with the police. Street thugs and small time dons were preparing to join forces.

Khanbaba was preparing for battle. He wanted a stake in Deva's empire. It would be a lucrative deal for him. That's what Yadav said was the latest word on the street.

Through their network, Onyx members were aware of a tsunami-size wave of anger spreading within the fabric of society. The news of the Taj had created a new reason to create fresh distrust. The widow had become the bait. When Deva kidnapped her, Khanbaba was waiting to hear of her death.

They didn't want to kill her. But her death implied the death of the scroll.

KD didn't want to reveal the seriousness of the situation. But on a scale of one to ten – it was an eleven. Manzil would be easily found, the dons had the largest network of contacts, from street cobblers to hotel guards and from secretaries to dabbawallas. The Onyx had warned that it would be difficult to send in the forces to protect them. They were vulnerable.

'How much longer?' she asked Yadav.

'About eight hours.'

Yadav slowed down the car and turned into a driveway of a truckstop for tea and snacks. Bir's Dabba was an open porch with plastic tables and chairs.

Their car faced the roadside and every vehicle that drove in or out was clearly visible. Yadav switched off the engine and studied the area. It seemed safe. 'We should have a quick bite and get back on the road,' he said glancing at Manzil.

'I need to wash my face.' She got out of the car slowly, grimacing at the pain that shot through her as she transferred her weight to her legs. Wobbly, Manzil leaned against the side of the car, and waited until she felt strong enough to move. Slowly, she headed towards the large signboard that said toilets. KD joined her. Manzil realised this wasn't going to work. She would have to find another opportunity to escape. She didn't have the energy to walk, let alone run.

'I'll order some tea and snacks in the meantime.' Yadav stretched his arms over his head and then forward, twisting from side to side.

'*Sahib*, we have fresh onion *bhajia*. You want some with tea?' the young waiter said. With one hand, he placed three glasses on the table, filled with water.

He waved the boy away, glancing around. 'Get me three teas and one plate of bhajias. And add plate of bun pav to that.'

The boy nodded. He wiped the table with a greasy napkin, swiped away a few crawling spiders. 'Where are you going, *sahib*?'

'Why?'

'Just asking, not used to see anyone other than truckers here.'

'We are going on a long pilgrimage.' Yadav said vaguely. He sat down and waited for the women, his eyes focussed in the direction of the washroom.

The waiter placed the order with the cook. Turning away, he hurried towards the phone at the back of the dhaba. He dialled and when it connected, he said three words. 'They are here.'

Chapter 54

Deva had fifteen minutes and he took full advantage of his time. Being in jail wasn't going to stop him from following his dharma. Deva's right-hand man listened intently.

'It is time for war,' Deva whispered.

The words seemed out of place in a prison. Deva explained the choice of weapons, the method of combat and their main enemy. 'Khanbaba will destroy everything. We have to get to him first, before he takes over. He needs to know I'm still in control. Have you informed Mahesh about the widow?'

'Yes. He is on his way.'

'Good. There is only one thing we need - the scroll. That is our trump card. Let me know when you find the widow. Her true blood has been discovered. She deserves to die.'

Chapter 55

Satish Kumar's sprawling home was in Kalyani Nagar, the newly developed section of Pune, the satellite town of India's financial capital Mumbai.

His house was at the end of the street of one of the largest complex of row houses in the area. It was also considered one of the safest. Ten feet high walls with another five feet of high stone masonry and high-tech solar-powered security fencing surrounded the whole half acre plot.

As they entered, a security guard checked their identity and double-checked with Satish if they were expected. As the turnstile lifted, they noticed three overhead cameras angled from flagpoles.

Yadav still didn't feel safe.

Security guards could be bought or killed. Speedbumps disrupted his pace and he drove slowly. The lush tree-lined landscaping on both sides of the cobblestoned road was spectacular, leading them to the main entrance. Satish Kumar's home was still not visible. They faced a wide electronic gate. Another guard house on the left side greeted the newcomers. The guard had a body of a boxer and an expression of a fierce dog.

Yadav began to breathe a bit easier. The security seemed impenetrable. But one never knew. The guard watched them keenly, probably a trained bodyguard, before he became a security guard of the famous film producer.

They were allowed inside only after the underside of the car was checked with an electronic device. A watchman guided them into a basement carpark. As they entered, they couldn't help notice the sprawling grounds, complete with waterfalls and miniature gardens encompassing a huge monument in the centre. It was a replica of the Taj Mahal.

'Great! That's all we needed.' Yadav muttered.

The exterior of the majestic house was designed for effect. But inside, the architecture and the layout was modern with high ceiling and rustic tile flooring. The main door was oak and six feet wide with door-knockers. Inside the foyer, was a hexagonal-shaped entrance. They entered a hallway. On both sides of the walls, huge window panes with iron framework ledges for plants, allowed a spectacular view of the swimming pool, garden with a fountain and a small outhouse.

A hundred yards ahead and the hallway opened to an L-shaped living and dining area.

'We are not safe here,' Manzil said, hugging herself as if cold. 'We are too isolated, far from civilisation, and that red-haired maniac is sure to turn up here.'

'Don't worry Manzil. This is a secure place,' Kanyadevi said. 'No one knows we are here. And it is best to stay away from the city for a while.'

The living room was sparsely furnished, the floor was white and grey and the walls textured. Like the original monument, there was an emptiness about it.

Felt like a mausoleum, too. Manzil shivered.

She had changed into a pair of elastic trousers and t-shirt which KD had picked up from a small boutique earlier that afternoon. Free-size, but not something Manzil was used to.

'I'm going to check the rooms.' Yadav said and disappeared through one of the doors. Manzil sat on the edge of a sofa as if waiting for a tragedy to befall her.

Yadav had been driving for twenty-eight hours with just four breaks. It had taken a toll on him.

His bloodshot eyes were clearly visible; he noticed when he was in the bathroom. He splashed icy water on his face. It helped soothe his burning eyes, but the exhaustion was getting to him.

There was a good chance that the dons would send their henchmen. He needed to stay alert.

He wandered through the house, checked the windows and sliding doors for the third time. It was sealed. For some reason, Manzil was edgy. He was bothered by her quiet discomfort. He could almost hear her brain ticking, and it wasn't just about the scroll. His instincts told him that there was more on her mind.

He heard the two women in the kitchen. He wanted some coffee, but settled on the sofa. He would rest his tired eyes for a few minutes.

When KD emerged from the kitchen with a tray of biscuits, sandwiches and coffee, Yadav was snoring lightly.

It was getting dark, and with it Manzil's fear increased. For all the trouble the dons had gone through, they were not going to give up, she guessed, she could be dead by the next day. On another more chilling thought, to make it easier for Onyx and the police, if KD and Yadav conspired to kill her, who would doubt their word that Deva or Khanbaba's men had done so. They were all alone in the boondocks.

'Can I take a look at the scroll now?'

KD pointed at a locked drawer by the dining table. 'I've put it there for safekeeping.' She handed her the key and returned to the sofa watching her as she sipped her coffee.

Manzil paused. She felt unsure. Should she trust KD, and Yadav – he was the good guy, went to her home, retrieved the scroll, saved her. KD was a part of the Onyx, and Parag trusted them. She shouldn't doubt them and wanted to believe everything they said.

But in the past few weeks, she had seen so much, heard lies, knew that a murderer was stalking her, how could she not suspect that they too might want her dead now that they knew her ethnicity.

Earlier, she had checked the bedrooms in the eastern wing, keeping in mind possible escape routes. Each of the four bedrooms led off to an outdoor garden area, complete with a jogging track skirting the fence around the mansion. The screen doors were locked down with huge padlocks. There were corridors that led off to different parts of the house. As much as the security was tight, the vastness of the mansion, and many access routes made her feel vulnerable.

Manzil removed the scroll from the drawer. She saw the small handgun next to it and knew this was a perfect opportunity. She hid the weapon in her pocket and returned to the sofa.

Yadav was awake and alert when he saw her with the scroll.

He sat up and helped himself to the tray of food, swallowed a sandwich in two bites and gulped down the scalding coffee.

KD chewed on her bread, she seemed distant, her mind stuck on some past incident.

Steam was still rising from the mugs. Manzil couldn't have her coffee so hot, but, she recalled, Parag could. She closed her eyes to the memory of her dead husband.

So much had happened, and so much more was going on. She was so focussed on the scroll, she had forgotten his birthday, yesterday. She might be able to wish him personally if things didn't go well, she reflected morbidly.

Manzil carefully removed the plastic wrapping around the gold encasing. She opened the top and removed the scroll. Carefully, she unrolled and studied the scroll, its meaningful loops and curves of the words, written with ink that must have been made from a special vegetable dye, it was smudged in places but legible after all these centuries. She wondered what it all meant. The professor was disturbed by its contents.

Why were people willing to kill over this five-hundred-year old text? Parag's darkened blood stain had left its mark on the scroll. Parag had died for this, information that could change the face of Indian history. The government-approved version of the story had been torn to shreds by the media. If Parag were alive, he would have handled the information cleverly. There wouldn't have been this kind of craziness.

'So what is it?' Kanyadevi asked, sipping her coffee.

Manzil looked at her blank.

'You said there was something important you wanted to check?'

Manzil was silent. She felt her fingers tremble as she carefully rolled up the scroll, returned it into the gold case, and then into the plastic pouch.

Silently, as they watched, she headed towards the dining area, turned away and then stood by the sliding door that led out into the swimming pool area. She turned to face KD and Yadav.

There was no other way to do this. 'I will leave now,' Manzil said, removing the gun from her pocket and pointing it at them. Yadav was on his feet in an instant. KD placed her mug back on to the coffee table and stood up slowly.

'Why are you being a fool?' Yadav asked.

'Stay back!' Manzil said with more confidence than she felt. Her hand shook.

'Listen Manzil, you are just in a state of panic. You are not thinking this through. Put down the gun and we will talk,' KD said, placating. 'I know you are scared, but everything will be alright.'

Manzil continued to move backwards, and aimed the gun at them. The scroll snug in her pocket, she had both hands on the weapon. With a determined shake of her head, she spoke. 'I won't hurt you. I just want to leave. I know you are going to get rid of me, because of my... background.' She unlatched the door, and slid it open, she took another step back.

'Manzil, don't do this... we are not going to kill you, and you're not going to shoot at us. What a stupid idea, and come on, you don't know how to handle a gun!' Yadav said in frustration. As the sheer white curtain swelled in the night breeze they couldn't see her for a few seconds.

'Even then, why should you put your lives at risk? And I need to work this out on my own. This is not your problem. The scroll is my responsibility.' She could see the two of them through the design of slivered blooms of the sheer drape, it reminded her of the looped floral carvings on the Taj.

'Listen Manzil, you have to start trusting us. We are not here to hurt you – we don't care which religion you belong to.'

Yadav turned, nodded at KD that she should keep talking. He edged closer.

'You are being irrational if you think we are the ones who will kill you. There are others out there, who at this very moment have possibly found our location and this very minute heading here. They are not interested in us. They want you. They know you have the scroll. We can protect you. You have to trust us.'

KD noticed her hesitation. Manzil felt a warm wind and with it the fragrance of mogra, the night jasmine offered a deceptively sweet comfort. 'I am not of your. . . faith.'

'What makes you think we will kill you for such a lame reason? ' KD pressed.

'And where will you go? All alone? You will be vulnerable. Think about it. Why are you acting so irrationally?' Yadav added.

Manzil felt her hands grow clammy. 'Irrationally? Death in riots are irrational. Because that's how my mother was killed. She was targeted because of her religious leanings . . . . My father doesn't want to come back here because the memories still haunt him, he blames this country. I don't know why I still have hope . . .'

The gun felt like a chunk of of iron, her forearms hurt from holding the weight upright. Manzil wanted to believe them. Yadav made sense. Where would she go? How far could she run? With the scroll? What would she do with it? She stepped back and her foot caught in the sprinkler on the patch of grass, she lost her balance and before she hit the ground, the gun went off.

In horror, she saw everything happen in slow motion.

Yadav rushing towards her. The bullet ricocheting against the marble wall and then slamming into his leg.

'Nooo!' She screamed.

Chapter 56

Rana was sure that Mahesh would be heading south to be with Kanyadevi.

'Where are you?' Rana asked.

'I'm at the train station. Going to Mumbai.'

'Another dig site?' Rana asked.

'Yes,' Mahesh said.

'I need to talk to you. It's about the dancer,' Rana said, surely that would catch his attention.

'What is it?'

'Cannot discuss on the phone. It's important. I will meet you in Mumbai.'

'That's not a good idea. I will be busy, travelling around the area. Just tell me what it is.'

'Do you want to know where the scroll is?' Rana decided to use the best unkept secret as bait.

Mahesh paused. He seemed to be considering the question. 'Yes. Meet me at the Chhatrapati Shivaji Terminus. Tonight.'

'Fine.'

Chapter 57

They helped Yadav into the house and slid the door shut. Manzil whispered 'sorry' a dozen times and sobbed uncontrollably.

'I shouldn't have acted so foolishly.'

'It's okay, I'm not going to die.' Yadav grunted as he hobbled towards the stool by the kitchen. He sat down and stretched his bleeding leg. 'Get me a pair of scissors,' he said. His face was dripping with sweat. Manzil frantically searched the kitchen cabinets and returned with scissors and a first aid kit.

KD cut the fabric of his trousers, split it apart and checked the wound. On the thickest part of his calf muscle, she could see a small jagged hole bleeding. 'It's not too deep.'

Yadav grimaced. 'Can you see the bullet?'

'First let me cleanse the area.'

The first aid kit contained a thick roll of white cotton gauze, cotton wool and a bottle of Dettol. Manzil was by his side, helping KD.

Using a kitchen towel, KD wiped away the blood and then with the antiseptic liquid, she carefully wiped the wound. 'I cannot see the bullet. We have to stop the bleeding first,' KD said, as she soaked the bandage with some antibiotic cream and wrapped his leg with it.

They helped Yadav to the sofa and gave him some painkillers. As he lay down, he fell asleep from exhaustion and pain.

Manzil looked at Kanyadevi sheepishly. 'I didn't mean to – '

'This is not the time to dwell on it. Luckily, the impact of the bullet wasn't strong. Yadav is tough, he will be fine,' KD said. 'What happened to your mother, Manzil?'

'My mother was an innocent. It was a small incident – an idol in a temple was vandalised. There was some rioting on the streets. And it happened at that time when my mother was heading to a shop near the local mosque. She was about to enter, and someone threw a glass bottle. It hit her; she fell on the marble step knocking her head. She died later in the hospital, fractured skull."

'Where is your father now?'

'In England, he copes with his loss by turning himself into a workaholic.'

'And you?' Kanyadevi smiled in encouragement. 'Why didn't you leave? Be with your father.'

'I . . . think, my mother was in the wrong place at the wrong time. It's hard to pin blame. . . .. But my father will not see it that way. And he left for that reason. I didn't leave because of Parag. He had this relentless optimism that he could fix the wrongs in this country. I was afraid for him, but deep down I was also very proud of his ideologies. Still am,' Manzil said. She was surprised she could talk about Parag without tears. 'I met Parag in college. He didn't care about my religious background, whether I was rich or poor. He just loved me, slightly stubborn with the habit of speaking my mind.'

They were silent.

'He was one of those students who wanted to change the social landscape of India.'

'Haven't we all tried?'

'Sometimes I think that we are making progress – the new generation are intermingling. Their belief system is more about changing in positive way. It's more about inner strength, than outdated beliefs – and the melting pot of these like-minded people will make a difference.'

'Spoken like a true Onyx member,' KD said.

'Trying to recruit me?'

'Yes,' KD admitted. 'We are trying to find people who can stand their ground, not sway easily by rigid beliefs.'

'Yes – that is the big picture – religion filters into every area of our lives, seeps into our hearts, our souls. On every street corner, in every home there's a shrine to a god.' Manzil hesitated and then she asked. 'You're an atheist?'

She shook her head. 'I believe in god. A higher power that doesn't have rules and regulations, that brings us together for a common good. It's a simple philosophy. Besides, I have my dance. It's a form of religion for me.'

'Not sure if everyone would agree, but I like the way you think.'

KD headed towards the door by the dining area. 'You said there's hope. So, let's live with that. Come help me make some more coffee.'

'Sure,' she stood up and followed KD. 'You know my life story, tell me about yourself.'

Kanyadevi smiled. 'When I was born, my mother abandoned me by the cliffs of Kanyakumari, hoping the tide would wash me away. My fisher parents, who found me, took me home. They needed an extra pair of hands, and used me to make money. Later when I was older I was sold to a pimp and worked as a prostitute before I managed to escape. I became a professional classical dancer by sheer determination. I am a survivor and I think you are the same.'

Manzil was silent for a minute. 'You have been through a lot. You are a very courageous woman. What surprises me more is not what you went through, but how you manage to tell me about your experience without wallowing in self-pity,' Manzil said as she opened the refrigerator and found a few packets of juice and a large tetra pack of milk.

She removed them and placed them on the countertop. 'I admire that tenacity to find a way out of the hellhole, finding your destiny,' Manzil said softly.

KD filled the kettle with water and set it to boil. 'Thank you. But I admit - it's not as easy as it sounds. It takes a lot to hold back the memories. I live with it everyday of my life. The secret is not to let it get to you, or blame fate, god, or anyone. The past should stay in the past.'

'I think you speak for the Taj too,' Manzil said and they both smiled.

Chapter 58

The most famous railway station in Mumbai, the Chhatrapati Shivaji Terminus, was previously known as Victoria Terminus in honour of the then reigning monarch of Britain, Queen Victoria. Built in 1888, it was a legacy of the British Raj. The detailed architecture bore resemblance to the St Pancras station in London.

Designed in the Victorian Gothic style, the station took ten years to complete and is an imposing structure. In 1996, in response to demands by the Shiv Sena, the station was renamed by the state government after Chatrapati Shivaji, a seventeenth century Maratha warlord.

Rana saw him first exiting the platform. Mahesh noticed Rana and before he could wave, Rana indicated the direction of the toilets. The man was behaving oddly. Mahesh followed. Obviously all was not well in the IIA.

As soon as Mahesh entered the toilet, Rana hung a 'closed for cleaning sign' and shut the door. Shoving him against the tiled wall, Rana glared at him with hatred. 'You bloody son of a bitch!'

Mahesh pushed him away. 'Back off, man! What are you getting all worked up about?'

'You bloody murderer! Why did you have to kill Dass of all people? Your boss, the assistant director? What did he do to you? Why did you get him gunned down?' He slammed him against the wall with every question.

Mahesh was shocked. 'Dass is dead?'

'Yeah, quit acting. Why did you do it?'

'For God's sake, back off. I had nothing to do with it!'

'You had everything to do with it. I heard you murder prostitutes too. Murder comes easily to you. You're some blue blood, right? Decides who lives and who dies, eh?' Rana said, venting his anger, punching him again in the gut.

Mahesh felt the sudden pain in his jaw and tasted blood. He was totally dazed. There was someone rapping on the door. Then it went quiet. Rana stopped bashing him up.

'Listen to me very carefully,' Mahesh said, his eyes puffy and his cheeks swollen. 'I had nothing to do with Dass's death. And I don't kill prostitutes. Someone has been feeding you lies. It has to be Khanbaba's men. I'm sure of it. In fact, the widow and the dancer must be in danger. He will go after them. He knows the scroll is with them.'

'How do you know?'

'Deva,' Mahesh replied. It was enough for Rana to back off. 'He contacted me. I know where the women are hiding and we have to go there right now.'

The fear of losing KD was killing him.

'I will come with you.'

'We have to save them. Khanbaba's men will stop at nothing and when he gets the scroll, he will not just destroy it but murder anyone who gets in his way. What he would do to those women, I'm afraid to think about. But he will make sure it is a lesson for Deva.'

Again they heard the distinct tapping, sounded like a police baton. 'Open the door, this is the station master.'

Chapter 59

Scraping sounds woke Manzil with a start. As her eyes adjusted to her whereabouts, she tried to figure out the source.

Yadav was sprawled on the sofa, his injured leg balanced on the armrest. KD was asleep. Manzil heard the noise again. It came from the sliding doors. With a sudden chill, she realised someone was trying to get in. Manzil panicked. She stood up quickly, thinking what to do.

The scroll was safely in one of the dozen drawers of the Rajput cabinet. She had placed a few rolls of paper, shaped like the scroll, wrapped in plastic, strategically around. One was on the dining table, one rested on the coffee table, hopefully it would be adequate distraction. The scraping continued.

Should she wake up the two? Better to check who was making that noise. But then it might be too late. She slid off her two-seater sofa and leaned to her right. KD was on a reclining chair.

Manzil pressed KD's hand softly. She didn't want her to make a sound. Her eyes fluttered open, 'What's wrong?'

'There is someone at the door,' Manzil whispered. 'We should hide.'

It was dark, but in the muted moonlight they noticed a shape outside using a sharp instrument on the lock. Before they could do anything, they heard the hiss of the door sliding open.

Yadav had the largest sofa and he was snoring softly. They couldn't help him. It was better that they let him be for now.

Manzil urged KD in the direction of the kitchen. They made their way softly.

They heard the squeak of the intruder's shoes. He entered the living room and then paused as if trying to adjust to the darkness. In a few minutes, he would notice Yadav.

Manzil was confident that they had enough time to escape from the kitchen door. The kitchen was darker than the living room. Rustling sounds came from the dark corners. She felt KD jerk, but she didn't make a sound. This was no time to be scared, beads of sweat spread down Manzil's neck.

Grabbing a knife from the cutlery stand, Manzil sneaked towards the backdoor. KD was right behind. They heard scuffling and muffled voices. The intruder must have pulled Yadav out of his slumber. KD noticed a sliver of light under the door. 'We better hurry.'

Manzil twisted the backdoor knob quickly. It turned easily. She pushed the small wooden door open. It made a slight squeak. Manzil nudged it slowly ensuring that it opened as quietly as possible.

Before they stepped out, they heard a large crashing sound from the living room. In a panic, they lunged outside. 'Shut the door slowly!' Manzil whispered.

'Tell me where they are?' The gravelly sound erupted from the living room.

'They are not here,' Yadav said loudly.

'You tell me now or I…'

Too late.

The backdoor slipped shut with a sharp squeal. The two women looked at each other and then raced towards the only other hiding place dead ahead – the basement carpark.

Chapter 60

Mahesh and Rana arrived at Satish Kumar's residence in the dead of the night. The sky was vivid with stars.

'Why are there no lights?' Rana asked as they snuck towards the guard house. The two men inside were dead, knifed.

'Looks like we have an intruder,' Mahesh said, as he entered the partially opened gate. He figured the assailant was inside. But he prayed KD was safe.

'Let's go towards the back.' Rana suggested as they hurried past the fountain with a statue of a mermaid with long flowing hair. The conch shells, scattered around, reflected the moonlight forming shadows that made the shells come alive, like giant snails.

The two men ducked under a window and then turned the corner.

'There must be the back entrance,' Rana whispered as he turned the knob of a small wooden door next to the swimming pool. It twisted easily. Rana pushed it outwards. He paused, waiting for a sound. He heard nothing. They crept inside and realised they were in a large changing room.

Then they heard a scream.

Chapter 61

They ran down a sloping curve. KD wasn't afraid but was equally surprised at Manzil's presence of mind. She was keeping her fear in check.

'This way,' KD said, grasping Manzil's hand and leading her towards the furthest and darkest section of the carpark. There were two doors on the left and a large glass sliding door along the right wall. One of them must lead back to the house and another to the lawn. Kanyadevi tried one of the doors. It was locked.

They heard footsteps.

'Come out, you two.' The man's sing-song voice echoed through the open space.

The deep baritone sounded oddly familiar. Kanyadevi froze for a second. Then she felt her hand tremble and an overwhelming sense of panic gripped her. Frantically, she tried the other door. It opened. She pushed inwards and they entered, shutting and locking it from the inside.

'What's wrong?' Manzil asked.

'I think... I've heard that voice before. We have to be careful. He will kill,' Kanyadevi said, breathing as if she had run a marathon.

'I recognise that voice. He is the one who killed Ramu,' Manzil said with a tremor.

They were inside an open room with mirrors all around. It was dark but all the fixtures of a circular room were clearly visible. A large silver ball hung from the ceiling. The centre was a dance floor, it was surrounded by ornately carved pillars. Large speakers were built into brackets on the walls, painted with a wavy design of gold and silver. Leather sofas and velvet seats was located around the bar area. A large mirrored wall had shelves filled with bottles of booze.

They moved towards the large bar where a velvet curtain hung behind the larger synthesiser system. 'There must be a way out from here,' Kanyadevi said, searching for an opening.

'Wait,' Manzil said. 'I need to tell you something.'

'Later, let's get out of here first.'

'Listen. Please,' she begged. 'The scroll. It means nothing to me. You understand, even though I am who I am, I only want to do the right thing. Do you believe me?'

KD stopped. She turned to Manzil and took her hands in hers.

'Manzil, I don't care which religion you belong to. I just believe in you, and your sense of what's right and what's wrong.'

She patted the young woman's back. 'Now let's get out of the monster's reach.'

KD parted the curtains, and noticed the small wooden door behind. 'Come on, there's a way out.' She undid the latch and pulled. The door opened into darkness. Then she saw that there was a circular ascending staircase that hugged the wall.

Anwar smiled as he entered the dark mouth of the carpark. The women were not very smart; they had found a perfect prison. They were trapped. He snickered.

Walking slowly towards the middle of the empty space, he noticed one car in the corner. It was covered with a thick layer of dust. Further to his left, there was a room with a glass door. He checked inside. It was a billiard room. He headed towards the two doors on the far end. Then Anwar stopped dead in his tracks. There was an exit from each room. He knew how to trap them. Anwar raced out of the carpark, across the lawn towards the front of the house.

The rectangular swimming pool shimmered in the moonlight. Mermaid statuettes reclined sexily at the four corners. Their eyes seemed to follow him as he bent low, moving against the wall of the house.

Sliding doors from the bedrooms provided a perfect view of the pool area. The ideal access from the carpark would be the foyer at the main entrance of the house. These women couldn't escape.

Using a long pole leaning against the wall, Anwar smashed the window. He pushed aside the glass still stuck to the sill and with one leap; he was back inside the house.

He had already cut the main power and no alarms went off. But he heard the hum of a generator. Emergency lights, he guessed. He was standing squarely in front of two doors. Both were from the carpark. He waited for his prey in the darkness.

Manzil's heart beat at a galloping pace. 'Are you sure this is the right way to get out?' Manzil said, hesitating as she reached the top of the stairs. She stared at the door.

'This is our only way out,' Kanyadevi was impatient.

'Okay.' Manzil opened the door carefully and stepped into the foyer.

The carpet glistened with broken glass. She turned towards the window and Manzil took a deep breath. She saw a glint of a weapon behind the screen, before she noticed the red-haired man.

Anger gripped her senses. It was time to act.

With the loudest voice possible, she screamed and lunged towards him with the kitchen knife.

Anwar was sharp, he caught her in an instant, moving the knife away, he twisted her around until she was caught in his elbow grip.

'That was a stupid thing to do, widow?' Anwar said, dragging her, keeping his back to the wall. KD retreated in the darkness of the staircase.

'Where is your girlfriend? Why hasn't she come to your rescue?' He pressed the knife in the hollow of her neck. 'Come out woman, or she is dead.'

Silence.

'Let me go,' Manzil shouted.

'Not unless I get the damned scroll. And it better be the real thing this time. You think you can con me, well here's something to teach you a lesson.' He clamped one hand over her mouth and with the other, he carved an x on her chest.

'Come out. Come out from where ever you are.'

Manzil let out a cry, but it was muffled. She squeezed her eyes shut, as courage seemed to desert her.

'Let her go,' KD said calmly.

Anwar smiled, as he backed slowly into the living room. She followed him.

'Give me the scroll first,' he said, pressing the point of the knife on Manzil's cheek. His face was flush with sweat. His dark red hair seemed to glow in the dim lights.

He narrowed his eyes, studying KD. 'Wait a minute. I know you.' He muttered, moving sideways. Yadav was lying on the floor, a dark bruise on his forehead. He appeared unconscious.

KD picked up the rolled up plastic from the table. 'Here, take it.' She threw it at him, hoping he would let go of Manzil on reflex. Anwar caught the object with one hand. He didn't need to loosen his grip and Manzil was still in his stranglehold. He shook it open and let the blank papers fall to the ground. He laughed. It was an eerie sound.

'You can't fool me twice.'

KD had shifted position. She was by the sofa where Yadav had been, her eyes focussed on the killer.

'You think I'm stupid?' Anwar pressed the knife to Manzil's cheek, she felt the burn as skin split. The pain was sharp. Blood trickled down her face and chin.

Anwar grinned at KD. And then he howled with pleasure. 'Now I remember,' he laughed, 'I know who you are. You are that girl, that one who escaped, ten years ago.'

Anwar raised his eyebrows and stopped laughing. 'I knew I

would find you one day. You slut, you are no better than me, you are a killer, a murderer.'

KD stared in shock. Yes, the face was familiar. Black hair then. And it came flooding back. He was the one who branded her, the one who carved her thigh.

'Shut up!' She screamed, clamping her ears. Her eyes full of terror.

Chapter 62

'Take this,' Mahesh gave Rana his pistol. 'I will go distract him.'

Before Rana could stop him, Mahesh entered the living room, holding a frying pan behind his back. He sighed in relief when he saw KD was safe. She looked at him blankly as he approached her. 'It's alright KD, I've come. Everything will be alright.' He said holding her in his arms. She trembled, and mumbled a few words.

'What is going on here? Who the hell are you? Don't you see what is happening here?' Anwar yelled, moving forward, his temper rising.

The knife pressing dangerously close to Manzil's neck. Her clothes were covered in blood. She tried to break out of his stranglehold. 'Let me go, please let me go. I'll give you the scroll.'

'Shut up!' Anwar prodded her cuts. Manzil squeezed her eyes as the pain grew in intensity and fresh blood dripped down her face.

Mahesh stared in horror as the crazy bastard pointed at Manzil's bleeding wound. Anwar watched KD. 'There is a scar on that whore's thigh. Don't tell me you haven't noticed?'

'Watch your tongue, sinner. You will burn in hell for cursing a goddess,' Mahesh shouted. Anwar and he were only an arm length away. 'Your goddess was a whore,' Anwar waved his knife at KD. 'And I'm not talking of a past life. She was a very profitable prostitute,' he said, watching for her reaction.

KD stared at him with unblinking eyes.

'I branded her with this very knife,' he savoured the words as if he was carving her naked body all over again.

'Shut up you foul-mouthed idiot! Or I will stitch it up myself,' Mahesh said in a menacing whisper. His hands tightened behind his back. He came close to Anwar, and caught him unawares when he struck the iron pan with all his strength. It hit Anwar square on the side of his face.

Anwar unclenched his hands and the knife clattered to the floor, skidding across the floor under the dining cabinet. Quickly, Manzil slipped out of his grasp and reached out for KD.

Anwar didn't falter much; he regained his balance and faced Mahesh with eyes as hard as coal. His cheek was turning into a purplish hue, but it didn't seem to affect him. The man should have been knocked out cold, but Anwar gripped Mahesh's shirt, pulling him closer. Mahesh, still holding the frying pan, pushed away hard and hit him across the other side of his face.

Dazed for only a second, Anwar slammed his fist into Mahesh's jaw, sending him and his weapon sprawling to the ground. Blood spilled from Mahesh's mouth, and he swore in pain.

Just then, Yadav limped forward and aimed a gun at them. 'Enough!' His voice was meant to come out strong. But it was a weak stutter. He broke out in cold sweat.

Anwar grinned at Yadav, 'You two-bit servant of the country. You would sell your mother for one small stack of bills. Look at you. Can't even stand straight.'

Anwar laughed as he made his way towards Manzil. Before she could scramble away, holding her by her hair, he pulled her head back like she was a ragdoll. He positioned his elbow around her chest, pressing into her old wounds. She mewled in pain. 'I can break this dainty neck before the bullet hits me, officer. Do you want to try your luck?'

During the standoff, KD slipped away unnoticed and recovered Anwar's knife from under the cabinet. She advanced towards him coldly. 'Go ahead, freak. You think by killing her you will win – you will lose and wish that you could slit your own throat in shame.'

'Well, well, well. The dirty whore has spoken some pearls of wisdom.'

'Dirty I maybe, but seeing you cower in shame will be a glorious revenge. It is worth the effort, just like I scooped out that pimp's eyeball – may he be restless eternally,' she cackled.

Mahesh stared at KD, his love, his devi. She was a stranger. Her face was streaked with dirt, hair in disarray, and her eyes shining and wide.

Was it true? KD a prostitute? He wondered. The thought felt like a shot of electric current passing through him. He felt it down to the tips of his fingers. He stared at his goddess crumbling before his eyes. Yes, he did remember the scar on her thigh. She said it was from an accident. He believed her. Just like he believed everything else she said. She had lied about being an upper caste.

He felt a sharp pain in his chest. And then the memory of their lovemaking flooded his thoughts. The warmth of that love lurked in his heart. Then he realised that his woman, his goddess was nothing more than a whore. He looked at her again. She brandished a knife and stared, wild-eyed.

Yadav was limping forward. The gun wasn't steady and his eyes bloodshot. He blinked rapidly, trying to stay conscious. Blood had soaked his left leg and was now dripping from his pant.

Chapter 63

As soon as Mahesh exited the kitchen, Rana crouched to the ground and pressed the messages button on his mobile phone. He sent a text. The situation was out of control. He got a response that whatever happened here would affect the outcome of the next twenty-four hours, that full-scale communal violence might erupt.

The news of the scroll had spread, and there were more bombings around the capital. The escalating anger was adding fuel to the fire of hate. It was time to curb the reason for the devastation – that scrap of paper had to be burned.

Absurdly, at that moment, Rana recalled his grandfather's stories of protecting the king, honouring the clan, while the enemy approached.

Rana trusted no one. Unlike his grandfather, who trusted the priest to protect the king, and ended up dead. Rana would protect those that needed protecting.

He had waited for Mahesh's signal. It had not come. He heard the screams, the threats and the clang of the frying pan. It was time to make his move.

'Here's the scroll,' Rana said, waving a very real-looking ancient artifact at Anwar.

Rana noticed Yadav's unsteady stance as he clutched a gun. KD, the beautiful dancer, appeared wild and disorientated as she waved a knife at Anwar. And Mahesh, dripping blood down his chin, simply stared at KD. His swollen lip and purplish bruise on his jaw didn't seem to affect him. Manzil's face was covered in blood and she was still in Anwar's clutches.

Shit. Things didn't look good. Rana held a cigarette lighter under the scroll. 'Let her go or I will burn this.'

'Who the fuck are you? How many more back there?' Anwar asked yanking Manzil's hair.

Manzil cried out. Her lips were turning purple.

Rana clicked the small device. A blue flame emerged. He held it close to the scroll. 'There is no one but me,' he said.

Mahesh glanced at Rana. Yadav lurched unsteadily and then fell back on the sofa. He held the gun with both hands, in a tight grip aimed at Anwar. 'And the army is on its way.'

Anwar looked at all of them. 'I don't have time to waste. Give me the scroll or I kill her.'

'You wouldn't dare! This woman prays to your god. Manzil is a Muslim! Like you!' cackled KD.

Anwar let go in shock. Manzil fell to the floor, coughing and sputtering.

KD's laughter filled the room. 'Revenge is sweet,' she said when she saw the look of horror on Anwar's face.

He leapt towards Rana but before he could get to the object in Rana's hand, Yadav fired.

Anwar slumped to the floor as the bullet hit him squarely in the chest.

At the same time, as if a sudden spurt of energy gripped him, Mahesh lunged forward and tried to grab the knife from KD's hand.

'No! Back off, Mahesh,' KD said towering above him, and then very slowly she turned the knife on her self. 'I'm tired of the memories that haunt me...' He didn't give her a chance, he grabbed it before she sunk the tip into her stomach.

'You can forget about the past KD, it doesn't matter. I love you and don't care about anything else,' Mahesh said. KD could hardly register the words of affection he spoke in her shell-shocked state.

Rana was at Manzil's side. She was unconscious. He checked her pulse. She was alive. He tried to revive her and helped her up as she coughed violently.

Then they smelled the fire.

Chapter 64

'It's over,' Junaid said quietly.

'The newspaper reports a fire burned down the producer's home, killing two assailants and a woman. All are unidentifiable. It is rumoured that the woman was Manzil Saxena, the wife of a famous reporter, Parag Saxena, claimed to have uncovered an important piece of evidence related to the Taj Mahal,' Pritam Bhalla read from one of his newspapers.

'Good alibi,' Saraswati Sen whispered. She showed them Professor Gupta's report on the scroll. 'It has stopped the religious riots.'

'Our country is not ready for unity,' Junaid sounded defeated.

'That's not true. We will continue to strive for it. This is the purpose of Onyx, of our common intent. We can make it happen.'

'Manzil is a brave woman.' KD added. 'She is in a hideout and is willing to join us, after she has received a new identity.'

Satish Kumar sighed. 'Where is the scroll? I lost one of my favourite holiday homes because of it.' Then he smiled. 'But no one is going to stop me from making movies.'

'The scroll is safe.' KD said mysteriously. 'We better let the archaeologists handle their job.'

'It's with Mahesh Bhakti?' Junaid asked.

'Yes.'

'Get me a drink, Satish,' Akash Sinha said. 'All this is too much to handle.'

They lifted their glasses. 'To unity.'

'To unity,' they chorused.

Epilogue

Bengaluru, Karnataka

The tiny art gallery was located on the corner of Cox Town. The 'back in 30 minutes' sign dangled at an odd angle from the door.

Manzil, or Manisha as she was now known, was in a coffee shop across the street. She took a deep breath and looked at her reflection in the glass window.

Her hair was short, laced with streaks of copper. The hairstylist had decided it would suit her. She wore black-frame glasses. It made her feel more comfortable. The scars on her cheeks were visible, but with the right foundation, it was hardly noticeable.

Instead of her traditional salwar kameez, she wore a white shirt and long floral skirt. It had been a few months since she 'died in the fire'. And another few months when the government had provided her with a new identity.

She missed her old life. Actually she didn't, except for Parag. When she was Manzil she was being hunted. They would not have rested until she was dead. Now that she was dead, her old life was dead too. She wished… then she stopped herself. There was the future ahead of her, and she would return one day. If nothing else, to visit the Taj Mahal.

'You're looking thin, what's wrong?' Yadav said as he sat down on the empty chair opposite her.

'I'm just not used to this life yet.'

He looked at her and smiled. 'You can't fool me, I know what you really want to do, Manzil.' He sipped his coffee.

'What?'

'You want to change the world.' He laughed.

She nodded. 'Yes, right, as if one person can do that!'

'Glad to see you alive. I was worried. Luckily, your bandaged face made it easier for you to remain unrecognisable,' he said gently.

She recalled the horrible day. The Onyx army had safely taken the survivors to another location. The police commissioner had been in on it. First she had to spend some time in a private clinic. Doctors' treatments involving a dozen stitches on Manzil's face, doped on painkillers, reluctantly she agreed to have some plastic surgery done.

Onyx sent out news that both Manzil and the scroll had been destroyed in the fire.

Yadav smiled. He passed her a small package. 'This came for you yesterday.'

'What is it?'

'Open it; I think you will be interested.'

The square box was filled with strips of paper. Nestled in the middle was a stone plate. There was writing on it. 'Looks like Urdu.' She handed the biscuit thin rectangular stone.

He shrugged. 'Mahesh said it's the basic principles of the Din Ilahi.'

'This is the religion started by Akbar, one of the greatest kings of the Mughal Empire, in the sixteenth century.' She said excitedly. 'He wanted to create a religion that encompassed all the teachings of the other religions. The Islamists boycotted him for it.'

'One more piece of Indian history that needs to be hidden,' he said, taking the object and placing it back in the box. Yadav slid it across to her.

'It's getting harder to admit the truth.'

'That's not true,' Manzil said as she stood up. 'I should go. There is a customer waiting outside the gallery.'

Giving him a wave, she turned, but not before she saw the tenderness in his eyes.

'Keep bringing them in. One day they will all be revealed as our heritage and everyone will be proud.'

Manzil smiled at him.

A peek into Shobha's forthcoming thriller

NINE *unknown*

Prologue
Bhubaneshwar, Orissa, 264 BCE

The odour of decaying flesh reeked around the Kalingan's dying body. He heard the piercing cries of circling and swooping carrion. Torn limbs lay scattered, some corpses clutched weapons and others crushed by the weight of elephants. The air was thick with the metallic smell of blood. It was from his body and those of his clan. If hell be on earth, then this is it.

Aware of each inward and outward movement of lungs, he waited as slowly his mind seemed to melt into the stillness of time. The battle sounds roaring in his ears disappeared. His inner senses heightened.

The river Daya flowed red. The strange mist rose and rolled towards the hills. There was more to see, a hundred thousand broken bodies spread across the battlefield in the valley. His men, the Kalingan warriors had fought bravely. He wished he could move his useless flesh, stand up and lead them to victory. But it was too late. He willed himself to get up, but only managed to drag one arm towards his face. He twisted onto his side, his head half-sank into the wet soil. Caked in mud, he saw that his third finger was bent at an odd angle, and a jagged red line oozed where his thumb had been sliced. The palm of his hand was covered with cuts and callouses from driving his spear into the enemy. A deep rumbling sound emerged from his throat. He pressed down on the earth. His vision turned dark, there were tiny rivulets of blood, dripping down from his battered face, and then the earth absorbed the liquid turning a fiery red. The Kalingan felt the strength seeping but he willed himself to stay alert, he cried out, his hand pressed down, harder and harder.

Deep in his soul, he felt the scream erupt, loud and coarse with anger and tears, he cursed the Mauryans – their King. His spirit was wild with fury. He was not one to give up, the blood of the Kalinga clan flowed through him and had fought the Mauryan dynasty for generations.

"I swear by the Kalingan blood on this earth," he cried, "I will get my revenge." He fell on his face. He heard the flapping of wings and he felt the carrion's claws sink into his flesh. He closed his eyes for the last time.

Chapter 1
2008 AD Hong Kong, China

Earlier it took Vayu King hours to get into the zone. But this time, he felt the power surging like waves through his senses within five minutes. He focused on it until he was the energy and nothing more. He knew he had the power, and he was more than just an ordinary human, that he had a greater calling. He had been given a new lease on life and it meant for something.

Vayu was at one with the ancient mystical energy, connecting with a life force, like an antennae tuning into the right channel. He focused on his inner energy centres. The seven primary chakras revolved at amazing speed, and located along the central vertical axis of the spine, formed a single white column of light emerging from the crown of his head. After one of his marathon channeling sessions, he felt such incredible strength that he once struck a five-foot brick wall, and cracked it right down the middle. Yes, he had the power. And he was meant to achieve great things, it was in his destiny.

There was an oddity about the present moment. He felt another power in the vicinity, like a buzzing fly that broke the centre of his focus.

His body was still, his breathing controlled, his mind was in a state of deep conscious awareness. And in the stillness, the subtle sound was clear.

Vayu surveyed his room through narrowed eyes. His futon bed was folded and tucked in one corner, and the rolled up straw mat leaned against the wall. The spent syringe was some distance from the mat. The sparse furnishings included one small stool and a side table for his basic necessities. The office table and chair were pushed to the corner. The unusual humming sound was perceptible, and yet there was no electronic appliance connected. He always made sure of that. Lead lined rods circled him like a fence, he used it to trap 'white noise', including random thoughts of others. A crisp fresh breeze of dewy air wafted through the small window bringing in an odd metallic aroma. Nothing was out of place and no intruder was physically present. In a split-second back flash, he was aware of what was here. Memories were not slave to time, a blink of an eye and an entire scene from the past came to light.

A sensation hit him like a gut-wrenching punch. There was nothing but pure red-hot emotion. His heart raced in unison with the anger that flowed like a wild gushing river, pushing into him, forcing his mind to relent. This was his destiny, he understood the ancient force was waiting until he was ready. And he let it take over.

Still seated in the lotus position, he felt a warmth in his hands. He looked down at his upturned palm. In the centre, he saw the lines deepen and curve. Blood pooled and like tiny tributaries filled and flowed between his fingers. Vayu didn't shift. He closed his eyes.

Then his mind was drawn to painful memories from his teen years.

Vayu was fifteen when he had almost died. He suffered terrible aches in his stomach, so bad, it brought him to his knees. The pain, along with diarrhea, vomiting and fever, interrupted his life and his parents' tried everything. He lost weight and often had to miss school. Doctors couldn't figure out why, they tried all kinds of medication. And at most times the symptoms only got worse. His father presumed it was the work of black magic. He had a gambling debt growing at a rate that strangers threatened him on the street. His mother, a lawyer, didn't believe in occult, nor was she aware of her husband's addiction.

Despite medication and other treatments, Vayu became weaker and weaker. One by one, his organs shut down. In a few months, he was in the intensive care unit, hooked up to tubes and machines. His parents wept helplessly in the corner, watching him die.

His guilt-ridden father had tried alternative therapies, crystal healing, spiritual healers and many more while his wife scoffed at his primitive beliefs. For her, science was God and there was nothing else that could save her son. Then Vayu's father wanted to try one more extreme ritual: psychosurgical healing. His mother threatened to sue him, if he brought a barbaric witch doctor to touch her son. Vayu could only watch, wishing he would die so that they would stop their arguments. But finally his mother relented. She was never the same again, Vayu realised.

Very late that fatal night, Vayu saw his father leave. He followed him. It was an odd sensation – Vayu was as light as air, weaving in and out of his room, sometimes he watched from the ceiling. He stood face to face, but his father didn't seem to notice his son. Vayu felt a sense of anguish and fear spread through him. He was a ghost floating away from his lifeless body. But, Vayu understood he still had a chance, his body was still alive, the heart pumping blood. He wished desperately to live. And promised he would do anything in return.

Vayu noticed his father moving quickly past the hospital gates towards a car waiting by the road. He spoke to the driver. And the rear window slid down.

There was a thin-framed old man in the car. He looked ancient with wrinkled dark skin and pale eyes, hair as grey and wild as his eyes. The man turned his head slowly and looked out of the window at Vayu's ghostly form. He smiled directly at him.

As if time didn't matter, Vayu was back in the ICU, watching his physical self die. He was hovering above near the ceiling.

The nurse stared curiously at the old man with Vayu's father. She didn't react until they entered the room and shut the door. The man took out a bottle of oil from his bag. While Vayu's mother stared in horror, the shaman spread his hands, palms down, above Vayu's body and began chanting words. As his voice became stronger and more energetic, his hands shivered and shook. He moved the cloth until Vayu's white flesh was visible. Without hesitation, the shaman's hands pressed deep and firm into Vayu's stomach. While the healer, kneaded with his fingers, blood surfaced, pooled and spilled out of

Vayu's midriff, flowing like a stream down the sides of the bed. Vayu didn't react. He was asleep. Or dead.

Vayu's mother froze and then let out scream. She shouted at the crazy man to stop killing her son. Her husband held her back. The nurse and a security guard were at the door trying to open it. But a steel chair held it in place. The ICU alarms were ringing. Nurses scattered trying their best to keep the patients calm, doctors were called in, two more security guards arrived. But the people could not enter the room. They could see what was going on through the square port hole in the door and the glass wall next to it.

Besides the healer, Vayu's father was the only other person not affected by the scene. He made sure nobody interrupted the ritual. The spectators watched in horror, afraid to break down the glass and affect the other patients in the unit. They had already created a commotion in a primarily silent environment.

And then it happened.

Besides the milling people, Vayu hovered and watched with horror as the healer's bloody hands dipped in and out of Vayu's stomach and with a final yank a writhing snakelike object was removed. He inhaled loudly, and the healer muttered more strange words, and dropped the black length of the organic bloody mass into his bag. He waved his hands in the air, beckoning at him to return and then he wiped away the blood. Vayu felt a strong forceful wind push him back into his body. The whole process took less than ten minutes. He moved away allowing Vayu's parents to clean him up. His mother, weeping silently, wiped away the residual blood and noted Vayu's unblemished stomach area. While the focus was on Vayu's midriff, the shaman leaned close to his ear and whispered. "You remember your promise, boy." And then without another word, he turned away. Vayu's father unlatched the door and moved the chair, and the shaman walked through the crowd of gaping men and women that parted like the Red Sea to let him out of the room.

Doctors and nurses rushed in. Their first concern was their

patient. The police, called in by security, arrested the healer at the hospital gates. Vayu, given up for dead by the doctors, was conscious and asking for water.

Vayu's parents bailed out Master Jon Lubo, the faith healer who saved their son. They gave him and his organization – the Lubo Spiritual Healing Agency – their support and donations.

When Vayu was out of the hospital, he went to visit Jon Lubo. "You don't need to thank me. You must thank the spirit. You are nothing but a slave to this angry ghost. I am telling you this, and know it will cost me my life but you must know the power of this spirit. It is going to use you for its purpose." Jon said, fixing him with those blind pale eyes.

"What spirit?"

"The one you asked to help, the one you made the promise to."

"I didn't make any promise to any spirit."

"You did. And he heard you, when you left your body, when you wanted to live.. He is so powerful he can destroy any one in a split-second. He has been restless for centuries. This one wanted you. He is the one who came through me to heal you," Lubo explained.

"But what does he want of me?"

"He will let you know when the time is right. Be careful. You are going to become what it chooses for you, you will become one with this entity." Jon Lubo had said. Three days later the faith-healer was dead.

And Vayu forgot about the incident until today. His destiny had arrived.
